THE 24TH LETTER

ALSO BY TOM LOWE

A False Dawn

THE 24TH LETTER

TOM LOWE

MINOTAUR BOOKS

A THOMAS DUNNE BOOK
NEW YORK

A THOMAS DUNNE BOOK FOR MINOTAUR BOOKS.
An imprint of St. Martin's Publishing Group.

THE 24TH LETTER. Copyright © 2010 by Tom Lowe. All rights reserved. Printed in the United States of America. For information, address St. Martin's Press, 175 Fifth Avenue, New York, N.Y. 10010.

www.thomasdunnebooks.com
www.minotaurbooks.com

Library of Congress Cataloging-in-Publication Data

Lowe, Tom, 1952–
    The 24th letter / Tom Lowe.—1st ed.
        p. cm.
    "A Thomas Dunne book for Minotaur Books"—T.p. verso.
    ISBN 978-0-312-37918-6
    1. Priests—Fiction.   2. Death row inmates—Fiction.   3. Judicial error—Fiction.
4. Murder—Investigation—Fiction.   I. Title.   II. Title: Twenty-fourth letter.
    PS3562.O88423A614 2010
    813'.6—dc22   2009041132

First Edition: March 2010

10   9   8   7   6   5   4   3   2   1

For my daughter Ashley

ACKNOWLEDGMENTS

One of my favorite parts of writing is recognizing and thanking the folks who've helped me—and there are many. The people at St. Martin's Press are extraordinarily talented, and I'm fortunate to have their guidance and experience. From the sales department to editorial, they are the best. My deepest thanks to Ruth Cavin, Thomas Dunne, Toni Plummer, David Rotstein, Elizabeth Kugler, Rafal Gibek, and Bridget Hartzler. A special thanks to production editor Bob Berkel for his assistance. He's still the wizard of words.

Other people who have contributed to this book include: Detective Sara Gioielli, Detective Aaron Miller, Dr. David Specter, Father Roger Hamilton, A. Brian Phillips, and my agent, Phyllis Westberg.

Writing, especially when it's done after the day job, takes a lot of time. My family has always been my greatest source of inspiration. I am forever grateful for their love and support. My thanks to my children: Natalie, Cassie, Christopher, and Ashley. You're all amazing and talented, and I am proud of you. I wanted to recognize and thank my son, Chris Lowe, for producing my book trailers and designing my

Web site. His creative production skills astound me. His company is found here: www.suite7productions.com.

My thanks and love to my wife, Keri, whose support throughout the novel-writing process makes a tough job easier. Her sense of story is extraordinary, and it is matched by her passion and encouragement for each book. You're my inspiration.

I appreciate the booksellers who have taken the time to introduce readers to my work. And my thanks to you, the reader. If you're just joining us, welcome aboard. If you're returning for the next part of Sean O'Brien's journey, I'm thrilled that you're here.

ONE

U.S. Marshal Deputy Bill Fisher had never done it before, and after that morning he swore to God he'd never do it again. Never had he let a prisoner have a cigarette before entering a courthouse to testify, but Sam Spelling had been cooperative and polite on the long ride from Florida State Prison to the U.S. district court in Orlando. And they were early. The news media were on the other side of the building, out front. Maybe, thought Deputy Fisher, it wouldn't hurt if Spelling smoked half a cigarette.

Spelling was to be the star witness in the government's case against a bank robber turned cocaine trafficker. Since Spelling was helping the government, at a possible risk to himself, what harm could a quick cigarette do? *Might calm the boy down, help his testimony.* Marshal Fisher and a second marshal escorted Spelling up the worn steps leading to the courthouse's back entrance.

At the top of the steps, Spelling looked around, eyes searching the adjacent alley, the delivery trucks and sheriff's cars parked along the perimeter. His dark hair was gelled and combed straight back. Two white scars ran jagged above his left eyebrow like lightning bolts—leftovers from a diet of violence. He had a haggard, birdlike face, beak nose with feral eyes, red-rimmed and irises the shade of blue turquoise. He squinted in the morning sun and said, "I'd really appreciate that smoke, sir. Just a quick one to relax my nerves. I gotta go in there and say things that are gonna send Larry to where I am for a helluva long time. State's promised me he'll go to some other prison. If he don't, it'll only be a matter of time before he shanks me, or has somebody do it. Right now a smoke would make my time in the witness stand a whole lot easier."

THE RIFLE'S CROSSHAIRS swept up Sam Spelling's back as he reached the top step. The sniper looked through the scope and waited for the right second. He knew the .303 would make an entrance hole no larger than the width of a child's pencil on the back of Spelling's head. The exit wound would plaster Spelling's face into mortar supporting the century-old granite blocks.

He didn't anticipate Spelling turning around at the rear entrance to the courthouse. Even better, now he could put one between the eyes. Through the powerful scope, he saw the flame of a cigarette lighter. Magnified, it looked like a tiny fire in the marshal's hand. He watched as Spelling used both his cuffed hands to hold the cigarette, bluish white smoke drifting in the crosshairs. Spelling took a deep drag off the cigarette as the sniper started to squeeze the trigger.

Then Spelling nodded and coughed, turning his head and stepping backward.

He lowered the crosshairs to Spelling's chest and pulled the trigger.

Sam Spelling fell like a disjointed string puppet. The gunshot sprayed tissue, bits of lung and muscle against the courthouse wall. Blood trickled in a finger pattern down the white granite, leaving a crimson trail that glistened in the morning sun.

TWO

Sam Spelling knew he would go to hell one day. He didn't know it would be today. The hospital emergency room staff patched the bullet wound in his chest, restored his erratic heartbeat, and pumped him full of chemicals. Then they left him chained to a gurney behind privacy curtains.

He tried to focus on the acoustic ceiling above him. *Concentrate on the little holes.* They looked like tiny black stars in an all-white sky. He couldn't remember the last time he had actually slept under the stars—or even seen the stars.

He could hear the constant beep from the heart monitor—the slowing.

Where are they?

He could feel the flutter in his chest, nausea in his gut, bile in his throat. His pores leaked the medicinal smell of copper and sulfur. The black stars were dimming. The sounds from the monitor were like the pounding of off-tune piano keys as Spelling's heart tried to jump-start life and catch up with losing time.

A man's not supposed to hear his own death! Where are they? Somebody!

The taste in his mouth was like someone had crushed a cigarette butt on his tongue. Sweat dripped onto the flat pillow.

Better pillows in the cell! His neck muscles knotted.

The pain was now connecting from his chest through his left shoulder and down his tingling arm. He tried to lift his head to see if the guard was still standing outside the drawn curtain. The continuous beep. *So damn loud.*

Why couldn't they hear? Somebody!

The room was swallowed in black and then it didn't matter to Sam Spelling anymore because he was gone. He was caught in a dark whirlpool sucking him into a vast drain—down into a sewer of total darkness.

When the nurse yanked back the curtain, she didn't know if Sam Spelling was still alive.

FATHER JOHN CALLAHAN NEVER got used to it. Performing last rites didn't come easy to a man who, at age fifty-seven, could drill a soccer ball dead center from midfield. He was competitive by nature. Death was to be fought—and for the young, it was to be fought hard. Never throw in the towel. People need time to get it right.

He thought about that as he walked through the rain, stepped over cables from a TV news satellite truck, and entered the hospital emergency room. Father Callahan had a chiseled, ruddy face, prominent jawline, and green eyes the shade of a new leaf in spring. He saw four police officers—one sipping coffee, the others filling out reports. A plainclothes man, an African-American, stood in a corner talking with an officer—Callahan took him for a detective. A blond TV reporter applied pink gloss to her lips.

A veteran nurse with tired eyes looked up from her desk as the priest fastened the cord around his umbrella. Father Callahan said, "Nasty day."

The nurse nodded and glanced toward the packed waiting room. She said, "The reporters don't make the job any easier."

"Why are they here?"

"A prisoner was shot on the courthouse steps this morning. He was supposed to testify in that big drug trial."

Father Callahan nodded. "How is Nicole Satorini? She was brought in earlier? Head-on collision. I heard she's in IC. Is the family with her?"

The nurse inhaled deeply. "I'm sorry, Father. She passed. I think the family left the hospital a little while ago."

SAM SPELLING GRIPPED THE doctor's white coat like a drowning man grasps a life preserver. "It's okay," the doctor said, holding on to Spelling's wrist. "You need rest. Lie back down. We re-started your heart."

The Department of Corrections guard started to enter, but the doctor shook his head and lowered Spelling's hand to the gurney. He looked at the digital numbers on the monitor and said, "Pressure ninety-fifty. Pulse thirty-nine. Start another packed-cell drip."

A nurse nodded and began following the doctor's orders.

Spelling lifted his head. The prison guard stood just beyond the bed, close enough to watch the proceedings. The guard was built like a linebacker, his forehead thick with bone, nose flat and scarred.

Spelling looked beyond the guard. He saw a man dressed in a black suit standing by the nurses' station. The man in the suit wore the collar of a priest. Spelling blinked, the tears spilling from his eyes. He smiled, his cracked lips trembled, his left cheek quivered from pulsating nerves and muscle.

"Father!" screamed Spelling.

As Father Callahan was leaving, he looked in the direction of the shouting.

"Father!"

The priest started toward the frightened man. The guard held up a large hand, as if he stood at a school crossing. "Hold it, sir."

"That man called out for me," said Father Callahan.

"That man's a prisoner." The muscle in the guard's lower jaw tightened.

"He's also a human being in need."

Spelling looked up at the young doctor through watering, pleading eyes. "Doc, please, can I talk to the priest? Just for a half minute?"

"You've had a second heart attack in less than an hour. You need rest."

"Please, Doc! I saw something I don't know how to describe. I can't go back there. I need to tell the priest—to confess. Man, I need God right now!"

THREE

The doctor swallowed dryly. "No more than a couple minutes, Father. He'll be in surgery soon."

The hospital personnel left as Father Callahan stepped past the Department of Corrections guard to Spelling's bedside.

"Father," Spelling began, looking at his trembling free hand, now with an IV taped near his wrist. "Look at me, shakin' like I'm comin' off a four-day drunk. Father, I haven't been a religious man most of my sorry-ass life . . . but I always believed in God."

Father Callahan nodded.

Spelling said, "I saw something a few minutes ago that scared the livin' shit outta me. Pardon my language, Father, but I think I died . . . died and went straight to hell. Man, am I a believer now. You mind closing the curtain? I want to make a confession."

Father Callahan nodded and stepped to the curtain. To the guard he said in a whisper, "Please give this man a moment of privacy to confess his sins."

The guard grinned and said, "Gonna take a lot longer than a moment."

Father Callahan pulled the curtain closed and turned to Spelling.

"Father . . . I ain't sure how to say this . . ."

"Simply say it from your heart."

"Heart's almost wore out, but I'll try. Can I ask your name?"

"Father John Callahan. I'm an Episcopal priest."

"Can I call you Father John?"

"Yes."

"Father John, maybe you can put in a good word for me above." Spelling cut his eyes up to the dots in the ceiling. "I've done a lot of bad things in my life. I hope God can see what caused me to do that stuff and forgive me for some of it. What I got to say, Father, it ain't about me. Maybe God will take pity at this stage of my sorry life. Any chances of that, really?"

"It is never too late to seek our Lord and his forgiveness. You wish to confess?"

"It's about makin' something right." Spelling paused, glanced at the digital impulses of his weak heart on the monitor. "There's a man on death row up at Starke. State of Florida's gonna kill him. He's not guilty. They say he raped and killed a girl—a supermodel down in Miami. Happened eleven years ago, but he didn't do it."

"How do you know?"

"'Cause I *know* who did it. I'd been sittin' low in my car in a condo parking lot when I seen the killer come out of one condo. I was there to sell some coke when I spotted this dude. Wasn't long after I'd seen this first fella stumble shit-faced drunk outta the same place. I saw where the second man hid the knife. I *got* the knife. I took it from the Dumpster when I saw the dude toss it. Wrapped in newspaper. Got a good look at him and even memorized his tag. I hid the knife. Girl's killing was all over the news. Nobody was arrested . . . so I got in touch with the dude. Told him for a hundred grand, his takin' out the trash would remain our little secret. He wanted the knife. I kept it as an insurance policy. Got the money, and it wasn't but a few days before they'd arrested somebody else for the girl's killin'. I figured I was

8

now an accessory to the whole f'd-up mess. In a year, I'd sucked the money up my nose . . . robbed a bank and got caught. They sent me to Starke for a dime. The guy on death row, Charlie Williams, is an innocent man. A *real* fuckin' innocent man. Forgive me for that slip again, Father John."

Father Callahan was silent a moment. He said, "You're doing the right thing."

Spelling glanced down at the floor toward the end of the curtain. He saw the large black boots of the guard standing as close as possible to the curtain. "Father, come closer. The murdered girl was Alexandria Cole. She was one of those supermodels."

"I remember the case. Who killed her?"

The heart monitor beeped. Spelling chewed at his cracked lower lip. "Father, I have sinned bad. . . . Will God set it right? Will he forgive me?"

"God will embrace you for your confession. The police may need more. Write down your confession, as many details as possible . . . name the person who did it and sign it."

"Is this in case I die?"

"What do you mean?"

"If I die . . . if you got it in writing, proves a dying man's confession is more than only your word, Father. No offense."

"None taken."

"Feds want me to testify real bad. I heard they are gonna keep me in here till I'm well enough to testify."

Two nurses and the ER doctor approached. He said, "Dr. Strassberg has arrived. We'll be taking the patient up for surgery."

Spelling's eyes popped. He looked up at Father Callahan. "Say a prayer for me, Father John. If the good Lord sees me through this alive, I'll write it all down. Names and places, and where the weapon is hidden."

The priest nodded and said, "I'll need to share this information with a close friend of mine. May our Lord bless you."

As they wheeled Spelling from the area, he asked, "What time is it, Father?"

Father Callahan looked at his watch. "It's exactly six o'clock in the evening."

"Time's runnin' out."

"I'll pray for you, son."

"I'm talking about Charlie Williams, the fella on death row. He's next in line for the needle. If it's six, by my calculations, he's got eighty-four hours to live, and he's gonna need more than prayers to save his soul."

FOUR

Sean O'Brien stood on the worn cypress wood of his screened-in back porch and watched lightning pop through the low-lying clouds above the Ocala National Forest. Each burst hung in the bellies of the clouds for a few seconds, the charges exploding and fading like fireflies hiding in clusters of purple grapes. He could smell rain falling in the forest and coming toward the St. Johns River as the breeze delivered the scent of jasmine, wet oak, and honeysuckle.

Thunder rumbled in the distance. The rolling noise, the burst and fade of light reminded O'Brien of the times he witnessed night bombing in the first Gulf War. But that was many miles and years in the past. He deeply inhaled the cool, rain-drenched air. The sound of frogs reached a competing crescendo when the first drops began to hit the oak leaves. The river was like black ink, whitecaps rolling across its dark surface.

As the temperature dropped, the wind picked up, bringing a wall of rain across the river and through the thick limbs of old live oaks, soaking the gray beards of Spanish moss. Within a few seconds, moss hung from the limbs like the wet fleece of lamb's wool caught in the rain and stained the shade of tarnished armor.

O'Brien sipped a cup of black coffee and listened to the rain tap the tin roof over the porch. The old house was built in 1945, constructed from river rock, Florida cypress, and pine. Wood too tough for termites, nails, or even hurricanes. The house sat high above the river, on the shoulder of an ancient Indian mound. O'Brien had bought the home after his wife, Sherri, died from ovarian cancer fifteen months ago. Following her death, he'd had a fleeting romance with the bottle and the genies it released in his subconscious.

He'd sold his house in Miami, quit his job as a homicide detective, and moved to a remote section of the river about fifty miles west of Daytona Beach. It was here where he repaired the old home and his life. His closest neighbor was a half mile away. The nearest town, DeLand, was more than twenty miles away.

O'Brien looked at Sherri's framed photograph standing on a wicker table near his porch chair. Her smile was still as intoxicating as a summer night, fresh, vibrant, and so full of life. So full of hope. He deeply missed her. He set his cell phone by her picture.

Max barked.

O'Brien looked down at Max, his miniature dachshund. "I know you have to pee. We have two options. I can let you go out by yourself and risk an owl flying off with you, or I can grab an umbrella and try to keep us both dry while you do your thing."

Max sniffed and cracked a half bark. She trotted over to the screen door and looked back at O'Brien through eager brown eyes.

"Okay," he said, grinning, "never delay a lady from her trip to the bathroom." O'Brien reached for an umbrella in the corner, lifted Max under his arm like a football, and walked out the door. He set her down near the base of a large live oak in his yard. Sherri had bought the dog as a puppy when O'Brien was spending long days and nights on a particularly extreme murder investigation. She named the dog Maxine and allowed her to sleep in their bed, something O'Brien discovered after he had returned home one night, exhausted, awakening before dawn to find Maxine lying on her back, snuggled next to his side, snoring. In a dreamlike stupor, he sat up, momentarily thinking a big rodent had climbed onto the bed. But Max had looked at him too lovingly through chestnut brown eyes. They'd made their peace, and now it was only the two of them.

He sometimes wondered if Sherri had known she was ill before she was officially diagnosed with terminal cancer, and she had bought Max for him. Maybe she knew a nine-pound dachshund could show a six-two, two-hundred-pound man a softer, more compassionate side of his own self. Sherri had that kind of wisdom, he thought.

O'Brien held the large umbrella over Max as she squatted, the rain thumping the umbrella, the frogs chanting competing choruses.

A foreign sound sliced through the air like a bad note.

O'Brien could hear his cell phone ringing from the table on his back porch. "Ignore it, Max," he said. "Go with the flow. No need getting a bladder infection. If it's important, they'll call back."

Max bolted from underneath the umbrella and sniffed fresh tracks left in the dirt near an orange tree O'Brien had recently planted. He watched rain pooling in the tracks. O'Brien knelt down and placed his hand over one imprint. He let out a low whistle. "Florida panther, Max, looks like it was running." O'Brien's eyes followed the tracks until they were lost in the black. Max growled.

"That tough-dog growl would certainly scare a panther. Not many of them left. But, boy, do we have black bears in that old forest. That's why you, young lady, have to eat the leftovers. We don't need bears rummaging through the garbage cans. Coons are bad enough."

The cell phone rang again.

O'Brien stood and looked up toward the house and porch. "Come on, Max, let's see who is it that needs our immediate attention."

Max sniffed the damp air, sneezed, and followed O'Brien up the sloping yard. She climbed the wet steps and stood on the porch to shake the rainwater out of her fur.

O'Brien picked up his cell at the last ring. "Hello."

Nothing.

13

"Maybe it went to voice mail, Max." O'Brien looked at the caller ID.

Not a good sign.

The caller was a close friend of his. Father Callahan had been there for him when Sherri died.

Now maybe the priest needed him.

FIVE

O'Brien hit the number left behind on his phone's register. It rang four times and went into message mode, Father Callahan's voice asking the caller to leave a message. "Father Callahan, this is Sean O'Brien. Looks like you were trying to reach me. I'm around, give me a call."

Max sat, her eyes following a mosquito that made it in before the door shut. O'Brien picked up a dry towel that he had hanging from a sixty-year-old nail driven halfway into a white oak support beam. When O'Brien bought the house, an old horseshoe hung from the lone nail. He had painted the porch, painted around the nail, cleaned and polished the horseshoe, and hung it back in the same spot. He kept a clean towel there for rainy days and a little wet dog.

O'Brien picked Max up, set her on the towel in the center of the porch, and dried her. He said, "We have to head to the marina. Are you ready to visit Nick and Dave?"

Max cocked her head.

"Maybe Nick has some fresh fish. I have to replace the zincs on the props this weekend or *Jupiter* might be sitting on the bottom of the bay soon."

O'BRIEN WAS ALMOST to the Ponce Marina when his cell rang. O'Brien pressed the receiver button. "Hello, Father."

"Sean, you're either a psychic detective or you have caller ID."

"It's all about the technology today."

"Oh, I don't know. You've always been exceptional at reading things in people that no machine can detect."

O'Brien drove in the heavy shower, the rain now falling in larger drops like schools of silver minnows pouring from the sky. He said, "Storm's moving on, Father. Good to hear your voice. It's been awhile. How are you?"

"You visited me more after Sherri's death than in recent times. Are you okay?"

"Yes, thanks. I don't get out as much as I'd like to. Fixing up my old house and boat keeps me busy. I'm heading to the marina now."

"I was at Baptist Hospital where I heard a confession. It came from a prisoner who was shot as he was being transferred to testify in court this morning. After he was stabilized, he suffered a series of heart attacks. He underwent surgery."

"I'm listening, Father."

"This poor chap believes he died on the emergency room table, and in the near clutch of the devil, he says he was resuscitated. Says he saw evil . . . absolute evil."

"Maybe it was just a bad dream."

"The man believes he's been given a divine chance to make amends. He saw something, Sean, something that led him to confess."

"It may have more to do with the brain in an oxygen-deprived state than it does with good or evil."

"No." Father Callahan lowered his voice. "He saw something eleven years ago."

16

"What?"

"A murderer. Saw him leave the scene right after the devil's work was done. And the man who did it was never caught."

"Why doesn't he go to the police?"

"He's a convict. It's complicated. Time's running out, and he's under the knife."

"Father, start from the beginning."

"The real killer is free, and the man accused of the murder is sitting on death row. The state is going to put him to death at 6:00 A.M. Friday. That's less than four days."

O'Brien could feel tightness in his chest. "What does this have to do with me?"

"You might be the best man to free the condemned man and catch the real killer."

"Why me, Father?"

"If it's true, Sean, it was you who caught the wrong man, and he's about to be executed."

SIX

O'Brien pulled in the oyster shell parking lot of Ponce Marina and shut off the Jeep's engine. The rain stopped and he unzipped the windows. "Wrong man? Who, Father?"

"Charlie Williams."

"Williams? That was ten, maybe eleven years ago." O'Brien's thoughts raced. In his mind's eye he saw the murder scene. Blood covered the victim's bedroom. Young. Beautiful. Stabbed seven times in the chest and throat. Her blood was in the ex-boyfriend's truck. His prints in her condo. His semen in her body. He was found drunk. Passed out in his pickup truck. He said they'd fought, but he didn't kill her.

Father Callahan said, "I remember the press coverage. You were at the top of your game as a homicide detective with Miami PD. It was followed closely in the media because the victim was an internationally known celebrity."

O'Brien was silent. A dull pain started above his left eye. The adrenaline flowed, and he could almost hear his blood rushing through his temples. "This man—this inmate—what's his name? What did he say?"

"Sam Spelling. Said he saw the real killer hide the weapon—a knife. Spelling fished it out of a Dumpster, and he then succumbed to temptation. Blackmailed the killer for a one-time payment of a hundred thousand. Spelling went through the money, bought a lot of cocaine, wound up in prison. He was supposed to testify in a big drug trial before someone shot him today. But his confession tonight with me, it related to your old case—the death of the supermodel and her ex-boyfriend on death row."

"I assume that whoever shot him on the courthouse steps wanted him dead before he could testify in a drug trial, a trial that has nothing to do with Charlie Williams on death row. Now, after a near-death experience, he wants to clean the slate and confess . . . provide the identity of the person who killed Alexandria Cole, right?"

"Amen," said Father Callahan. "That's it."

"Who'd he say killed her?"

"He didn't say. Just told me the name of the victim. Soon as he gave me the victim's name, I remembered the case, and I wanted to call you. I asked that he write out the full confession—name names. As you know, St. Francis is within walking distance to the hospital. I'm going back there after he's out of recovery to pick up the statement."

"I need to see that statement."

O'Brien pinched the bridge of his nose. He had never heard of Sam Spelling. Most jailhouse snitches were repeat losers. Habitual liars. Cons used by corrupt defense attorneys to say they heard someone, someone other than the attorney's client, brag about committing the crime. O'Brien couldn't remember one doing the opposite—confessing that another inmate, especially one on death row, was innocent.

"Are you there, Sean?"

"You said he was going under the knife, right?"

"I spoke with the doctor. Spelling's in bad shape. Bullet barely missed his heart."

"Father, does anyone else know what Spelling told you? Does anyone know he's going to sign his name to a statement that reveals the killer's identity?"

"Don't think so. He whispered the details to me—the victim's name, where he found the murder weapon." Father Callahan paused. "I don't know if it's anything, but a reporter with *The Sentinel* approached me. He said his name was Brian Cook. Said he saw me speaking with Spelling. He wanted to know if Spelling knew who shot him."

"What did you tell the reporter?"

"Nothing. I said what was shared with me remains confidential."

"Did Spelling tell you where the murder weapon, the knife, is now?"

"He's putting that in his statement, too."

"If the knife still has detectable traces of the victim's blood, then we can tie it to the murder. If it has prints that match the identity of the person that Spelling says did it, we could have the killer."

"And the disbelievers say divine intervention isn't real." Father Callahan chuckled.

"Assuming Spelling is not lying, if he makes it through surgery, when the story's in the press whoever shot Spelling will know he didn't kill him. If the guy who hit Spelling is a pro, and there's a big payoff from taking Spelling out so he can't testify in the trial, the hit man might come back. He may kill Spelling before he can write out the details of who killed Alexandria Cole. That's if any of what he told you is true. I'll meet you there."

"If you're at the marina, you're an hour from the hospital. I'll call and see when Spelling's out of recovery, give him time to write the statement, and get with you. It'll probably be past dinner by then. Tell you what . . . you need to have the physical copy of this statement or letter. I'd like to see you. Meet me at St. Francis at eight o'clock tonight. I'll give you whatever Spelling wrote. You can take it from there."

"Okay, thanks."

"Good to hear your voice, Sean. I want to see you at Sunday service more often."

"I'd like that, too, Father, I really would."

O'Brien set his phone on the dashboard. He looked at Max, who stood on her hind legs, nose testing the marina air through the Jeep's open side window. The storm had passed and the sky was clear; a golden light clung in the air like an aged photograph, creating a temporary world without shadows. It was about forty-five minutes before sunset, and a three-quarter moon was already climbing above the marina bay.

O'Brien thought about the man he sent to death row—Charlie Williams. Was he innocent, and would he live long enough to see another full moon?

SEVEN

O'Brien locked his Jeep and started toward gate 7-F, the dock that led to where he kept his old boat moored. Max ran behind him, stopping to investigate the world with her nose. He walked by the Tiki Hut, an open-air bar disguised as a restaurant, which was adjacent to Ponce Marina. He could smell the scent of blackened grouper, garlic shrimp, and beer. A dozen tourists sat at the wooden tables, ate fish sandwiches, sipped from longneck bottles of beer, and watched seagulls fight for pieces of bread tossed in the marina water. The isinglass, which was lowered on rainy days, was rolled up, allowing a cross-breeze to carry the scent of seafood over the marina.

"Well, hello stranger," said Kim Davis, an attractive brunette who worked the bar. She was in her early forties, radiant smile, deep tan, and jeans that hugged every pore from her navel down. She smiled at O'Brien. "You look like you could use a beer."

"I'd like that, Kim, but I don't have time right now."

She wiped her hands on a towel, stepped out from behind the bar, and knelt down to greet Max, handing her a tiny piece of fried fish. "You are so darn cute!" Max's tail blurred as she gulped down the fish in a single bite. Kim stood, her eyes searching O'Brien's face. "So, if you don't mind my asking, did you attend a funeral?"

"An old case of mine has resurrected. I'm just trying to make sense of it."

"You want to talk about it? I'll be off in an hour."

O'Brien managed a smile. "I appreciate that, but I have to run. Come on, Max."

"If you get thirsty, I'll deliver to your boat." She smiled.

O'Brien smiled and stepped to the gate. He worked the combination lock and waited for Max to trot by him. As they walked down the long dock, O'Brien watched the charter fishing fleet churn through the pass. The party boats were filled with sunburned tourists who would soon be posing next to their catches.

O'Brien's boat, *Jupiter*, was a thirty-eight-foot Bayliner he'd bought for ten cents on the dollar in a Miami DEA auction. It was twenty years old when he bought it. He'd restored the boat, doing much of the work himself.

Docked two boats up from *Jupiter* was *Gibraltar*, a 42 Grand Banks trawler. Its owner, Dave Collins, bought the boat new and spent half his time on it, while spending the rest of the time in a beachside condo, the remnant he retained from his ex-wife during a territorial divorce war.

Collins was in his midsixties, thick chest and knotted arms from decades of exercise, full head of white air, inquisitive blue-gray pewter eyes, and always a four-day stubble on his face. He was chopping a large Vidalia onion in the galley when he saw O'Brien coming down the dock. Collins stepped onto his cockpit.

"Who's following whom? Miss Max and Sean, just in time for dinner. Is this the weekend you're replacing the zincs on *Jupiter*?"

"*Jupiter* needs some quality time, but now something's come up, and Max needs a dog sitter."

Collins chuckled. "You don't even have to ask. Hi, Max."

Max leaned in toward Collins, her nose quivering.

23

Dave said, "She smells the sauce I'm brewing. Nick Cronus gave me his special Old World recipe when he was in with a catch last week. I've got some fresh grouper to ladle it on. Come aboard. We'll eat and drink. Not necessarily in that order."

"I can't drink. I have to meet a priest tonight. Booze probably wouldn't go over too well, although I have plenty of reasons to get hammered." O'Brien knelt down by Max and scratched her behind the ears. He looked straight at Collins, his eyes searching his friend's face. "Dave, what's the biggest mistake you've ever made?"

"You want the top-ten list or just the one enormous fuckup I've thought about for the last few years?"

"Yeah, that one sounds like a qualifier."

"Staying too long at a job I didn't believe in anymore. Everybody is dealt the same deck of time, twenty-four/seven. If you're real dumb, you waste that deck, holding the cards too close, afraid to really gamble and do what you should. So you stay in the game too long and in the end you've only cheated yourself." Collins sipped his glass of red wine and added, "All right. Since we're fessin' up. Let's hear your mistake of a lifetime, although I've had considerably more time to screw up things than you."

O'Brien said, "In less than eighty-four hours, I could be the reason an innocent man dies."

EIGHT

D ave Collins put his wineglass down on the table in the center of the cockpit. He rubbed the end of a finger across the stubble of his right cheek, his eyes filled with challenge. He said, "We're talking about mistakes that have already happened, in the past tense. It sounds like yours is in the future. It's not a mistake yet."

"It's a horrific domino effect. The last one that falls is the execution of a potentially innocent man. The first one that started this was when I arrested the man eleven years ago. State's giving him a lethal cocktail. I have to do something to stop it."

Collins inhaled through his nostrils like a vacuum cleaner, his big chest swelling, and as he exhaled, a slight whistle sound came from his pursed lips. "Step aboard. This sounds like some deep defecation, my friend. I'll shut up and listen while I'm preparing 'Grouper Cronus Style.' You can begin at the beginning."

O'Brien lifted Max up, stepped into the cockpit, and followed Collins into the galley.

• • •

MAX SAT PATIENTLY, WATCHING Collins's every move as he prepared the food. He squeezed a cut lemon over a large piece of grouper as O'Brien was finishing the story. O'Brien left nothing out, telling him everything he could remember, from the murder scene to the jury returning with a guilty-as-charged verdict.

Collins closed the door to the small oven, sat on a bar stool, swirled the Syrah in his glass. "Okay, Sean . . . you believe this con, Sam Spelling, saw the killer, found the murder weapon, hid the knife, and blackmailed the killer eleven years ago?"

"Considering the circumstances, a deathbed confession with a priest I know well and trust, the fact that somebody took a shot at Spelling . . . maybe."

"But, as you said, you don't know if that shot was linked to Alexandria's murder . . . especially after more than a decade. It's probably to keep Spelling's testimony out of the drug trial. What else? I sense something beyond the confession."

"I always wondered if I got the right guy."

"Why?"

"The case was too easy. Some of the points didn't quite add up. The case against Charlie Williams was clean-cut, maybe too clean."

Collins sipped his wine, swallowed thoughtfully, and said, "Well, as you know, crimes of passion often are clean-cut in a dirty way. They usually don't start out to be a murder. The argument escalates, and the killer goes crazy. He or she usually shoots more than they have to. In the event a knife is the weapon of choice, they'll often repeatedly stab the victim beyond a single, fatal wound. The crime scenes are sloppy, but the trail leading to the killer is seldom sloppy, it's damn obvious."

"I think that was it. It was too obvious. Williams fit the profile, an agitated and jilted lover. A man desperate to have his true love back. He gets in a fight with her and kills her. With the exception of a bartender, who remembered serving him three fingers of straight bourbon near the time of Alexandria Cole's murder, he has no alibi to fit the time line. The forensic evidence leading to him was overwhelming."

O'Brien stood and walked around the boat's salon. A small color TV was on in the corner. The sound was turned down. O'Brien said, "And that's it!"

"What do you mean, 'that's it'?"

"That's what bugged me then about the investigation. Charlie Williams is a farm boy from North Carolina. He may have killed and butchered a few hogs on the family farm, but now I don't believe he killed Alexandria Cole. I think he was set up. The real killer is someone who knows forensics, a perp that's so good he can make it look like Williams did it."

"If so, what do you do now?"

"I meet Father Callahan. Get Spelling's written statement, assuming he can write after coming out of recovery."

"That's assuming he makes it to recovery."

"I know. I'm waiting for Father Callahan's call. Then I call Miami PD and let them quietly pick up whoever is named in the statement. Then I call the governor's office. He issues a stay of execution, and Charlie Williams is released. We put the real killer on trial, and I finish a bottle of Irish whiskey and try to forget why I ever got into law enforcement in the first place. If I did send the wrong man to prison . . . how the hell do I make that up to him?"

Dave said nothing, his eyes filled with thought.

O'Brien looked at the television. He saw a reporter standing in front of Baptist Hospital. "Where's the sound?"

"Second button on the right."

O'Brien turned up the sound in time to hear the reporter say, "Police still don't know who took the fatal shot that killed Sam Spelling, a man whose testimony was, according to prosecutors, key in the high-profile bank robbery and cocaine trial of Spelling's former partner, Larry Kirkman, and three other men believed tied to a Miami crime family. Despite undergoing three hours of surgery, Spelling died later in his hospital room due to complications from a rifle bullet that officials said hit him in the chest. Now police have a homicide on their hands with very few clues to go on at this time. This is Jeremy Levy, News Eleven."

O'Brien reached for his cell phone, quickly hitting buttons.

"What's the urgency, Sean? You calling that reporter's boss, something he said?"

"Yes, it was something he said. I'm not calling the television station, I'm calling Father Callahan."

"Why?"

"Because Father Callahan was supposed to call me when Spelling went into recovery, or at least when he was coming out of it."

"It looks like Spelling never recovered. It happens."

"But why hasn't Callahan called? That worries me. The reporter said Spelling died after surgery in his hospital room. I want to make sure Spelling died from a gunshot wound."

NINE

Detective Dan Grant, African-American, tall, broad shouldered, light skinned, held a television remote control. He pointed it toward a TV as another detective and two officers watched the newscasts from a doctors' lounge in the hospital. Grant flipped through channels and saw the story on the other stations. He turned to the detective, a smaller wiry man, and said, "Let's hope this buys us time. We'll keep an officer at Spelling's door."

SAM SPELLING'S RIGHT HAND trembled so much he didn't know if he could finish the letter. An IV was taped to the back of his hand. He was glad he'd started writing in block letters. A kindly nurse, a few months shy of retirement, had given him a pad of lined paper, legal size. Spelling wanted to keep what he had to say to a single page. After surgery, after recovery, his chest felt as if an iron vice were squeezing it. *You brought me outta there alive, God. I'm gonna do my end. Get this done for Father John.*

As he started writing, he heard muffled talking outside his hospital room door and the sound of a chair sliding on the tile. The deputy who had stationed himself there was probably being replaced, he thought. Spelling looked at the bandage across his chest. In the center, near his heart, he could see a rust-colored spot the size of a quarter. He could smell the coppery odor of wet blood and adhesive. He continued writing.

A pain shot from his chest to his jaw. His heart fluttered. The monitor on the left side of the bed sounded. Then his heart jumped into sync, a steady beat, and the machine silenced. Spelling felt like he had sand on his tongue. With his left hand cuffed to the bed, he used his right hand to hold the pad of paper in place on the tray as he wrote.

The door opened. Spelling glanced up to see that the guard, Lyle Johnson, had returned. Before the door shut, he saw a deputy in the hall yawn and stretch.

As Johnson stepped inside the small room he said, "D . . . O . . . C back on duty." The guard held a large foam cup of steaming coffee. "Kinda funny how the abbreviation for Department of Corrections is short for doctor."

Spelling said nothing. He continued writing.

Johnson snorted and stepped to the window overlooking the parking lot. "Writing your last will and testament, huh? All your worldly possessions, something like that?"

"Why don't you get outta here?"

"You cons are all the same. Still think you're entitled to privacy in lockup."

"Look man, I've been shot. I had surgery. I'm chained to the fuckin' bed. My heart is sick. I'm not goin' anywhere. Just leave me be, okay?"

"That's called justice, what's happened to you, Spelling."

There was a knock at the door.

"It's open," said the guard.

Detective Dan Grant entered the room. He lifted the right side of his sports coat, displaying a gold badge clipped to his belt. "Dan Grant, homicide, Volusia County."

"I ain't killed nobody, and I ain't dead yet," Spelling said.

Grant smiled and stepped toward the bed. "No, you're not. But for the sake of your protection, we'll pretend that you are. Whoever took a shot at you wanted you dead." He looked at Johnson. "Would you excuse us?"

The guard took his time securing the plastic lid on the foam cup, glanced at the paper under Spelling's hand, and left the room.

Grant turned back to Spelling. "Who wants you dead?"

Spelling sighed. "I guess I've made my share of enemies over the years. FBI finally caught my partner in the last bank job we pulled. He managed to stay hid till he got sloppy. I'm sure you know I was being taken to the courthouse to testify against him. Maybe Larry or one of his scumbags hired the hit. He's been in jail for more than eight months waiting trial."

"Maybe he had somebody on the outside to plan it, someone to arrange a hit."

"Possibility. We weren't friends. Business partners, that's all."

"He just managed to stay in business longer than you, right?"

"Larry liked selling lots of dope, too."

"Who else might want you dead?"

Spelling looked at the paper he'd finished writing. He was silent, his eyes flat. "Who knows? All I really know is, there's lots of evil all around us. It's a tragedy for a man to go to his grave never knowing who he really is. We're too stupid to get it right until it's about all used up. I ain't afraid to die. No sir, not now. Not after what I saw."

As the evening sunset broke through a patch of pewter clouds, light seemed to flow into the room like organic energy. Spelling looked toward the window and smiled. He saw a sparrow alight on the windowsill outside the room. "Bird's hurt."

Grant looked at the bird.

Spelling said, "Missing a foot. Little fella has to stand on one leg. He's a peg leg, but he's still got his wings."

Spelling signed his name on the bottom of the paper beneath his hands. He folded the paper and wrote on the outside in bold block letters:

CONFIDENTIAL: FOR FATHER JOHN CALLAHAN

Spelling held the paper. "Detective Grant, this is my ticket."

"Ticket?"

"It's my ticket to fly just like that little bird out there on the window. Don't know if I'll fly to heaven, but I'm hopin' this will get me my wings."

"What is it?"

"It's something a priest asked me to write. It's nothing about Larry's trial. More like my own personal confession. Priest is comin' to get it. Detective, would you be kind enough to drop this in that bag with my clothes. All I got left in this world is what's in that sack." Spelling smiled through cracked lips. Blood, the color of dried tobacco juice, lined his lower lip. "But that's all I really need."

Two nurses entered the room. One said, "We have to change bandages and give the patient medication. He must sleep now."

Detective Grant nodded. He took the piece of folded paper and dropped it in the bag. As he started to leave the room, Spelling said, "Detective, anything happen to me . . . if I don't make it. You go see Father John Callahan. And do it real quick."

As the nurses hovered around Spelling, attending to his wound, he looked at the sparrow just beyond the window glass. The bird hopped on one foot to the ledge, stretched its wings, and flew toward the light in the western sky. Sam Spelling smiled.

TEN

Guard Lyle Johnson waited twenty minutes. Spelling ought to be sleeping about now, he thought. Johnson swallowed the last bit of cold coffee in the foam cup and walked into Sam Spelling's room. Johnson's Department of Corrections black shoes made a hollow sound as he stepped to the nightstand.

The caffeine and Dexedrine put him on edge. His hands were moist, mind racing. *A con getting better medical treatment than most taxpayers. All because he was shot. Nineteen years wearing a corrections officer uniform—a job that wouldn't get a private hospital room. Maybe it's 'cause of the damn media—the shooting—all over the news. Maybe it was 'cause nobody gives a shit about the nobodies.*

He peered into the brown sack, reached in, and lifted out the folded paper. Johnson looked over his shoulder at the closed door. He opened the paper and began reading. The further down the page he got, the wider his eyes became. Johnson let out a low whistle and mumbled, "Un-fuckin' believable."

"What are you doing?"

Lyle Johnson spun around. Father John Callahan stood at the door with his arms folded over his chest.

"Nothing," Johnson said, lowering his hand with the paper.

"What do you have there?"

"Nothing."

Father Callahan stepped closer. He could read his name on the yellow legal paper. He said, "As an officer with the state, I would think that security, confidentiality, would mean something to you. That's marked for me—confidential."

"With all due respect, preacher, no such thing as personal property for an inmate."

"You're not holding personal property, you're holding a private letter, a confession, addressed to me. I asked that man to write it. As a spiritual confession, it's a sacred trust between God and one of his children."

Johnson said nothing. He made no effort to move.

"Give it to me. That man, regardless of his past, is trying to make amends with our Lord. This could be his last statement—his last wish on earth. I won't let you deny him, because right now God's law supersedes your regulations."

Johnson's eyelids lowered, a red patch forming on his bull neck. He slowly lifted the piece of paper. "Take it. I didn't read it anyway."

Father Callahan took the paper and placed it between the pages of the Bible he carried. He glanced down at Spelling, who was in a deep, drug-induced sleep, his breathing slow, the mechanical pulses thumping. Monitors filled the room with a bluish tint. He looked at Johnson's name tag and said, "I'm praying for this man. He's more than a prison number. His name's Sam Spelling. And, Mr. Johnson, I will pray for you, too."

Johnson snorted, turned around, and left the room. Father Callahan watched Spelling sleep a moment. He placed his hand on Spelling's forehead and whispered, "Our heavenly Father, you kept this man well under surgery. You have a larger purpose for him, I pray, and I pray that he will live the rest of his life in service to you. Amen."

ELEVEN

Lyle Johnson sat in a remote corner of the hospital snack bar and rewrote what he remembered reading in Sam Spelling's letter. There was only one other person sitting at a table, a woman finishing a piece of pie. She got up and walked to a coffee dispenser less than twenty feet away. Johnson saw that she had left her book and cell phone on the table. He strolled by the table, lifted her phone, and exited the hospital.

Outside, Johnson stepped into a memorial garden with blooming roses and a three-tiered water fountain that splashed into a concrete base dotted with coins. There were no patients or family members outside. He was alone. He sat on one of the benches and thought about what he would say. Not often does an opportunity like this fall into a workingman's hands. *No way to live the rest of life—retiring on a state pension and having to work security for Walmart until you die.*

He would do it. He could do it. After all, a stupid con like Spelling had done it, and he'd kept the secret for years. Johnson lifted the stolen cell phone out of his pocket. He knew where the person worked. *Spelling had spelled it all out.* All he had to do was call—one call to change his life. *Easy. Fuckin' A.* Then why was his hand shaking so much he thought he would drop the phone?

Get a grip!

JOHNSON WAS SURPRISED. The voice on the phone was calm. Too calm. After he introduced himself, Johnson said, "You seem like a very reasonable man."

"You have the wrong person, Mr. Johnson."

Johnson nodded. "I knew you'd say that on the phone. So I'll do most of the talking. I'm not greedy. I just figure, according to Sam Spelling's note, if you gave him a hundred grand to keep quiet eleven years ago, your secret ought to be worth even a little more today. You know—inflation—cost of doin' business."

"I'll play along with a prank call for a moment. How'd you get my number?"

"Spelling had your number, pal. In a lot of ways he had your number. Now I got it, but I can be forgetful, very forgetful, just ask my wife. Here's the deal: you get the written statement I stole from Spelling's room. I get two hundred grand to go away forever. The state executes Charlie Williams in a few days. A few weeks later, nobody remembers his name."

"Who else have you shared this prank—this alleged letter—with?"

Johnson was silent a moment. "Nobody, except maybe that priest, Callahan. And I didn't share shit with him. He's the priest that heard Spelling make a deathbed confession. Exactly what he said, I don't know. But this is a hard-core priest, one of 'em guys who keep spilled shit between them and God. Nobody else. Don't sweat it. I have the shit on paper, the statement in Spelling's own handwriting."

The voice on the phone was silent.

Johnson said, "Meet me tonight. Midnight. Bring the money."

"Where? I ask this only because I may send the police there."

"Sure you will. Listen, asshole. Be there! It's an old pioneer village

36

at the corner of State Road 46 and 76 near Pierson. It's under rehab. There's a replica of an old general store. Meet me on the store's porch. In that letter, Spelling says where he found the murder weapon—your murder weapon. And he tells where it's been hidden all these years for safekeeping. I know where to find it. Don't be late."

Lyle Johnson disconnected, a smile working at the corner of his mouth. He fished out a quarter from his pocket, tossing the coin in the fountain. "My wish is comin' true."

TWELVE

Father Callahan walked quickly down the long hospital corridor. Turning the corner, he almost ran into the ER doctor he'd met earlier. The doctor was walking with another man, older, white hair, tired but compassionate eyes. Father Callahan said, "Congratulations on the successful surgery of Sam Spelling."

The ER doctor nodded and said, "It was Dr. Strassberg here who performed the operation."

Dr. Strassberg looked at the priest. A tiny speck of dried blood was in a lower part of the doctor's glasses. He said, "I always ask for a little help upstairs, Father."

"Indeed. What is Mr. Spelling's prognosis?"

"Bullet was a clean shot. Hit no major arteries. But the heart was long suffering from atherosclerosis. We did a triple bypass. He'll live. How long, though . . . Father, you're closer to that answer than me. But he'll be okay. He'll walk out of here."

"I'll pray for his recovery."

The doctors left, and Father Callahan started to dial his cell phone. He saw the tiny battery icon. It was down to the last bar. Two men approached. One was a uniformed officer. The other was African-American, tall, sports coat and tie. His jacket had a slight budge on the left. Callahan recognized him from the ER lobby area.

"Excuse me, Father," said the plainclothes man.

"Yes?"

"I'm Detective Grant, investigating the attempted murder of Sam Spelling."

"It looks like the offender wasn't successful. The doctor just told me Sam Spelling is going to pull through. He's turned the corner with his life. And our Lord had a bit to do with it."

"Then we don't have a homicide, only a shooting. A nurse said you were in his room earlier."

"I was in the emergency room earlier, too. Not long after he'd been shot."

"Did he tell you anything?"

"You mean who tried to kill him?"

"That's a good start."

"No. He did ask for forgiveness. I listened to a private confession."

"Might any of that confession lead us to the shooter?"

"I'm not a police investigator, but I highly doubt it. His concern was more of seeking our Lord for strength, love, and ultimate forgiveness for his sins."

"Did he suggest who might have shot him?"

"No."

"Father, if you are approached by the media—there are still some TV trucks in the lot—please don't say anything that will indicate Spelling is still alive."

"Why?"

"We don't want the shooter to know he failed."

"I can't lie."

"I'm not asking you to."

"What are you suggesting, Detective?"

"Spelling's testimony is crucial in the trial. If his shooter believes

39

Spelling did die, then he won't try again. Spelling can heal in a safe area and be brought in to testify in a couple of weeks. Working with the Florida Department of Law Enforcement we've indicated his recovery was not successful."

Father Callahan was quiet for a moment. He said, "I see."

"Thank you, Father."

As the detective and the officer turned to go back down the hall, Father Callahan said, "I was approached by one reporter in the ER earlier, a man."

"Oh, what did he ask?"

"I think he saw Sam Spelling making a confession to me, and he wanted to know what he said. Of course, I told him that was confidential. The reporter is with *The Sentinel*. Said his name is Brian Cook."

Detective Grant looked up at a security camera for a second. He said, "The guy must be new. I know their crime reporters. Don't recognize the name. Do you have a card?"

"I do. Here you go. My lips are sealed, Detective. Good night." Father Callahan started to walk down the corridor. Then Grant asked, "Father, there was a Department of Corrections officer posted at Spelling's door. He's not there. Have you seen him?"

"Maybe he took a break. Sam Spelling will be in recovery for some time."

"No doubt. It's just that Deputy Gleason is here to relieve the guard."

"If I see him, I'll pass that along."

As Callahan walked down the hall, Deputy Gleason noticed that the priest had a slight limp. The left foot. Almost undetectable, but it was there.

THIRTEEN

Charlie Williams paced in his tiny world like a trapped animal. He walked from the steel bars to the thick wall of reinforced concrete, back and forth. A cage, eight by nine feet, had been his home for more than ten years. Soon they would be moving him to another cell, this one closer to the death chamber. At thirty-three, he felt like fifty-three. Face and body now a scarecrow. His hair had turned gray. The dark circles under his eyes never faded. His stomach burned as if a pipe constantly leaked acid. He could feel his rib cage under his skin. Weight dropping because food seemed almost obscene as the state readied him to die.

He stopped pacing and looked at the picture of Alexandria Cole. It sat next to a photograph of Charlie and his mother. In the picture, he was a boy holding his mother's hand on the banks of the New River in North Carolina. It was where the family went weekends in the summer. It was where Charlie Williams learned to swim—where he was baptized. Now he felt like a man drowning.

He stepped to the small steel shelf and picked up the picture of Alexandria and said, "You know I didn't do it. You're probably the only one who knows that—just you and the bastard who really did it. But you can't tell a soul. I miss you, Lexie. Looks like I'll be joining you soon, baby. Maybe I can get it right with you in the next world."

A single tear rolled down his cheek and splashed across the forever smiling face of Alexandria Cole.

FATHER CALLAHAN WALKED OUT of the front entrance to Baptist Hospital, said good night to a security guard, and looked around for any reporters. Two TV news satellite trucks sat in the parking lot, their diesels humming, engineers adjusting antennas while reporters scribbled notes and spoke loudly into cell phones.

Father Callahan carried his Bible in his pocket and an umbrella in one hand as he walked from the hospital down the city streets toward his church. Dark clouds rolled over the moon as if a candle had been snuffed out. Lightning flickered in the distance. He opened his cell phone to dial Sean O'Brien's number. Before he could punch the keys, the phone rang.

"Hello," Father Callahan said.

"Father, this is Detective Grant. I wanted to make sure I heard you correctly. What did you say was the name of the *Sentinel* reporter?"

"Brian Cook."

"I just called *The Sentinel.* The only Brian Cook they have is the food writer."

"That's strange. I'm sure that's the name he gave me. He looked legitimate. Carried a copy of the newspaper folded under one arm. Had one of those reporter's notebooks and a pen."

"He probably got the name of the food guy right out of the paper. He's an imposter."

"I don't follow you, Detective."

"I think the guy you spoke with is the man who tried to kill Sam Spelling."

FOURTEEN

Father Callahan disconnected with the detective, stopped under a street lamp to see the numbers on his phone as the battery grew weaker. He punched in Sean O'Brien's number. "Sean, are you near? My phone battery's about to die."

"Be there soon, Father. Bad storm's moving your way. It blew down a tree across State Road 44. I'm in my Jeep. I'll go around the cars and cops. I'll just be a few minutes late."

"I just spoke with a detective. He said the reporter who approached me in the ER lobby was an imposter."

"What?"

"The detective said he believes the man was the same person who shot Sam Spelling. Spelling's letter says . . . Sean, can you hear me?"

Between the storm and the weak battery O'Brien lost contact. The broken connection gave him an eerie feeling and he stepped on the gas.

DEPUTY TIM GLEASON WAS hoping to get a final refill of his coffee when he saw a priest approaching, walking down the long hospital corridor. There was something different about the way Father Callahan walked. The slight give to the left foot was gone. Now he moved with an aggressive step. He had a more determined gait than when he'd spoken with Gleason and Detective Grant earlier.

Deputy Gleason could then see the man approaching wasn't Father Callahan. This man wore a fedora hat. Could be because of the pouring rain, thought Gleason. The priest had wider shoulders, neatly trimmed dark beard, and black frame glasses.

Maybe priests have a shift rotation, too. Maybe he is from a different church.

The priest stopped a few feet away from the door to Spelling's room.

Deputy Gleason stood and said, "He's still out of it, Father."

The priest nodded. In a low whisper he said, "Sometimes just a voice, the word of God, can penetrate a sleeping man's soul. The power of prayer aids recovery."

The veiled black eyes held on Gleason. The deputy felt tension and embarrassment at the same time. There was something about this priest that didn't seem right—but he was a man of God, and who was Gleason to judge him?

"Father, I'm a firm believer in prayer for healing the sick."

"Bless you, my son."

"Thank you, Father." Deputy Gleason stepped aside. "You can go on in."

"Thank you. Please open the door. I hurt my wrist playing tennis."

FIFTEEN

Sam Spelling dreamed in shades of red, pink, yellow, and purple, like film processed in morphine and projected through stained glass onto the front of his brain. He saw himself in waders fishing a Montana stream, the cool air traveling deep into his lungs. He pulled a bull trout from the water, the iridescent colors bright and alive. Spelling removed the hook and lowered the fish back into the clear stream.

He smiled and slowly opened his eyes. The morphine dripped from the IV into Spelling's bloodstream, and it was as if he were looking though opaque glass, smoky, clouded.

A man dressed in black stood next to Spelling's bed.

"Father?" he asked. "Is that you, Father John?" Spelling smiled. "You said you'd come back." He coughed. His chest pounded, his vision growing watery.

"Yes, it's me. Good to see you again, Sam."

The voice.

Even through the fog of drugs, Spelling could tell the voice didn't come from Father Callahan.

Spelling opened his eyes as wide as he could. *Focus.* The man wore a hat and a priest collar—but the face. He couldn't see the face clearly. Vision blurred from drugs. But the man's voice was there. He remembered where he'd heard it. "It's you!"

"Who else?" The man stepped closer and leaned over the bed.

"Get away from me! Guard!" Spelling's lungs were too weak to scream. He could only whisper. "Why are you here?"

"I think you know why. You are the reason I'm here. You decided to talk after all these years, eh? I'm so disappointed. I compensated you. We had a nice little agreement. Then, after you blew all the money, wound up back in prison, I get a note from you. Clever how you got your letter mailed out of prison without raising eyebrows. Your coding was exceptional—suggesting that I visit your mother's home to exchange Christmas gifts. Impressive. After I read it, though, I knew you were about to cause me a lot of trouble, and I'd never be safe with you alive because you violated our agreement. Too bad the rifle bullet didn't take out your heart. I aimed for it."

Spelling wanted to crawl out of bed. "It was you! You shot me?"

"Even you find it hard to believe. That's good. The police will never figure it out. When the marshals delivered you to the courthouse to testify in a drug trial, it gave me the perfect opportunity to take you out. No one, not even you, would have suspected it was tied to a murder years before. Timing is almost everything in life . . . and death. You've got a really big mouth that must be sealed . . . forever."

Spelling looked to his left and then to his right, his eyes searching. *Where's the emergency button?* "Get away from me!" Spelling's heart hammered in his chest, the pain crushed him in a vice, the taste of metal erupting from his stomach like butane.

"You've become quite a liability, Sammy. Having little heart palpitations, are we? Perhaps it's time for our bedside prayer."

"No!"

"You can say a nice prayer in the time it'll take you to die. And you should begin right now. Shhhh, it's painless. You will go to sleep. This is how I seal big mouths."

Sam Spelling struggled as the man placed a wide hand over his mouth and pinched his nose. His lungs burned. His blood was so flooded with drugs, his heart rate barely increased, but his nervous system raced. *Where were they? Somebody!* The single handcuff restrained his free arm. He struggled and felt stitches rip in his chest, the heat of his blood flowing across his stomach like warm soup. He could see the digital white light from the monitor reflecting off the killer's wide eyes—eyes the blackness of coal. He could see his own heartbeat beginning to slow, the reflection fading from the eyes like a flashlight dimming. His mind flashed back to the evil in the eyes he saw when he was dying in the emergency room. Now he saw the bull trout's eyes, its mouth gasping for air, its body thrusting. He held the trout under the stream, a calmness returning to the fish. Then he released it and watched the trout swim into the cool translucence.

Spelling smiled. The little sparrow with the lost foot had returned to the windowsill. Spelling saw himself open the window. He reached down and cupped the tiny bird in his hand. It was as light as a cracker and its heart raced. *"You're okay, little bird. You've got wings. I do, too."*

Sam Spelling jumped from the windowsill, soaring over the parking lot, flapping his wings, feeling the heat of the morning sunrise as he flew toward the light.

SIXTEEN

Father John Callahan stood in the sanctuary of St. Francis Church and lit seven candles. Lightning, from a storm blowing off the Atlantic coast, illuminated the sanctuary's massive stained-glass windows. The priest stepped toward a marble statue of the Virgin Mary, made the sign of the cross, and whispered a prayer. He reached inside his coat pocket and retrieved the letter. He wanted to read Sam Spelling's letter one more time before Sean O'Brien arrived.

As he finished reading, Callahan stood next to the pulpit and folded the letter once in the center of the paper. He opened the large Bible that sat on the podium, and he carefully placed the letter in the reading of The Revelation of St. John, slowly closing the Bible.

Lightning struck close to the church, the sound of thunder exploding and rumbling like echoes bouncing off canyon walls in the night. The lights in the church flickered and faded out. Father Callahan found a lighter, lit a candle, and picked up the church phone. No dial tone. He lit more candles. He plugged his cell phone in the charger just as he heard a noise. He looked up to see the back door to the sanctuary open, the wind blowing rain into the dark alcove.

"Thought I locked that," he said, walking toward the rear of the church to close the door, the chill of wind and the smell of rain meeting him.

Lightning popped and the wind blew rainwater into the hall. Father Callahan glanced in the direction of the alcove to see a man step out from the shadows, the burning candles tossing a soft light on the left side of his face.

"Who enters the house of our Lord?" Father Callahan asked.

The man was silent.

Father Callahan assumed the bearded stranger, who wore a hat pulled down low, was homeless, someone needing a dry place until the storm passed. He had always extended a helping hand to the homeless, but as he walked toward the new arrival, he could tell the man was not a homeless person.

He was a priest.

"Welcome," Father Callahan said. "Glad you could duck out of the rain on a night like this. Just took me ol' nerves back a notch. Most folks come in the front door."

The man said nothing.

O'BRIEN LOOKED AT THE GPS navigation map on the screen in his Jeep. He signaled, pulled off the highway, and drove on the right shoulder. Drivers hit their car horns. One man in a pickup truck gave O'Brien the finger as he sped past.

O'Brien pulled completely off the shoulder, driving through a pine thicket, the limbs slapping at his window, the birds scattering. He looked at the navigation map, cutting the wheel to the right, following under the clearing of a high-tension power line for less than a half mile, and then he drove down a slight embankment that connected to a paved road, SR 46. He tried the priest's cell again. No answer.

SEVENTEEN

Father Callahan's cell rang as he turned toward the stranger. "Regardless of your point of entry, I'm delighted that a fellow priest is visiting. Not the best of nights for a social, but please enter our Lord's house. You must be soaked. I can put on some tea, shot of brandy perhaps. I have a change of clothes that ought to match yours well. What brings you to St. Francis?"

Still, the man said nothing, the sound of the rain pelting the parking lot.

"Would you'd be good enough to close the door? At least you can step from the shadows and show yourself. All we have is good old-fashioned candle power, but for hundreds of years it was all the church needed."

The man said, "No need for tea or brandy. No need to shut the door, for that matter. I won't be staying long." He stepped out of the recess, the long shadows from candlelight dancing off his face. Father Callahan could not see the man's features.

But he did recognize the voice.

Stall him. Sean's almost here.

Father Callahan said, "I detect a very slight accent. Are you from Greece?"

"That's impressive, Father. Very few people can pick that up. I was born there. One of the islands."

"I've studied linguistics and art history. Which island?"

"Patmos."

"Indeed, the sacred island. The place where Saint John wrote Revelation."

The man said nothing.

"Odd," Father Callahan said, "that you're Episcopalian rather than Greek Orthodox."

"I'm neither. Where's the letter?"

"Letter? What letter?"

"The one Spelling wrote."

"Perhaps you're mistaken."

"Where's the letter? Answer me!"

"So you're the one who took the life of the young woman, Alexandria Cole."

"I'll also claim yours. Give me the letter!" The man pulled a pistol.

"Please, like a confession, it's in God's ear . . . and his forgiving heart."

Father Callahan's cell rang, the sound ricocheting in the farthest reaches of the old sanctuary. Father Callahan turned to run to his phone. The intruder fired two shots into the priest's back. Father Callahan fell, the bullets hitting him like sledgehammers.

Father Callahan lay on the marble floor a second. He slowly crawled in the direction of the altar. He knew he was going into shock. The darkness was descending—the cell ringing reverberating in his ears. He could crawl no farther, stopping at the first marble step, the right side of his face now against the chill of the stone.

Father Callahan felt his wallet being removed from his back pocket, coat pockets searched. Lying on his stomach, he sensed the man step over him, approaching the altar. There was the sound of crashing. He could hear the coins and dollars stolen from the poor box.

Father Callahan fought the rising darkness.

He's making it look like a robbery.

Sweat stung his eyes. He could feel his blood pumping onto the floor. He knew one bullet had exited through the right side of his chest, his body fluids seeping across the white marble. In thirty seconds, the blood pooled close to his face.

The shooter opened the door to Father Callahan's study and began searching through his desk. He pulled out drawers and rifled through papers.

Father Callahan felt his heart racing. *Stay awake. Sean O'Brien will be here soon. Hold on. Just breathe. Easy. In and out . . . breathe.*

He could taste the blood in his mouth; the gases, fueled by fear and adrenaline, boiled in his gut. Father Callahan dipped the end of one finger into his blood. He began to write on the marble. His hand shook and he concentrated hard to control his trembling finger. Sweat dripped from his face. He could not get enough air into his lungs. Slowly, his finger moved across the marble, leaving a note in blood.

The man in the priest's study saw car lights rake across the window. He ran from the study, bolting by Father Callahan, the sound of his shoes hitting the marble floor hard as he sprinted to the back door. The man stepped into the dark, leaving the door open.

As Father Callahan wrote, he whispered, "Our Father, who art in heaven . . . hallowed be thy name . . . thy kingdom come . . . thy will be done on earth as . . . as it is in heaven . . ."

Thunder boomed with the ferocity of a mortar round exploding outside the church. The rain sounded like hail pelting the roof.

". . . give us this day our daily bread . . ."

Stay awake. Write!

His strength was fading, the energy—the life—seeping out of his pores. He could move only his eyes. He looked at the stained-glass windows, backlit from lightning.

". . . and forgive us our trespasses . . . as we forgive those who trespass against us . . ."

Father Callahan felt the chill of the night air, the dark and dampness blowing through the open back door, brushing like ghostly fingers against his face. The draft caused candles to flicker, light and shadow dancing across the sanctuary.

An explosion of thunder shook the foundation of the church. Father Callahan looked up at the stained-glass window as streaks of lightning ignited dark sky. Through the radiance, he could see the face of Christ in the glass.

"And lead us not into temptation . . . but deliver us from evil. . . . Amen."

The pulse of lightning ended, but the face on the stained glass lingered in Father Callahan's mind for a few seconds, then faded like a dream. His index finger quivered a beat and became still.

A single drop of blood fell from the tip of Father Callahan's finger and splashed onto the marble.

EIGHTEEN

O'Brien drove through the St. Francis Church parking lot and thought about the last time he attended service. It was a couple of months after the death of Sherri.

He had moved back to central Florida, trying to reconnect with those things he knew growing up. Father Callahan was one of those things—one of those people. He was a special man—a man who loves unconditionally and lives large, splicing his covenant to God into his relationship with people. When O'Brien was trying to come to grips with his wife's death, Father Callahan had been there for him.

"*It's all about loving and being loved,*" O'Brien remembered Father Callahan telling him. "*It's in your heart, Sean. That's what made you a good detective. Justice begins in a virtuous heart. It's one thing that won't leave you. Talent will. Even memory will drift, however, character of heart remains true to you, because it is you.*"

Somewhere along the line, somewhere between the war in the Gulf, the body counts on the streets and the heinous evil in the dull-eyed killers he tracked down, the death of his wife—somewhere in it all, O'Brien had lost something. Father Callahan had tried to help him find it.

Maybe he still could, O'Brien thought.

Maybe Father Callahan was sitting in his study knocking back an Irish whiskey and didn't hear his cell phone.

Maybe all of O'Brien's cop instincts—the signs—were wrong. Maybe Sam Spelling really had died from complications caused by the shooting.

Maybe if he'd gotten it right eleven years ago, he wouldn't be trying to save a kind, loving man's life—a priest's life. *God, let me get there in time!*

O'Brien shut off the Jeep's engine and rolled to a quiet stop beneath an oak tree in the east side of the parking lot, the farthest corner away from the sanctuary.

He chambered a bullet in his Glock, got out of the Jeep, and crouched by its rear bumper for a few seconds. He wanted to listen beyond the rain: to listen for anything moving, someone running, a car starting, a dog barking.

There was only the patter of rain off the canvas top of his Jeep.

O'Brien started toward the annex section of the church, keeping away from the streetlights and hanging close to a row of shrubs. He ran along the wall of the building, coming to a breezeway that separated the two structures. Something moved.

O'Brien leveled his pistol as a cat bolted from the breezeway and ran behind a Dumpster. He saw Father Callahan's white Toyota in the parking lot. There were no other cars. There seemed to be a dim light, possibly coming from burning candles inside the sanctuary, the light barely illuminating the stained-glass windows.

O'Brien held the Glock in his right hand and slowly opened the sanctuary door with his left. Then he gripped the pistol with both hands. He listened for the slightest sound. Sweat dripped through his chest hair. He moved silently down the entrance foyer and around the atrium that led to the sanctuary. He could smell burning candles. There was the lingering smoky scent of incense and something else. He could almost feel it. It came to him after years of shifting through crime scenes, a sixth sense of sorts—an inner sonar that detected death before he saw it. It was the way time stood still at a murder scene. The spool of life caught in a macabre freeze-frame. The grisly still image often laced with the coppery smell of blood and the inherent odor of death.

O'Brien's heart raced. As he stepped around the corner of the vestibule, he held his breath and listened. There was only the sound of rain. Nothing he had investigated in the past prepared him for what he saw as he entered the sanctuary.

Father John Callahan was lying facedown in a pool of blood.

The flickering candles caused shadows to move eerily across the paintings of saints and angels, a marble statue of the Virgin Mary, Moses with the Ten Commandments, and images of Jesus Christ on the cross. Lightning in the distance backlit a stained-glass window depicting three wise men following a star in the sky near the town of Bethlehem.

O'Brien wanted to run to Father Callahan, but, even from across the sanctuary, he could tell his old friend was dead.

O'Brien labored to control his breathing. He pointed the Glock in corners and at darting shadows cast by the candles. Nothing else moved. He could hear the rain falling near an open back door, the drops thumping the gutter and falling into parking lot puddles. Instinct told him the killer was no longer in the church. Probably fled the way he'd entered, through the rear door. Nevertheless, he still checked darkened crevices, tried locked doors. Nothing.

O'Brien ran to Father Callahan. He could see the wallet tossed on the floor. He remembered a gold cross that adorned the altar. It was gone. O'Brien wanted to scream. His head pounded. He felt a wave of nausea travel from his stomach to his throat. His friend was slaughtered in a church.

O'Brien knew it wasn't a robbery. He knew it because the same man who killed Alexandria Cole eleven years ago had left a deliberate trail to an innocent man, and now he had killed one of the most compassionate men O'Brien had ever known.

As he came within a few feet of the body, he stopped and placed a finger on Father Callahan's neck. Two bullet wounds to the back. No pulse. O'Brien fought the urge to scream, to curse. How could this happen to this man? A man of God? O'Brien spotted something scrawled near the left hand. Father Callahan's thumb and small finger were bent under his hand. Only his other three fingers were extended. And next to his hand was a message Father Callahan had managed to scrawl in his own blood. O'Brien felt the message was left for him—a clue and warning.

O'Brien slowly stood. A milky shaft of diffused light seemed to float through the skylight in the high ceiling. The rain stopped and the dark clouds dissolved in front of the moon. A soft beam fell across a statute of the Virgin Mary near the altar, illuminating the face. O'Brien looked into the unblinking eyes of Jesus' mother. Then he looked down at the body of Father John Callahan. O'Brien wanted to pray, and he wanted to scream, but he could do neither. He felt empty. Very alone.

His hand shook, eyes now welling with tears, as he slowly reached out to touch the priest's shoulder. "I am so sorry, Father . . . sorry this happened to you . . . it is unforgivable . . . and I'm to blame." He stood, holding his clenched fists by his side. His eyes closed tight, trying to shut out the aberrant, the absolute isolation he felt as the horror of Father Callahan's murder fell around him with a numbing silence of moving shadows cast by candle flames.

A cloud parted from the moon when O'Brien looked up at Mary's face, the light hitting her eyes. It was a connection that locked into something deep within O'Brien. It was ethereal and yet caring. His eyes burned for a moment as he looked at Mary's face, and he felt a single drop of sweat inching down the center of his back.

O'Brien turned and walked out of the church into the cool night air. He lifted his cell off his belt and sat down on the steps to dial 911. Where would he begin the explanation of the scene inside the church? What did the message mean . . . the circle drawing? The 666 and the letters P-A-T with the letter omega from the Greek alphabet? Were the numbers 666 supposed to be the biblical "sign of the beast"? Was *Pat* the killer's name, or his initials? The crude drawing? What had Father Callahan meant? *Think*.

The clouds parted and the three-quarter moon revealed itself. O'Brien could see it was slightly more rounded than yesterday. It would be a full moon this time next week. Unless O'Brien caught a killer, Charlie Williams would be executed before a full moon rose over the Atlantic.

NINETEEN

The howl of a dog was soon replaced with the wail of sirens. O'Brien sat on the church steps and listened to the cavalry approach. They came from all directions, a disjointed parade of blue and white lights—the out-of-sync blare of police cruisers, fire and rescue trucks, ambulances, and a sheriff's helicopter.

They were all too late. One was not.

O'Brien watched the coroner's car pull through the maze of emergency vehicles and stop. He could see a man inside the car with a cell phone to his ear.

Three uniformed officers raced up the church steps. They looked at O'Brien, their eyes wide, breathing heavy, adrenaline pumping. O'Brien said, "Inside."

One officer stayed on the steps while the others entered the church. He pulled out a notebook. "You call it in?"

O'Brien nodded.

"What did you see?" asked the officer.

As O'Brien started to answer, the sheriff's helicopter circled the church. The rotor noise echoed off the concrete steps. The sound took

O'Brien back to a night rescue in the first Gulf War. He glanced up at the sheriff's helicopter as the prop blast blew trapped rainwater out of gutter corners, the smell of rust and decaying leaves raining down on O'Brien and the officer. From the belly of the chopper, a powerful spotlight moved over roofs, trees, cars, apartments, and houses in the surrounding area.

The CSI people, coroner, and one of the three detectives walked past O'Brien. Two detectives didn't. A white-haired detective with a ruddy, narrow face was flanked by another man who resembled the actor Andy Garcia. Both men looked as if they had just sat down for dinner when they got the call. The white-haired man had a fleck of tomato sauce in the corner of his mouth. He introduced himself as Detective Ed Henderson. His partner was Detective Mike Valdez.

"Sean O'Brien?" Detective Henderson asked.

"That's me."

"Tell us what you saw."

"Unfortunately, I didn't see a lot. I found it, though. If I'd been here five minutes earlier, Father Callahan might be alive."

"Were you meeting Father Callahan?"

"At eight."

Henderson looked at his watch. "It's going on eight now. You're not late."

O'Brien cut his eyes toward the detective without turning his head. He waited a beat. "I said if I'd been here earlier, he might be alive."

"Why were you meeting the priest?"

"To pick up a confession."

"A confession? You mean you were here to confess something?" Henderson's mouth stayed slightly open.

"No. I came here to get a statement—a written statement. Father Callahan was witness to a dying man's confession, a near-deathbed confession. If it's true, it'll prove a man sitting on Florida's death row with"—O'Brien looked at his watch—"a man with eighty-two hours to live, is innocent."

Henderson glanced at his partner. Both were at a loss for words.

A man approached. Someone O'Brien recognized. Detective Dan Grant climbed the steps. Grant looked between Henderson and Valdez to the man sitting on the top step. Now Grant, too, was at a loss for words.

"Hello, Dan," O'Brien said. "It's been a while."

TWENTY

The other two detectives turned toward Grant. Valdez scratched at a spot above his right eyebrow. He looked across the lot toward the growing mob of media, dropped his voice a notch, and said, "It's getting weird. You know this guy?"

"Yeah," Grant said. "I know him." Grant extended his hand to O'Brien, who stood, and they shook hands. "It's been more than a year since we worked together."

"Worked together?" asked Henderson.

"Not in an official capacity," Grant said. "Sean O'Brien, retired Miami PD, homicide. One of the best. He offered a little assistance to Leslie Moore and me when that serial killer Miguel Santana was stopped."

"So you're the one . . ." Henderson's words faded like a distant radio signal.

Valdez said, "They never found Santana's body, right?"

O'Brien said nothing.

Grant said, "Let's go into the church where it's less noisy. Sean, you can take us from the beginning. How you wound up here tonight, on a night when a priest is murdered in his church."

They stood in a corner of the vestibule, ignoring the parade of forensic investigators, medical examiners, assistants, and police officers. O'Brien explained the circumstance leading up to the meeting with Father Callahan. All listened without interruption—Henderson and Valdez, with an incredulous look in their eyes, stopping to glance at their watches when O'Brien again noted the time remaining until the state would execute Charlie Williams.

Detective Grant said, "Sean, you mentioned a letter, a written statement. The priest was going to hand it to you?"

"I think it would have given us the killer's ID. Enough to get Charlie Williams a stay of execution until the perp was picked up. Father Callahan said Spelling was going to reveal the place the murder weapon's been hidden for eleven years. If it's got prints or DNA, it may match the person named in the letter. Then Charlie Williams is a free man."

Grant said, "The letter you're talking about is probably what Sam Spelling asked me to drop in a paper grocery sack at his bedside. He had it marked 'For Father John Callahan, confidential.'"

"You should have opened it," Henderson said. "You were conducting an investigation into Spelling's shooting, for Christ's sake."

"Yeah, but you should have seen the look in Spelling's eye when he asked me to drop it in the bag. Like he had an epiphany happening. I planned to go back in his room to read it when he went to sleep. The nurses were giving him something to make him sleep. When I did go back, the letter was gone. I figured the priest came back in and got it."

Valdez turned toward O'Brien and asked, "When you found Father Callahan's body, guess there was no sign of any letter, huh?"

"No, at least not in the open. Lots of spilled stuff on the floor. Briefcase rifled. The perp made it seem like a burglary/murder. I didn't want to turn the body over to go through Father Callahan's pockets until forensics worked the scene."

The detectives nodded approval. Henderson asked, "Why do you think it wasn't a burglary? Could be some asshole high on drugs, breaking into a church to steal to support his habit."

"Because of what Father Callahan told me."

"Sean's right," Grant said. "Sam Spelling told me something."

"Told you what?" Henderson asked.

"Spelling said if anything should happen to him, if he should die, I needed to see Father Callahan as fast as I could. But now Father Callahan's dead instead of Spelling."

O'Brien asked, "Is Spelling's room under guard?"

"Of course," Grant said.

O'Brien nodded. "You might want to double the guard. This guy's good."

Grant shook his head. "Public thinks Spelling's already dead. Soon as he recovers, he'll testify. We'll explain the fake death later."

O'Brien said, "Dan, call whoever's posted at the room. Have him check on Spelling."

Grant sighed, opened his cell, and made the call. "Yeah, I'll hold," he said.

Detective Valdez looked at his watch. "While Dan's checking on the patient, we've got a body in there . . . inside a church, for Christ sake. Let's do it."

O'Brien glanced toward the atrium leading to the sanctuary. "In there," he said. "We need to find the letter. Maybe Father Callahan hid it before the killer walked in."

"And maybe the perp found it on the priest and stole it," Henderson said.

O'Brien nodded. "Possibility, but Father Callahan left his own note, and he left it in his own blood. We have to figure out what he was trying to say before he died. We don't have much time to solve this puzzle or another man, Charlie Williams, will die."

"What!" Grant yelled into the phone. "Are you sure?" There was a short pause. Grant lowered his tie a notch. He closed his cell phone, his eyes distant. Then he looked at O'Brien and said, "Sam Spelling's dead."

TWENTY-ONE

A TV news helicopter flew above the church. O'Brien waited for the chopper to pass. He said, "Dan, seal Spelling's room! Don't let them remove the body until you can get an ME there. The perp—"

"Wait a minute!" Henderson interrupted.

Grant held up his hand. "It's okay, Ed. Sean's right. Right now Spelling's hospital room, like this church, is a fucking crime scene. Let's go inside."

ANITA JOHNSON OPENED the door to her mobile home, let the skinny cat out into the night, and turned back toward the television. She lit a cigarette, adjusted a frayed terry cloth belt around her robe, and sat on the edge of a plastic chair to watch the events unfolding on television. She pushed a strand of unwashed blond hair behind one ear and touched the tip of a finger to the bruise under her right eye.

Gotta leave. No more. Take the baby and just get the hell out.

Anita Johnson's thoughts were interrupted by scenes on TV. She reached for the remote to turn up the sound. A stoic reporter stood outside St. Francis Church and said, "What we know at this time is Father John Callahan, a man beloved by his parishioners, has been brutally gunned down in his own church. I was told that paramedics got here within a few minutes of the call, and Father Callahan was found dead on the floor of the sanctuary."

The picture cut to a news anchor in a studio. His brow creased as he leaned into the camera and asked, "David, do police have a motive for this heinous crime?"

"Police did say it looks like the church was burglarized. Some religious artifacts are reportedly stolen, and the poor box was rifled and found on the floor."

Anita Johnson crushed out her cigarette and lit another one. She mumbled under her breath, "World's gone straight to hell."

The reporter continued, "One source, who asked not to be identified, said he saw where the priest had left a note on the floor, apparently scrawled in his own blood. Police aren't releasing the content of that message, but investigators hope it'll lead them to the person who murdered one of the best-known and most beloved priests in the city, Father John Callahan. This is David Carter reporting."

The phone rang. Anita Johnson jumped. She lifted it off the coffee table and held the remote in one hand to turn down the sound.

She looked at the caller ID and asked, "Where're you?"

LYLE JOHNSON sat in his car in the parking lot of a closed post office. He sealed an envelope and began writing an address on it. He said, "You sound jumpy."

"Phone scared me. Lyle, a priest got blown away in a church tonight. Happened at St. Francis, right off Tilton Road. That's not far from here. Judy takes her kids there."

"Criminals don't have boundaries."

"Where're you? Dinner's cold."

"Gonna be late. Might have to work a few more hours at the

hospital. They'll probably rotate me out tomorrow. County will keep a deputy on Spelling."

She was silent.

"What's wrong?"

"Don't lie to me."

"I'm not lying. Got to work."

"On the TV news they said Sam Spelling died. If your prisoner's dead, why are you still at the hospital?"

Johnson ran his hand over his scalp. His voice softened. "Anita, look, baby, I know I ain't been much of a husband recently. I want to make it up to you. I'm sorry about the other night. I'm swearin' off booze. Look, I ran into something. I can't tell you over the phone, but it's gonna take care of our money problems." He paused, sighed, and said, "If you really think about it, the lack of money has caused all our problems."

She bit her lower lip and said nothing.

"Anita, I want to make things up with you. I'm doin' a deal, all legit, with a guy that will help us get our finances straight."

"What deal? What guy?"

"Can't go over it on the phone. I just happened to have some information dropped into my lap that he's willing to pay for. It's that simple, baby. He gets what he wants. I get paid. But it's got to happen tonight. I'll be back by one thirty."

Johnson got out of the car, held the phone to his mouth, and walked to a postal box. He dropped the letter through the slot. "Love you, Anita. Everything is gonna be beautiful, just like you. You wait and see."

"This don't sound right. I'm taking Ronnie to Mama's for a few days—"

"No! That's not gonna happen. Nothin's more important than family."

Anita touched her trembling fingers to the bruise on her face.

Johnson lowered his voice. "Anita, listen. We'll go away. Take

Ronnie to the beach. Things are about to change. I don't want to worry you, but anything worthwhile has risks. If I'm not home tonight . . . you go on tomorrow and take Ronnie to your mother's. But make sure you check the mailbox."

"What do you mean? I don't like the way you—"

"Just do it, okay? Now I gotta go." Lyle Johnson hung up, got back in his car, turned on a country radio station, and drove off in the night.

Anita moved to the tattered couch. She lay in the fetal position, knees pulled up to her breasts. A single tear rolled down her swollen cheek and was absorbed by worn cloth on the couch, the tiny spot indistinguishable from the others before it.

DETECTIVE MIKE VALDEZ STOPPED and made the sign of the cross as he approached the body of Father John Callahan. Valdez said, "Holy Mother of Christ . . ."

The forensics team, the detectives, and the coroner all worked in hushed tones, a sign of reverence for the place and what occurred in it. They snapped digital photos and examined the body. Father Callahan's head was bent at an odd angle, his eyes fixed on the stained-glass window. A pool of blood had seeped into white grout.

Detective Dan Grant stood next to O'Brien and looked down at the message scrawled in blood. Grant said, "Six-six-six . . . I've tracked a lot of criminals. Met a lot of degenerates along the way, but I've never had to hunt the devil."

TWENTY-TWO

Father Callahan left us the first clue," O'Brien said. "The three sixes might be a reference to Satan. What does that drawing mean? The letters P-A-T could be a name or someone's initials. The symbol omega is the last letter in the Greek alphabet. If I remember my ancient Greek history right, omega means the end."

"Definitely the end for the priest," said Grant, his voice almost a murmur.

"But it might be the beginning—the clue that points us to the start of this," O'Brien said. "Father Callahan was a linguistics and art history genius. Let's put ourselves in his shoes—his frame of mind after he was shot twice. He's dying and he knows it. He's going into shock. Doesn't have much time. He struggles to write this. Probably began with the drawing—could be a cloaked figure against the moon or sun. Then the six-six-six . . . followed by the omega sign . . . ending with P-A-T . . . after making the T, it looks like he lost consciousnesses. The T is closest to his fingers."

O'Brien hovered over the bloody message, and then he knelt down and touched the back of Father Callahan's left hand. "The killer's identity is in there before us, written in the blood of a priest before the altar of God."

The medical examiner's team lifted Father Callahan's body, lay it down carefully on the gurney, and started to pull a white sheet over the face.

"Wait a second," said O'Brien. He stepped to the gurney and used two fingers to close Father Callahan's eyes. "We'll find him . . . I promise," O'Brien said in a low voice.

The forensic crime scene investigators took a few more photographs of the blood smears and patterns as the coroner made notes on a clipboard. One of the forensic investigators said, "There was nothing on the body. Found his wallet about ten feet over there. Money and credit cards are gone."

O'Brien knew the answer to the question before he asked it. "You found no papers in his pockets, a letter maybe?"

"He was clean."

The coroner stepped over to the detectives and said, "You don't have to be a religious man to know whoever did this has a date with the devil."

Dan Grant looked at the body. "May have been the devil himself—six-six-six, the initials P-A-T, a drawing, and some Greek letter."

O'Brien said, "Father Callahan has already given us a big clue."

"And what would that be?" Detective Henderson asked, his tone skeptical.

Valdez said, "Maybe the priest didn't know the perp's name. Otherwise he'd have written it, or at least part of it, right?"

"Not if Father Callahan thought the killer might see it," said O'Brien.

"What about the initials?" Henderson asked. "Could be the perp's."

O'Brien squatted down near where the body had lain. He was silent for half a minute, his eyes locking on every detail—blood patterns, religious relics scattered across the floor. O'Brien stood and followed the blood trail away from where the body was found. He walked slowly, tracking, his eyes looking for the smallest specks of blood.

When he was about forty feet away, heading in the direction of the rear exit, he turned and said, "Father Callahan was shot about here. This is ten to fifteen feet from the first sign of blood. After he was shot, he turned and started in the direction of the altar." O'Brien walked back toward the detectives. He knelt down. "He fell here first. There's a bloody palm print. Then he got up and staggered toward the altar. He crawled to within a few feet of the steps—his last breaths were taken at the first marble step. That's where he died. Why would he crawl in this direction?"

"Maybe to get to a phone," Detective Valdez said.

O'Brien looked to his left. "The church offices are that direction."

"Cell phone," Detective Grant said.

O'Brien lifted the cell phone off his belt and punched in numbers. A phone rang. The detectives looked in the direction of the sound. Detective Grant walked toward a small old table in a dark corner of the vestibule, near the entrance door to the church. The cell phone was sitting at the base of a large pewter bowl.

O'Brien disconnected. "If Father Callahan's cell is lying over there on the table, why wasn't he crawling in that direction? Why wasn't he trying to dial nine-one-one?"

The detectives were silent, and then Henderson mused, "Phone was too far away."

"Then why was he here? Why was his body at the base of the altar?"

Detective Grant said, "When you are dying—right at the cusp of death—people try to get right with God." Grant gestured with a hand in the direction of the burning candles, the statue of Mary, and the figure of Christ hanging from a cross above the altar. "Maybe the priest was saying his last prayers in a place that he knew best."

O'Brien said, "Why would a man so close to God feel a need to redeem himself in his last minute of life?"

No one spoke.

"I think he was crawling in this direction for another reason," O'Brien said.

Detective Valdez said, "Maybe the Father was crawling in that direction because he was in shock. And as Dan said, he was trying to get in the vicinity of the altar—a very holy spot to pass into heaven."

"Those things are symbols. I knew Father Callahan well," O'Brien said. "He could be as close to God on a boat as he would in his own church."

O'Brien stepped up onto the altar. Except for the artifacts tossed on the floor, all else looked intact. He looked behind the dais and beneath it. There were two incense burners, half a dozen church books, and a stack of printed agendas from last Sunday's service. He removed a pen from his shirt pocket and used it to leaf through a few pages of the large Bible that lay open on the dais stand.

"Pardon me," said a woman dressed in a navy blue jumpsuit with CSI VOLUSIA COUNTY on it. She held two boxes of fingerprint equipment. Another investigator climbed up from the back of the altar. He held a portable light and stand.

O'Brien nodded and moved to the front of the altar, then slowly descended the steps. He looked at the message written in blood. "What was he trying to tell us? The rough drawing—could be a circle and face. Who? The Greek letter omega—the end? The letters . . . P-A-T. Is it the name Pat? Patrick? Patricia? Or is it something else?"

"Could be a warning," said Grant. "But if it is . . . then who was he warning?"

"Dan, you said that Spelling told you if something happened to him to see Father Callahan immediately." O'Brien stared at the message in blood.

"He was adamant about it."

"Meaning, as Father Callahan told me, the identity of the killer is on that written statement. If Spelling happened to use a pad of paper when he wrote it, he might have pressed down hard enough to leave an impression on the next page. Even if it's only a few words—enough letters to spell a name—we might have something."

"You mean as in P-A-T?" asked Grant.

"Exactly. We need to get to the hospital now."

"I was just heading that way. ME is a busy man tonight, too."

"Call your officers. Don't let them remove any notepaper."

"Paper?"

"The killer's ID could be on the sheet of paper that was under the original—the one he wrote for Father Callahan."

O'Brien looked at the figure of Christ on the cross. He watched as a dark cloud passed over the moon. He thought about Charlie Williams locked in a place where light from the moon, stars, or the sun never penetrates. O'Brien walked faster.

TWENTY-THREE

Lyle Johnson pulled off Highway 29 onto the gravel road leading to the old pioneer village, reached across the seat, and felt for his pistol. He turned off the headlights and slowly made his way about a half mile until he came to the entrance. There was no gate, only an old Florida cracker house the Volusia County Historical Society used for an office. The faded sign read:

Volusia Pioneer Village & Museum
An Authentic 19th-Century Replica of a Florida Farm Community
Open Monday–Saturday 10:00 A.M.–4:00 P.M.

Johnson was an hour early. He wanted to arrive in plenty of time to stake out the grounds. One street lamp hung near the office; the light illuminated a few of the old buildings scattered nearby. The rest of the grounds and buildings were in black and white and shades of gray, silhouettes standing under the oak trees in the moonlight.

From the gravel road, Johnson could see the replica of an old country store, a Burma-Shave sign painted on one wall. Not far from the store was a hewn cypress barn. A steam engine sat frozen in time on rusty rail tracks beside a reproduction of a train depot. The sign hanging from the side of the depot read: DELAND, FLORIDA, POP. 319. The rest of the grounds consisted of cracker shacks, a tiny white clapboard church, a one-room schoolhouse, and a small barnyard where a cow and a pony stood quietly. Johnson could see two large peacocks pecking at a corn husk. A few chickens roosted under an A-frame platform that looked like a doghouse for birds.

Johnson parked behind some bushes, beneath a lone pine tree. He pulled the overhead bulb from the dome light in his pickup truck. He worked the pistol under his belt, gently opened the door, and got out.

There was movement.

A bat flew in and out of the light cast from the street lamp. It attacked large moths that orbited the light.

Johnson's heart beat faster. His hands were damp and clammy as he folded a copy of Sam Spelling's letter and put it in his button-down shirt pocket. He walked across the gravel road to the side entrance. His eyes scanned the shadows. The gate was unlocked. Johnson pulled it toward him. The rusty hinges made a squeaking noise. An owl, sitting on a wooden fence post, lifted its wings and flew into the dark. The pony snorted and walked a few steps before standing like a statue in the long shadows.

Johnson swallowed dryly, a mosquito whining in his ear as he walked through the open gate and headed toward the general store. He hesitated when he came to the store's front porch. On the heart-of-pine porch were three chairs and a long wooden bench. There was a bushel of Indian corn near one chair. Garden tools from a century ago, the metal ends turned up, sat in a wooden barrel. There was a hoe, a shovel, and a pitchfork.

Johnson looked around, his eyes searching the dark paths between the aged buildings. A breeze blew through the trees and turned the blades of a wooden windmill. The windmill groaned and stuttered, like the creaking hinges and slats on a barn door. The wind nudged the blades, and the shallow water pump sputtered and coughed, then burped up tannin water from under the sandy soil. Johnson could smell the odor of sulfur as the water trickled down an open pipe and spilled into a horse trough.

He glanced at the moon shining through the windmill's slowly turning blades.

The pony whinnied.

Hang tough. Remember what the Marine Corp taught. Know your enemy. Approach him with respect and surprise, if possible.

Johnson stepped onto the porch, the slats of pine groaning under his weight.

Just sit tight and wait. You have the goods. You've mailed the insurance policy.

A peacock shrieked. Johnson pulled the pistol out and pointed it toward the sound. The call was a long, mournful cry. Johnson's heart raced. His hand trembled. He felt a drop of perspiration roll from one armpit and down his side.

"Hold both hands up!"

TWENTY-FOUR

Johnson felt nausea deep in his gut. He started to turn, to face the man who issued the order.

"Don't!" the voice said. "There's a nine-millimeter bullet pointed at the back of your skull. And I think you know I won't hesitate to blow your head open like I'd shoot a pumpkin out here. . . . Do as I say and you might live to see your wife, Anita."

"How you know my wife's name?"

"I know all about you, Corporal Lyle Johnson—your history with the Department of Corrections. The three times you were written up for abusing inmates. Twice deputies were dispatched to your home on domestic abuse calls. Oh, I'd say you have a slight anger problem, Corporal. Now stay exactly where you are and lower the gun."

Johnson did as ordered.

"Drop the gun."

"Why? You gonna shoot me anyhow."

"Haven't made my mind up. Drop the gun and kick it across the porch."

Johnson dropped the gun by his right foot and kicked it a few feet.

"Good. Now sit in the chair closest to you and look toward the streetlight."

"What—"

"Do it!"

Johnson slowly sat down and looked in the direction of the light.

The man walked to the steps and climbed onto the porch. Johnson could see only the man's silhouette and the tip of a barrel pointed toward his face.

"Why the gun? Thought we'd make a simple trade and go our separate ways."

"Why'd you bring a gun, Corporal Johnson?"

"Always carry one. Protection mostly. Only shot it at the range."

"Where's the letter?"

Johnson reached in his shirt pocket and retrieved the letter. A hand appeared from the dark and took it from him.

A tiny penlight came out of the man's pocket. Johnson watched as the light traced over the letter, the unseen eyes reading each word.

"Sam Spelling had quite a novel imagination. Come on, Corporal Johnson, do you really believe that years ago I could have killed that poor girl? And all this time an innocent patsy has been sitting in prison under your own watchful eyes. You must appreciate the irony. Now Charlie Williams is going to die. Courtesy of the governor. Williams can protest his innocence as they drag him from his cell and strap him in to die, but nobody will believe him. They didn't years ago . . . and they won't now. Something about the biblical eye-for-an-eye philosophy. Justice or just revenge. Let's do a little inventory— Sam Spelling is gone—his secret is right here in my hand. And that priest, the one who had to hear the confession, is dead . . . so that only leaves one person alive who knows my name."

"You killed the priest?"

"And I have you to thank. So now that brings me to you, Corporal Johnson. When you die, so does the secret. When Charlie Williams dies on death row, so does the whole story, and the public forgets quickly. Amazing, really. Try to recall the name of the last person the state put to death."

Johnson was silent.

"You can't, Corporal. And you work there."

"You kill me and you'll be exposed," Johnson said, his voice rising.

"Why is that, Corporal?"

"Because I've mailed an insurance policy. I've mailed your name and what Sam Spelling said you did. I mailed it to a person of authority. Now, I can intercept that letter and destroy it before the police get it. But I have to be alive to do it. So why don't you just give me the money like we agreed, I go away, pick up the letter before it's opened, and burn it. You won't never hear from me again . . . ever. I swear to God."

"To God? Does that impress me? You'll have to do better than that. Do you really think you're smarter than me? No one is! Do you think this is some kind of chain letter game? No, Corporal, it isn't."

The figure stepped back to pick up Johnson's gun off the porch. Johnson stood quickly. He pulled the pitchfork out of the barrel and lunged at the man. The pitchfork ripped the man's shirt, scraping his rib cage.

The pistol barrel was shoved into the center of Johnson's forehead.

"Sit down!" ordered the silhouette.

Johnson held up his hands and slowly took half a dozen steps backward, feeling for the chair with both hands and sitting down. A mosquito alighted on Johnson's cheek. As it began sucking blood, Johnson swatted at it. He missed. From the dark, the man caught the insect in midair, crushing it in his hand and wiping the remains on his pants. He said, "You're not fast enough, Corporal Johnson. Nice gun you brought."

The wind blew, causing the old windmill to spin. Johnson saw the moon flickering between the blades, the light creating a bizarre strobe effect in his adrenaline-pumped mind. Then Lyle Johnson saw a white flash and the moon exploded. He slumped back in the wooden chair, a mosquito alighting on his neck.

The shooter ejected all but one remaining bullet in Johnson's gun. He picked each one up, wrapped Johnson's right hand around the pistol and fired a round into the night sky. Then he let the gun drop to the porch, bouncing once and stopping next to a dark spot that grew larger as blood dripped onto the century-old heart pine.

TWENTY-FIVE

O'Brien met Detective Dan Grant at the emergency room entrance to Baptist Hospital. As they entered, O'Brien said, "Maybe we can find some coffee here. Dan, try to remember everything Spelling told you before he died. Father Callahan told me what Spelling had revealed to him—except for the identity of the shooter. Maybe there's something, probably small, Spelling mentioned that might fit the puzzle."

Detective Grant glanced to his left and right in the ER before responding. "Look, Sean, as I was leaving the church, Henderson and Valdez questioned me about you."

"Questioned?"

"You know, how'd you get involved? Stuff like, if you're a retired cop, then why don't you retire. More territorial than anything else, but you're not even carrying a PI license. You might think about that if—"

"I'm not going to put a condemned man's life on hold while I run out and get a license. I didn't choose this. Father Callahan called me after he heard what Spelling told him. It was a deathbed confession.

Callahan wanted it in writing because he knew Spelling might not make it. He called me because I was a friend, and he knew I was the cop who caught and convicted Charlie Williams."

"Look man, I'm on your side. I'm damn glad you're on our side. Henderson and Valdez don't know you. They know of you, but that's it. Maybe when they saw you walk though that media herd and all the media tossing questions at you, the reporters remembering you from the Santana case, maybe it's a pissing contest for them."

"I just lost a dear friend. We have an odd set of new clues and less than seventy-nine hours left to catch a killer. As you saw, this guy's the worst of the worst. And he's smart."

"You're no dummy, either. How'd you miss him the first time around? How'd Charlie Williams take the fall?"

"I missed him because the perp wanted me to and I didn't recognize it. He set a trap, a path to Williams. I had an agenda. Wanted notches on my gun. I had a heavy caseload, and I didn't look beyond Williams once we found the vic's blood in his car. His semen was in her. Fingernail cut on his face. My gut told me it was too easy and that bothered me, but there were two other murders that came in the week I was working the Alexandria Cole case—one case that really pulled at me. It was a serial pedophile, and the average age of his vics was nine. We were short-staffed, and I guess I made excuses." O'Brien felt fatigue growing behind his eyes.

"Man, it's a lot easier to go back and say the what-if's after time's passed. So Williams, the guy on death row, was set up. But why, after a decade, is the real killer comin' out? I mean, Spelling's confidential confession to a priest . . . how'd the perp know about that? How'd he slip in here and whack Spelling, if he did do it?"

"Because there's a connection here . . . somewhere."

"I'm gonna need more than that, Sean. So will you if you have any hope of getting the DA to reopen this thing. People forget. Witnesses die."

"Sam Spelling never forgot."

"And he's dead."

O'Brien inhaled deeply. "Look what's gone down the last couple of days. Someone took a shot at Spelling. Why? My guess is Spelling somehow reconnected with the killer, probably related to money. Father Callahan said Spelling told him he blackmailed the real killer eleven years ago to keep the killer's ID secret. Maybe Spelling had tried doing it again, this time from his cell."

"If Spelling were getting out of prison soon, he'd need the money immediately. Then it would make perfect sense. I'll check to see if he had a release date coming up."

"It's all about timing because the perp somehow knew Spelling was supposed to act as state's witness in a cocaine and bank robbery trial. So, the killer resurfaced and used the opportunity to hit Spelling. If Spelling survived, he would think, and so would everyone else, that the hit came from someone connected to the drug trial—an ordered hit, mob style."

"And, all the while, the guy who killed your vic a decade ago was taking Spelling out for something no one knew about—"

"Except Spelling."

"And Father Callahan. He's there by default and his good graces."

"Father Callahan told me something else." O'Brien paused. "He said there was a guard, a guy from DOC, who was trying to eavesdrop on Spelling's confession. Apparently the same guy was posted outside Spelling's room for the first few hours."

"Yeah, I saw him. Seemed preoccupied. Like he was in a hurry to clock out. At the end of his shift, we put a deputy on Spelling's door."

"We need to find that guard immediately."

TWENTY-SIX

D r. Silverstein, phone call, Dr. Silverstein" came the announcement over the hospital's PA system.

Detective Grant looked at O'Brien and asked, "Why do we need to find the corrections guard immediately?"

"Because the guard was eavesdropping when Spelling was confiding—confessing to Father Callahan. If this guard heard enough, meaning enough information to link back to the person who killed Alexandria Cole—maybe he spoke with Spelling when he was partially sedated, somehow managed to get even more information from him. I don't know, but I'm thinking that now he might have the identity of the man who killed Spelling and Father Callahan."

"Maybe the guard is somehow tied in with the perp. He could have knocked off Spelling and killed the priest."

O'Brien shook his head. "I don't think so. But it's plausible that if he somehow discovered the perp's real identity . . . just maybe he could have contacted him."

"But why would a Department of Corrections guard do that?" Grant asked.

"The same reason that Sam Spelling did . . . greed." O'Brien pinched the bridge of his nose. His eyes burned. "Let's walk and talk as we head to Spelling's room."

ANITA JOHNSON DIDN'T FEEL the hand touch her shoulder. She lay on the couch with a knitted blanket pulled up over her shoulders, the bluish light from the television flickering across the room. An open bottle of sleeping pills was on the coffee table. A few pills were scattered across the glass top. One of the pills had turned into a milky liquid and lay dissolved in the condensation left from a sixteen-ounce can of Budweiser.

The hand touched her shoulder again, this time more forcefully.

"Mommy, I'm scared," said the two-year-old boy. He stood at his mother's side and tried to keep from crying. Summer storms were rolling in again, the approaching thunder sounding like bombs in the distance, growing louder.

"Mommy, wake up."

Anita Johnson slowly opened her eyes and tried to focus on her son. "Hey, baby . . . what you doin' up, huh? You supposed to be sleepin'."

"Thunder scares me."

"It's okay, sweetheart. You can crawl under the blanket with me."

"Where's Daddy?"

Anita felt her heart jump. She tried to focus on the digital numbers glowing from the DVD player. She closed one eye. 1:37 A.M. "Oh, God."

"I'm sleepy, Mommy."

"I know, Ronnie. Let Mommy stand up and check on something, okay? You sit here and keep our spot on the sofa warm, okay, baby?"

The boy nodded and climbed on the couch.

Anita got up, steadied herself against a wall, and walked into the kitchen. She slowly pulled back the curtains and looked out onto the dirt driveway.

Lyle Johnson's truck was not there.

Anita touched her fingers to her throat. She felt sick. Darkness and nausea rose around her like a flash flood. Her sealed emotions broke as her eyes filled and tears flowed, bursting like trapped water through a cracked dam.

He's not comin' back. He's never comin' back.

She could hear the sounds of frogs calling as the rain grew closer. She flipped on the porch light and looked through the parted curtains again. Only her seven-year-old Toyota was in the driveway.

There was something in the road. Maybe it was the outline of a parked car. *Is it really a car, or are the damned pills causing hallucinations?* She strained to see the object as a blanket of clouds engulfed the sky.

Then the mobile home was covered in darkness.

Thunder rolled like a distant drum.

"Mommy, I'm scared."

TWENTY-SEVEN

The medical examiner pulled the sheet above Sam Spelling's head. He turned to O'Brien and Detective Grant and said, "This man might have died from the gunshot. I spoke with Dr. Strassberg and he said there were no complications. The patient was resting and a full recovery was expected."

"Now he's heading to the morgue," Grant said, looking around the room.

O'Brien pulled back the sheet near Spelling's handcuffed hand. He looked at the skin around the handcuff. "Whatever happened to Sam Spelling, it looks like he wasn't sleeping peacefully when it occurred, unless he was having one hell of a nightmare. Skin's broken and bruised around the wrist here at the handcuff. The other cuff has scratched the metal bed railing. Looks like Spelling was using what strength he had left to escape from something."

The ME said, "You're right. Let's get the cuff off. We'll get the body into the lab and open him up."

The medical examiner and his two assistants left as the body was wheeled from the room. Three deputies were at the door and in the hall. Deputy Gleason and one CSI investigator were in the room.

"Deputy Gleason," O'Brien said, "you found Sam Spelling dead, correct?"

"Yes."

O'Brien said nothing. He studied the man's eyes.

"I relieved the DOC guard. I've been posted here all night, sir."

"Besides the hospital staff, has anyone entered this room?" O'Brien could see the deputy's pupils open wider, a slight change in his stance, thumbs cocked in his gun belt.

"Only person that entered the room was the priest."

"Father Callahan?" asked Grant.

"No, sir, not the priest you and I spoke to. Different one. I figured Father Callahan was off duty because another priest was making hospital rounds. Thought he was from the same church, that St. Francis. Said he wanted to say a prayer for Spelling."

O'Brien asked, "How long after this man left was it before Detective Grant called and you found Spelling dead?"

"About twenty minutes, give or take."

"What did this priest look like?"

"About my height. Real black eyes. He wore a hat, so I couldn't see his hair. Probably dark because he had a dark beard."

"He wore it to hide his identity. Probably fake. Anything else?"

"No, sir." The deputy paused. "It might be nothing . . ."

"What is it?" asked O'Brien.

"The priest had a bad wrist. Said he hurt it playing tennis. He asked me to open the door for him."

"That's because he didn't want to leave prints," O'Brien said. "There's a surveillance camera at the end of each hall. Call security. We need to see what that camera saw. Dan, let's have them check any other security cameras—lobby, parking lot, entrances, and exits before and right after Sam Spelling's untimely death."

Grant turned to Gleason and said, "Get hospital security here immediately."

"Yessir."

Grant looked at O'Brien and pointed toward a paper grocery bag. "That bag, Spelling told me the stuff in it was all he had left in the world. Then he looked up at me and said it was all he needed. It's like he was the happiest guy on the planet. Probably leftover endorphins from his near-death trip and confession to Father Callahan. Spelling seemed like the character in that old movie . . . you know—the one with Jimmy Stewart."

"It's a Wonderful Life."

"Yeah, that's it."

O'Brien opened the paper bag. He emptied it on the unmade bed. The bag contained Spelling's Department of Corrections–issued clothes—a pair of pants, blue button-down shirt, white socks, and a pair of lace-up black shoes. There was a small, brown Bible, pages worn. O'Brien opened it. An aged picture of a woman and little boy fell from the pages. In the faded image, the woman stood with flowers in one hand, holding the child with her other hand. Behind them was a statue of an angel and many trees. The picture looked to have been taken in a park.

Grant said, "I'll have the stuff and the room dusted in the morning."

O'Brien said nothing.

"Sean, after I dropped the letter in the sack, they came in to treat and sedate him. The note—he'd folded as best he could, like he'd tried to seal it—could have been the written confession for the priest. That's why I waited for him to go to sleep before I came back in to read it. Figured the priest visited and took it."

"Maybe Father Callahan did, but if this DOC guard read it, then he knows the perp's identity and whatever details Sam Spelling revealed about the killing. The guard could have taken it, copied it . . . could have given it to his superiors to contact the police . . . or he might have decided to blackmail the guy like Spelling originally did. Maybe he's an honest guy who decided to do something very dumb."

"If he did, might as well have called his executioner."

O'Brien felt around and beneath the mattress. He pulled a yellow legal pad from behind the flattened pillows and bunched sheets. He lifted the top sheet of paper by the edge, turned on the bedside light, and held the paper toward the light. He examined both sides. "This is the paper Spelling used, isn't it?"

"Yes. Legal sized, lined."

"If we're lucky, we might get something from it. Even with the naked eye, I can see where he made an imprint on this sheet, especially the first paragraph or so. He was either angry when he was writing it or his strength was better when he began. See? It's more pronounced on the first third of the page. And if he mentioned the killer's name there, we might have him."

Grant looked at the page. "I'll have to get it to the state crime lab."

"We don't have time, Dan. I have an FBI contact. She'll help. But first, I'm going to see Charlie Williams."

Grant grinned. "Our man on death row. Bet he'll be real happy to see you."

TWENTY-EIGHT

The hospital security center was on the first floor, hidden through a labyrinth of corridors. Two security technicians sat in front of forty monitors, all taking live video feeds from every floor in the hospital—lobby, cafeteria, parking lots, and rooftops.

O'Brien looked at the identifying locations superimposed on the bottom of each monitor. "Why monitor the roof?" he asked.

The man at the console said, "To spot jumpers. We had two guys do swan dives to the street the last couple of years. I'm glad they double-locked the door to the roof."

"What do you have on our elusive priest between seven and eight o'clock?"

"I cued it up for you. All digital. Stored in some pretty hefty hard drives. Archived and erased at the end of ten-day cycles. It's done automatically unless we tell the computers to store it. Camera nine caught a priest."

The man pressed four buttons and the time of day appeared at the bottom of the screen. It was calculated in military time, down to the second. O'Brien, Grant, and the other two security officers watched in silence. On the screen, they saw nurses making their rounds, a custodian pushing a mop, a family huddled at the far end of the hall, and a man dressed as a priest walking toward Deputy Tim Gleason.

O'Brien leaned in toward the monitor, his eyes searching every facet. Although the images were in color, the shot was too wide to see much detail. The man wore a fedora hat, collar, glasses, dark church-issued suit, and black shoes.

O'Brien studied the man's body language. He wasn't animated. Movements more conciliatory. Brotherly love. Head nodding. He moved a Bible from his left hand to his right and reached out to touch the deputy on the shoulder. "Why is he carrying a Bible? Catholic priests usually carry breviaries. Can you back it up about fifteen feet before he approaches the deputy?" O'Brien asked.

"Sure."

"There, that's fine. Play it. Can you get any closer?"

"Some. Cameras don't have high resolution. You'll see some loss of quality when I push in." The security tech zoomed in on the image. "Look," O'Brien said, pointing. "See that, Dan?"

"See what?"

"The perp knows there's a camera, and it's not an easy camera to spot. He looked toward it just a half second. That's why he turned profile. He moves the Bible from his left hand to his right—the right hand is supposed to be hurt, remember? He scratches his left cheek while he's talking. Doesn't want his lips read. Can you go in any closer?"

"Just a notch," said the technician. "Pixels in the picture start to come apart."

"That's good. See that, Dan?"

"I see his hand."

"Look closer. I don't know many Catholic priests who are married."

Dan Grant leaned in toward the monitor. "Wow, he's wearing a gold ring."

"I wonder if the lady of the house knows she's sleeping with a killer."

TWENTY-NINE

B y the time O'Brien got back to the marina it was a few minutes after 3:00 A.M. As he walked down the dock to his boat, he could see a mist rising over the estuaries, moving with an eerie crawl across the water. The humid night air carried the scent of mangroves, salt water, barnacles, and fish. Nothing moved. The silence could be felt. It was one of the rare times O'Brien could hear the punch of waves breaking a quarter mile away. The tide was rising.

Jupiter groaned against the ropes as it played tug-of-war with the incoming tide. O'Brien stepped over the transom and onto the cockpit. The floor was damp, wet from a heavy dew. He unlocked the salon door, kicked off his shoes, and entered.

Max sat up from her bed on the salon couch. Her tail thumped against the leather. She whimpered and coughed a slight bark as O'Brien stepped inside the salon.

"Hey, Max. You been holding down the fort? I bet Dave fed you like a princess before he had to go fix a broken moat, right? I missed you today. Want a snack?"

Max danced in a circle on the couch before jumping off and following O'Brien down two steps into the galley. In the refrigerator, he grabbed one of the last two bottles of Corona from a six-pack he'd shared two weeks ago with Nick Cronus.

O'Brien tossed two aspirins in the back of his mouth and took a long pull from the bottle. He tried to remember the last time he had eaten. He broke off a piece of cheese, sliced an onion, wrapped the cheese and onion in pita bread, and laced it with hot mustard. He handed a nibble of cheese to Max.

O'Brien sat down at the small table in the galley. He was physically exhausted, almost too tired to eat. His mind kept playing back the events that unfolded after he received Father Callahan's call. Sam Spelling killed in his hospital bed with an armed guard outside. Father Callahan killed in his church with God inside. O'Brien thought about the message on the bloody floor. He looked at the image from a picture he'd snapped on his cell phone.

What does it mean?

He bit into his sandwich, gave Max a piece, opened his laptop computer, typed in "omega," and clicked on a link that took him to a Web page, Religions of the World. In reference to the Greek letter omega, it read: "Omega (Ω), the last letter in the Greek alphabet. Often meaning the end, something final. The opposite is the first letter in the Greek alphabet Λ, Alpha. Jesus used these two symbols, the Λ and the Ω to say, 'I am the beginning and I am the end.'"

O'Brien rubbed the back of his hand over his chin. The stubble felt like sandpaper. He keyed in "666."

"Two million pages. That narrows it down." He sipped his beer and started reading, his eyes scanning the first few pages. He stopped and reread a sentence: "666, often referred to as the mark of the beast. First attributed to Saint John in his description of the Apocalypse, as seen in a vision from God when Saint John lived in exile."

Okay, he thought, popping the second beer. He mulled over the information, trying to see a connection. ". . . and I am the end." One half of a Jesus parable . . . and some guy called Pat . . . or the initials, P-A-T.

"Saint John lived in exile." O'Brien stared at the sentence. Reverse the spelling of *lived* and we have . . . *devil* . . . *devil in exile.*

"Father Callahan, what were you trying to tell me?" His voice sounded hoarse.

O'Brien's eyes were heavy, he was nodding off. He looked at his watch and was too tired to calculate the hours left in Charlie Williams's life.

He tried to think back eleven years ago, searching his memory for scraps that might have fallen between the cracks—the smallest pieces of information that he might have missed at the time. Who would *want* Alexandria Cole dead? And why was the killer resurfacing a few days before Charlie Williams's date with death? O'Brien thought about the odds, the time it normally takes in a typical murder investigation. Then he thought about the time left to prove Charlie Williams's innocence. What would he tell Williams? What could he say? How could he ever right the wrong? "If I don't sleep, Max, maybe I can track this bastard down. Want some fresh air?"

She wagged her tail. He turned off the laptop and headed for the salon door, Max following him to the cockpit. O'Brien picked her up. She licked his face as he held her and climbed the ladderlike steps up to the flybridge. He unzipped the isinglass window, sat in the captain's chair, propped his feet up on the control console, and finished his beer. Max jumped in his lap. He scratched her behind the ears, her eyes half closing.

"Max, what would I do without you, little lady?" She kept her eyes closed as O'Brien spoke. "There's a bad man out there. Human life means nothing to him. I've got to find him, and I'm running out of time. I have to try to save another man's life. It's my responsibility. I'll be leaving soon. . . . You be good, and don't let Nick pour any beer in your bowl, okay?"

O'Brien watched the fog rolled off the Halifax River, blanketing the mangrove islands and hanging over the marina like clouds descending. He could see a shaft of light from the Ponce Inlet Lighthouse rotating every minute, its beam giving the fog a momentary illusion of dimension, the figment of ghosts swirling over the sailboat masts as if dancing albino marionettes were pulled by unseen hands.

Soon the ghosts faded and the real nightmares began. In his dreams, O'Brien saw the dead body of Alexandria Cole. She was lying on her bed, seven stab wounds in her sternum and breasts. Her eyes staring at the ceiling.

He saw a young Charlie Williams, the expression of disbelief in his eyes when the jury read the guilty verdict. The chilling echoes of his pleas as two deputies led him out of the courtroom, his mother weeping in a back row, her eyes hot and lost.

O'Brien saw Father Callahan lying facedown on the cold marble of the sanctuary. His three fingers extended, touching the very edge of a postscript written in blood. His eyes locked on art in stained glass, paintings of salvation backlit by the fractured pulse of lightning. Images of deliverance cast in a dramatic tragedy, flickering, as in a silent movie, off the wide pupils of Father John Callahan's unmoving eyes.

THIRTY

Max heard the throaty sound of the twin diesels first. She cocked her head around the bridge console, peeked through the open isinglass, and barked once.

"Hey, hot dog!" came the voice, coated with a Greek accent thick as olive oil.

O'Brien opened his eyes. He steadied himself in the captain's chair, now regretting he had fallen asleep on the bridge. His back ached, the muscles constricting between his shoulder blades, his foot tingling from the lack of circulation.

Max wagged her tail, jumped on O'Brien's lap, and licked his whiskered chin. "Max, thanks for the wake-up kiss," he said, smiling. He rubbed her head and set her on the bridge floor.

She looked at him through wide, excited brown eyes, trotting to the steps leading down to the cockpit.

O'Brien stood, squinting in the morning sun rising over the Atlantic Ocean. He looked at his watch. 7:39 A.M.

A little more than seventy hours remaining.

"Hey, Sean" came the Greek accent. "Got plenty of grouper and snapper."

O'Brien waved toward Nick Cronus, who eased his forty-eight-foot fishing boat, *St. Michael,* into the marina with the skill of an Argonaut. Cronus stood in the wheelhouse of the *St. Michael,* a boat blessed by a saltwater pedigree going back two thousand years. He wore dark sunglasses, his skin the color of creosote, a mop of curly black hair styled by the wind, bushy black mustache, and forearms like sides of ham. A life at sea, pulling nets and anchor ropes, diving for sponges, and riding out storms had sculpted a man of steel. Even at age forty-three, Nick Cronus showed no signs of slowing down. He worked hard. Played harder. He smiled with his eyes. O'Brien had once saved Nick's life, a debt Nick said he would honor forever.

O'Brien lifted Max under his arm and carried her down the steps to the cockpit. He headed toward Nick's slip, which was on the opposite side of Dave Collins's boat.

Nick backed the *St. Michael* into the slip as easy as a New York cabdriver can parallel park. He cut the diesels and brought twenty tons of boat to a gentle stop.

O'Brien helped tie the boat to a second piling. Max scampered up and down the dock, her eyes darting with excitement, the tip of her small tongue showing as she panted in the morning humidity.

Nick pushed his sunglasses up on the top of his head. "Sean, you look like hell."

"And good morning to you, too."

"Somebody roll you? Take your money or what, man?"

"No, Nick. Nothing like that."

"You tie one on without ol' Nicky to join you, huh?" Nick looked at O'Brien, eyes playful, eyebrows arched, and a toothpick in one corner of his mouth. He knelt down to pick up Max. "Hot dog, I miss you when I go to sea almost as much as I miss the ladies on two legs. And even when I'm here, I don't see you enough. Tell your papa, Sean, to bring you to the docks more, yeeaah."

Max wagged her tail and licked Nick's salt-and-pepper stubble. "I pick you up now 'cause I know you won't pee on me. Sean, remember that time I held hot dog up over my head? We were on your boat, I did a Greek dance with her, and she peed all the way down my arm."

"And if you don't want a repeat, don't pick her up. She hasn't hit the grass yet."

Nick laughed. "She made me jump in the bay. I didn't know what's cleaner—the marina or little Max's pee pee." He set Max back on the dock. "Let's eat. You couldn't have no breakfast lookin' the way you do."

"Nick, I don't have a lot of time. I have—"

"You have to eat, man. You gotta learn to relax more. I met a girl, and she has this gorgeous sister. Big tits and—"

"Father Callahan was killed last night."

"What?"

"Murdered."

"Murdered?"

"Killed in the church sanctuary."

Nick made the sign of the cross. His mouth parted, a sound like a cough lost in his throat.

O'Brien said, "There were no witnesses. I'm trying to find who did it."

Nick looked out at the water, then back at O'Brien. He rubbed his mustache with a thumb, the smile gone from the corner of his mouth. He said, "Can't believe it. I remember when the priest came to the docks. I was cleaning fish when he asked me, where's your boat. I told him, and then I asked him to bless my boat. He say a little prayer, and said next time he's gonna bring holy water. You two were supposed to go fishin', but it stormed and you drank Irish whiskey with the Father. I brought some ouzo. We played cards, the guitar, and sang some good tunes. Dave Collins was there, too."

"I remember."

"Cops know who killed him?"

"No, but it's related to an old case."

"What case?"

"I don't have time to get into it, but it's erupting from an old case I had in Miami years ago. Two people are dead within the last twenty-four hours, Father Callahan and a man who confessed to him about a murder eleven years ago."

"This man killed someone?"

"No, but he knew who did it. And, in a deathbed confession, he told Father Callahan. Somehow the killer found out and murdered both the guy who confessed and Father Callahan. To make matters worse, an inmate on death row is going to be executed in a few days unless I can prove he didn't commit the murder eleven years ago."

Nick shook his head. "No wonder you look like hell, you're livin' there."

"I have to walk Max, grab a shower, and hit the road. Father Callahan left a message on the church floor where he died. He scrawled something in his own blood."

"What?"

"He wrote six-six-six, a circle drawing, the Greek letter omega, and the letters P-A-T. Nick, you grew up in Greece. In a few minutes, tell me all you know about omega."

THIRTY-ONE

Dave Collins sat in a faded canvas deck chair on Nick's boat and sipped from a mug of black Greek coffee. He looked over the rim to see O'Brien approaching, with Max trotting down the dock behind him.

O'Brien said, "Thanks for taking care of Max and putting her inside *Jupiter* before you left. Did you fix your daughter's plumbing leak?"

"After some trial and error. Slept in my clothes on her couch. You were right. You said Father Callahan might be the next target. Nick told me what happened. I'm so sorry to hear that. Although I'd only met him once on your boat, he was the kind of person that made you feel you knew him a long time."

Nick yelled from the galley. "Sean, get some coffee. I'm makin' fish and eggs."

Max barked once and darted toward the galley, following the smells of frying fish, feta cheese, and black olives. "Good morning, hot dog," Nick said, tossing Max a small piece of fish.

O'Brien looked at Dave and shook his head. He said, "No leads, at least not yet."

"How was he killed?"

"Shot to death."

Dave held both hands around the large mug and inhaled the steam from the coffee. He said, "You saw it coming."

"But I couldn't get there fast enough to prevent it." O'Brien told Dave everything he could remember. He went over the details of the crime scene and Father Callahan's last conversation with him.

Dave was silent, his mind working. He finished his coffee and said, "The message Father Callahan left . . . it's in there . . . somewhere. I'm wondering why he didn't try to write out something more definitive. The killer's name, if he knew it, a physical description. You don't need to crack a code to save Charlie Williams's life. You need evidence. I can see the DA asking, 'What's the connection to Charlie Williams?' "

Nick yelled from the galley. "Food's ready."

The men sat around a small table and ate pieces of grouper fried in olive oil and mixed with scrambled eggs, feta cheese, and onion. Nick poured dark coffee into three cups and said, "I say a prayer for Father Callahan. Lord, help our friend Sean O'Brien find the man who did this terrible thing to one of your teachers . . . amen." Nick made the sign of the cross and shoved a large spoonful of eggs in his mouth. "I could use a Bloody Mary."

O'Brien said, "I don't have time to sit here, but I'm not sure what path to follow."

Dave sipped his coffee and leaned back on his wooden bar stool. "Sean, I remember Father Callahan as an excellent art historian and a man with a keen ear for linguistics. There's something in this last message related to his expertise."

"What do you mean?" O'Brien asked.

"You said the last thing Father Callahan wrote was six-six-six, the letter omega, a circle with something that may or may not have been his attempt at a woman's profile, and the letters P-A-T—the T smeared, indicating he lost consciousness at that point."

Nick chewed his food thoughtfully and said, "Spooky stuff. The six-six-six is from the Bible, the sign of the beast. Omega, well, in Greece it's our last letter—the twenty-fourth letter. But it's more than a letter. Like alpha, which represents the beginning, omega means the end of something. The end of a love. A life. The end of time, whatever. Gone, man. Poof! Maybe that's why Father Callahan wrote it . . . the end of his life."

"But it doesn't explain the other things he managed to scrawl," Dave said. "Do we try and read it left to right, like reading a sentence, or are the symbols and letters emblematic of a whole picture that will point you directly to the killer? Sean, can you sketch it out on this paper towel, as close as you can remember, the way Father Callahan wrote the message?"

"I can do one better than that. I used my cell phone to take a picture of what Father Callahan wrote on the sanctuary floor. I can e-mail it to you from right here. On a larger computer screen, it might make it easier to read."

As O'Brien reached for the phone on his belt, it started ringing.

"Does that always happen when you retrieve your phone?" asked Dave as he bit into fish, eggs, and cheese wrapped in warm pita bread.

O'Brien looked at the caller ID. He didn't recognize the number.

"Sean, this is Dan Grant. The ME confirms what the surveillance camera pointed us toward when we saw the fake priest enter Sam Spelling's room. Spelling was asphyxiated. We have a very smart, fast, and extremely dangerous killer out there."

THIRTY-TWO

O'Brien looked over to Dave, who raised his eyebrows. Detective Grant continued on the phone, "Normally I wouldn't think twice about something like this, but under the circumstances—"

"What do you have, Dan?"

"The guard's name is Lyle Johnson. Tried to reach him at the Department of Corrections. Supervisor said Johnson is on first shift—seven o'clock to three in the afternoon. But he didn't report for work this morning. Super tells me that Johnson is always punctual, but today, no call. No nothing."

"Did you try to reach Johnson's home, his wife, maybe?"

"I called her. Didn't get much."

"What'd she say?"

"Not a lot. She sounded like she was on some strong medication or coming off a few drinks too many. But she said something odd, too."

"What?"

"Said she was going to call in a missing-person report . . . but she knew the department wouldn't do anything until her husband had been missing for forty-eight hours. I told her she was correct. Then, out of the blue, she laughed. It was a painful laugh, know what I mean? The kind that feels fake and all wrong."

"I know what you mean."

"She said she might as well skip the missing-person report and wait for them to find his body because she knew he wasn't coming back home alive."

"Did you ask her why?"

"She said it was just a feeling she had."

"Was the call taped?"

"All our calls are taped. Why?"

"Because she may have incriminated herself in a murder."

"We don't have a body. And I doubt that she killed her husband."

"I do too," O'Brien said. "But she's obviously spoken with him . . . and he apparently told her something. If he managed to read Spelling's letter or overhear the confession with Callahan, then he may know the perp's name. He might have tried to contact him to cut a financial deal like Spelling had."

"And if he did?"

"Then he might be as dead as Spelling. You need to talk to her now. If she thinks she could be tied to her husband's disappearance, she just might tell us everything he told her. Check phone records, bank accounts. See if Johnson had probable cause to contact the perp, then we're one step closer to finding this guy." O'Brien looked at his watch. "We have about sixty-nine hours to stop the execution of an innocent man. When I was a detective like you, I'd work an investigation by the book, the gut, and the mind. In this investigation we don't have a lot of time to trace leads."

"What are you saying, Sean?"

"I'm saying that unless we get something very fast, maybe a read on an imprint from the Sam Spelling paper or a name that Lyle Johnson may have given to his wife . . . Charlie Williams is good as dead." O'Brien paused. "Dan, I'm telling you this because we worked together. I trust you—trust your confidence. I'll need your help."

"No problem, but what do you mean?"

"I might have to force some people to talk. It'll be the fastest way to the truth. I don't like operating this way, but if I don't, Williams will die. I can't let that happen."

Dan said, "I'm going to question Johnson's wife. Where will you be?"

"In prison. It's time I spoke with Charlie Williams."

THIRTY-THREE

Starke, Florida, is one of America's death capitals. Starke is the home of Florida State Prison, a place where the death penalty has been challenged and upheld more times than in any prison in America. Some of the more notables listed on the roster of death include Ted Bundy and female serial killer Aileen Wuornos.

It took Department of Corrections guards about fifteen minutes to bring Charlie Williams to meet O'Brien. He was escorted by three guards, one on either side and one behind him. Chains kept his stride to a minimum. His hands were cuffed.

O'Brien almost didn't recognize Williams. He walked with a rhythm of distrust in his body language. Suspicious eyes. Shoulders rounded. Skinny. His spirit now nothing more than a defense posture. Eleven years in prison—eleven years on death row—had turned the raw farm boy from North Carolina into a man with a hard face and apprehensive eyes.

Both men took seats on the opposite of the no-contact glass. O'Brien could see a faded scar leading from the left side of Williams's forehead and vanishing into his thinning hair, turning gray before its time.

O'Brien picked up the phonelike receiver first. Williams sat there, staring though the thick glass. Finally, he slowly lifted the receiver.

O'Brien said, "I'm glad you agreed to see me, Charlie. How you holding up?"

"How do you think I'm holding up?"

"Look—"

"What the fuck do you want, O'Brien?"

"To save your life."

"You're a little late, Detective."

"I'm not a detective anymore."

"Then what the hell are you? Why are you here?"

"I believe you didn't kill Alexandria Cole."

Williams let out a mock laugh. "It only took you eleven years to figure that out?"

"A horrible mistake was made. I want you to know that I feel awful about that. The evidence was so compelling. I want to tell you how sorry I am for—"

"Bullshit, man! You wanted me here. It's because of you, Detective O'Brien, that I'm here. It's because of you that I've been beaten, stabbed twice, raped, and now they're gonna stick needles in my veins and let poison slowly shut my organs down. All because you wanted another closed case."

"You have every right to be angry, but listen to me a second. Please. Just listen. We don't have time—"

"We don't have time! What are you—"

"I'm saying we—you and me—have to stop this execution. I know you didn't kill the girl. To set you free, I'll need your help."

"Leave me the fuck alone! What'd you do, find God or something, huh?"

"No, I found two people dead."

THIRTY-FOUR

Charlie Williams's dry lips parted. Eyes filled with confusion. "What?"

O'Brien said, "Two people dead. What they had in common was this: they knew who killed Alexandria. One was a priest, a close friend of mine. The other was an inmate. Did you know Sam Spelling?"

Williams was quiet a long moment. His eyes focused on the handcuffs around his wrists. Then he looked up through the glass at O'Brien. "Sam Spelling. The guy who was shot when they were taking him to testify in the coke trial?"

"That's the one."

"I'd seen him around. He hung with more of the sleazeballs than I was comfortable with . . . not that you have a good bunch of normal people in this shithouse."

"Tell me about Spelling. Did he ever talk with you? Can you remember conversations . . . anything about your past or his? Did he prod you about the murder?"

Williams thought, his eyes searching. "One thing nobody really talks about in prison is why they got here. The sexual deviants, the ones who molest children, they find out about them. But the others . . . everybody's innocent, right?" Williams sneered.

"Think!" O'Brien almost shouted, embarrassed by his tone. "Can you think of anything Spelling may have casually mentioned, or something you might have said, that may give me a clue as to who murdered Alexandria?"

"Sometimes I'd catch Spelling looking at me, when they let me get some exercise. Thought he was gonna shank me. So one day, I asked him what his deal was. He said I didn't *look* like I really belonged here. Told me his mother had him reciting Psalm Twenty-Three when he was four. He said if I memorized it, believed it, then there was no way I'd be alone when they strapped me to the gurney."

"Charlie, Sam Spelling knew who killed Alexandria."

"How'd he know?"

"He saw the real killer hide the weapon. Spelling blackmailed the killer."

Williams was quiet. He closed his eyes and inhaled deeply. "Why me?"

"In a deathbed confession he told a priest that you were innocent. The priest asked him to make a statement in writing. Spelling did. He was killed."

"I heard he died from the shooting. Shot so he couldn't testify."

O'Brien told Williams why he believed Spelling was killed and added, "The perp found out Spelling had revealed his identity to the priest, and the location of the murder weapon. Spelling was killed in his hospital bed recovering from surgery. And the perp then left the hospital, went to the church, and killed Father John Callahan."

"How'd Alex's killer come out after so long to whack Spelling and this priest?"

"Father Callahan said the guard, a guy from right here assigned to transporting Spelling, overheard some of the confession in the emergency room. I believe he stole the statement Spelling wrote for Father Callahan, and he contacted the perp."

"Why would he do that?"

"To blackmail him or her."

"So let's get these iron bracelets off me and let me walk outta here."

"I need something I can take to the DA. Some physical evidence that will prove who really killed Alexandria."

"You got two people dyin', what more do you need?"

"But I can't directly tie them to Alexandria's murder. The fact that Spelling made contact with you shows that somewhere in his mind his guilt was bothering him."

"Yeah, but obviously not enough to tell anybody I was innocent."

"Charlie, think back to the time of Alexandria's death. Did she confide in you then? Maybe mention something that was bothering her? Scaring her?"

"Not really. But her attention span seemed different."

"How?"

"I don't know, kinda like she was looking over her shoulder all the time."

"Do you think she was afraid of her manager, Jonathan Russo?"

"He was definitely using her, like a tick in a mare's ear. I hated the bastard."

"I don't know why Russo would kill someone he was using as a cash flow."

"Alex told me she was firing him. She had a new agent lined up in New York."

Williams used the back of his cuffed left hand to wipe perspiration off his forehead. He said, "Since I've been here, they've executed seven men and one woman. Every one they led outta their cell was scared shitless. You can memorize any Bible verse you want, but when you're strapped down, they open those curtains so others can watch you suck in your last breaths. All that really matters, O'Brien, is what you are inside. You can tattoo a Bible verse on the inside of your eyelids. But unless it's inside your heart—not some last-minute finding-God crap, then you might was well take a seat at the devil's table. Now I'm gonna be sacrificed in a place that the devil's blessed—the execution chamber. And I'm innocent!"

O'Brien shook his head. "I know you are, and I'm going to get you out of here."

"How, man? I got sixty-seven hours to live! They're telling me to decide what I want for my last meal. And guess what, O'Brien . . . it can't total more than twenty dollars. My lawyer's given up. He told my mama he'd help with the funeral arrangements. So, what the hell are you gonna do to keep the state from killing me? Tell me, huh?"

"I'm very, very sorry for what's happened to you. I'm going to do everything I can to right a terrible wrong. If you can think of anything that might—"

"I can't even think, O'Brien! Can't sleep. I'm scared, man. And I'm innocent!" Tears streamed from Williams's eyes.

O'Brien said, "I'll find who did it."

"Bullshit, man! You got sixty-seven hours till they poison me. How are you going to find the killer in that time? Huh? Tell me? Took you eleven years to find out I didn't do it. What the hell can you do in sixty-seven hours?"

O'Brien said nothing.

"Tell me, O'Brien!" Williams screamed. "Are you gonna work as hard to get me out as you did to get me in?" He dropped the receiver, blinking tears out of his eyes, lower lip trembling, saliva in the corner on his mouth. Two guards ran over and lifted him, kicking, out of the metal chair. As they dragged Williams back to death row, O'Brien could hear him screaming, "I loved her! I loved Alex! What're you gonna do now, O'Brien! Tell me!"

THIRTY-FIVE

In his rearview mirror, O'Brien could see the white buildings, guard towers, and razor fence of Florida State Prison as he drove away. O'Brien lifted his cell phone and called information. "Connect me, please, to the office of Florida's attorney general."

"Hold for that number."

After being transferred three times, O'Brien reached the attorney general's executive assistant. "May I help you?"

O'Brien explained why he was calling.

"Hold, please."

After he had listened to more than one minute of a tape-recorded message from the governor, the assistant came back on the line. "Attorney General Billingsley is in a meeting. Then he has a cabinet meeting. May I take a number?"

"Time is running out for Charlie Williams. If the attorney general is busy, please get me the deputy attorney general."

"Hold, please," her voice now agitated.

O'Brien listened to a recorded message of the governor discussing his accomplishments in education and job creation. Then a man's voice came on the line. "Carl Rivera, can I help you?"

"Are you the deputy attorney general?"

"No, but I am an assistant attorney in this office."

O'Brien fought the urge to throw the cell phone out the Jeep window. "I'll be quick and to the point."

The assistant attorney listened without interruption. He said, "Mr. O'Brien, as tragic as the murders are, it's not within the capacity or jurisdiction of this office to intercede. The original case was tried in Miami. I'd suggest you begin there."

"The attorney general's office is the first to hear a capital case appeal."

"Indeed, but this isn't an appeal. It's a stay of execution. Only the governor can issue that order."

"I've been listening to his tape-recorded message every time someone in your office puts me on hold. Stay on the line and put me through to the governor's office."

"I can do that, but I can also tell you that Governor Owens is out of the country. He's in Saudi Arabia on a fact-finding trip."

"The facts in this case spell death for an innocent man. The governor needs to know it. Media could have a field day while he's away. I'm leaving you with my cell number. I need to speak to the attorney general. He can at least examine the new revelations in the case and make a call to the governor. We have satellites and phones; all it takes is someone to make the call."

"What's your number, Mr. O'Brien?"

O'Brien gave it to him, disconnected, and immediately called the Miami FBI headquarters. As his call was being put through, he thought about what the attorney general's assistant had said. He also wondered how the cabinet could be meeting without the governor in attendance.

"Special Agent Miles," said the voice on the line.

"Lauren, this is Sean O'Brien. How are you?"

"I'll be damned . . . if it's not Sean O'Brien . . . maybe Miami PD's best dropout. What do I owe the privilege? Last time you resurfaced was the Miguel Santana case. After you two met, we never even found a trace of his body."

"And I spent seven days in a hospital, too. Lauren, I didn't ask to investigate Santana, but I had no choice. I have no choice in another very urgent matter, either. I could use your help this time around."

O'Brien heard her inhale quickly. "I don't know. What do you want?"

"I'm bringing something to you. Don't have time to explain on the phone. I'm catching a flight to Miami today. I'll come by your office this—"

"Wait a minute, Sean—"

"Lauren, please. It is truly a matter of life and death. I'm e-mailing a picture I took of a message left in blood."

She sighed and said, "I'll be here."

"Thanks, Lauren." O'Brien hung up and called Miami PD for Ron Hamilton.

"Detective Hamilton, homicide."

"Ron, this is Sean."

"Hey, ol' buddy. You're supposed to be moving on with your life. Aren't you teaching at UCF or running a charter boat by now?"

"I wish. Remember the murdered supermodel Alexandria Cole?"

"Sure, how do you forget a loss and a face like that?"

"The kid I arrested and convicted didn't do it."

"What?"

O'Brien gave Hamilton a quick rundown of the events and then said, "I'll explain more when I get there. I'm catching a plane for Miami today. I need a big favor."

"Name it."

"Pull the old case file for me."

"Sean, what's going on?"

"Two people have died since last night. Both knew the ID of the real killer. Charlie Williams, on death row, is set for the needle in sixty-six hours. A prison guard who may have known the killer's ID is MIA. Is Don Guilder still the DA?"

"Guilder retired. Stanley Rosen took over."

"Rosen, I remember the name. Guilder was the original prosecutor. Can you get me in to see Rosen immediately?"

"See what I can do. But this better be something we can sink our teeth in, because if it's not, I'm the one that's going to get snakebit."

"Okay. Ron, one other thing. I'm sending a package overnight to your home."

"What's in it?"

"My gun."

THIRTY-SIX

The district attorney for Dade County, Florida, said he could give Sean O'Brien fifteen minutes. O'Brien thought about that as he parked his rental Jeep in the county's parking garage and caught the elevator to the eleventh floor.

"Fifteen minutes," Ron Hamilton had said. "That's all I could get you on short notice, Sean." Hamilton had to testify in court and couldn't meet O'Brien until after five.

O'Brien looked at his watch as he rode the elevator up to the eleventh floor.

Sixty-two hours left.

The DA's office was furnished in earth tones, lots of plants in the lobby, framed pictures of the Dade County courthouse and the Florida Supreme Court justices. It had a subdued feel. Young attorneys in dark suits walked from one hall to the next. Some stopped at the receptionist desk to pick up messages and take a mint from a silver bowl that sat next to small stacks of business cards.

"Mr. Rosen will see you now, Mr. O'Brien," said the petite receptionist between the soft buzzing of incoming calls. She pointed to her right. "It's at the end of the hall, to the left . . . the double doors."

O'Brien followed her directions and met Rosen's secretary, a woman with a warm smile. She said, "Right this way, Mr. O'Brien."

District Attorney Stanley Rosen didn't bother to stand up behind his massive desk when O'Brien entered his office. O'Brien recognized Rosen. He was in his midfifties. His hair, now fully white, parted on the left side in a boyish style. He had a sailor's deep tan. O'Brien remembered Rosen as one of the state prosecutors in a murder trail involving a woman who shot her husband six times, the final shot hitting him in the groin. She had been the victim of abuse for more than twenty years.

Rosen typed on his computer keyboard, looking up once, offering O'Brien a cursory smile. "Mr. O'Brien, please take a seat. Be with you in just a moment."

The secretary left, quietly closing the door. O'Brien sat in one of the two chairs in front of the big desk. He looked at the framed pictures of Rosen with Governor Owen, with the mayor of Miami, and one photo with actor Sylvester Stallone at a golf tournament.

Rosen stopped typing. "Ron Hamilton mentioned it was urgent. Said you'd explain. I remember some of the highlights of your career with Miami PD. You seemed to have had an excellent arrest and conviction record. I also recall media accounts of Internal Affairs investigating some allegations of improper interrogation and arrest techniques you may or may not have used. Is your trip to this office related to that?"

"If you're asking me whether one of my convictions is suing the county for something, the answer is no." O'Brien leaned forward in the chair. "There have been two murders in Volusia County in the last thirty-five hours."

"What's that have to do with Miami-Dade?"

"The murders are a direct result of an arrest and murder conviction in Dade County eleven years ago. The man convicted, Charlie Williams, is innocent. He was found guilty after I arrested him for killing his girlfriend, Alexandria Cole."

"What would you like this office to do, Mr. O'Brien?"

O'Brien gave Rosen the details of the events, including his meeting with Charlie Williams. He concluded by saying, "The case needs to be reopened and a brand-new investigation launched into finding the real perp. I don't think he's finished killing. The DOC guard hasn't been found, and he's the direct link between the killer and what happened to Father Callahan and Sam Spelling."

"But you can't prove that," said Rosen.

"I will."

"I need more."

"You'll get it."

"When you bring it to me, we'll talk further."

"There isn't time to go on a scavenger hunt. I need you to help get a stay of execution until I can find the perp."

Rosen sat back in his large leather chair, crossed his fingers, pursed his lips once, and said, "Mr. O'Brien, these murders are horrific. I don't want to come across in a fashion that in any way seems to diminish the gravity of what you are telling me. However, I'm suggesting to you that without something concrete, something I can take to a jury and get a conviction, I'm not in a position to reopen a capital case, especially one that's so high profile. I can't reopen something predicated on what amounts to a former detective using speculation and deductive reasoning, based on information garnered from witnesses that can't be corroborated because they are dead. I apologize if that sounds callous, but it is fact. You haven't told me, or given me, something I could take to a grand jury or even a criminal jury in a murder trial. These events, in and of themselves, are heinous crimes, but are they related to the murder of Alexandria Cole eleven years ago? Maybe. Will they prove that Charlie Williams did not do it and point the way to the person that did? No."

"This is the prosecuting office of Dade County," O'Brien said, his voice rising. "Is it because this was such a high-profile case that you're gun-shy? You have a moral obligation to reopen this case. If you don't, and if Charlie Williams is executed, this office and you will be held culpable parties to his murder. Because that's what it will amount to—an innocent man killed when it could have been prevented. Prove to me that doesn't fit the definition of murder, Counselor."

Rosen stood. "Perhaps that temper of yours was why IA flagged your file three times during your career in the homicide division. O'Brien, I'm not opening a closed case to let the media play ball with it. Taxpayers deserve better."

"Charlie Williams deserves to live!"

"Unfortunately, I'm running behind. Thank you for coming to see me today. If Ron Hamilton and MPD want to crack this open, by all means. When they, or even you, bring me something I can use . . . we'll talk. Good-bye, Mr. O'Brien."

"You want something physical? I'll bring you the killer . . . then you can hang his mug shot up on the wall with the rest of your souvenirs."

THIRTY-SEVEN

Driving to the Miami FBI headquarters, O'Brien called Ron Hamilton's cell phone. Hamilton answered in a whisper. "Sean, I'm in a hall outside a courtroom. Just finished testifying. Let me walk over to a corner window."

O'Brien said, "Let's meet."

"Where?"

"Denny's on Ocean Drive. Around eight."

"Okay."

"Bring a copy of Alexandria Cole's case file and the package I sent you."

"How'd it go with Rosen?"

"Not good. I'll tell you more when I see you later."

O'Brien picked up the thin file folder and locked the car. From the moment he got out of his rental Jeep in the garage of the federal building, he knew his every move was on camera. The feds did a good job hiding cameras. The ones they wanted you to see were decoy cameras, blatantly hanging in visible places like metallic piñatas.

At the reception desk, a uniformed guard told O'Brien to sign in and wait. He also had him roll his right thumb in nonvisible ink and make an impression on a portable device with a glass surface. The machine looked like a small photocopier. It made an electronic swipe of O'Brien's print.

The guard rang through to Lauren Miles. "There's a Sean O'Brien in the lobby. Says he has an appointment with you."

"Be right down."

A tiny green light flashed once on the machine and the guard mumbled, "Looks like you're good to go."

O'Brien half smiled and nodded. He stepped over to the tall vertical glass windows and looked at the traffic zipping by on Second Avenue. He thought about the investigation he conducted eleven years ago. He remembered where he was when he got the call. He had taken his wife, Sherri, to dinner. It was their first anniversary. Before they could order, O'Brien received the call—a homicide in a South Beach condominium—the death of an international supermodel. Sherri said she "understood." She was that way, flashing that winning smile of hers even when the result of evil raised its ugly head time and time again.

"Hello, Sean O'Brien. Welcome to the FBI."

O'Brien turned and faced Lauren Miles. She smiled wide, reminding O'Brien of Sandra Bullock—inquisitive brown eyes, dark shoulder-length hair.

"Thanks for seeing me on such short notice, Lauren."

"So, what's the life-and-death scenario?"

O'Brien opened the file folder and took out the blank piece of paper.

"What's that?" she asked.

"Maybe the ID of the perp who just killed a priest and an informant."

"Talk to me, Sean. I see nothing on the paper."

"This was the sheet directly beneath a written confession an informant was writing out to give to a friend of mine—a priest who'd heard the informant's confession in an emergency room. I want your lab to see if it can raise the imprint of the handwritten confession. It's related to the death of supermodel Alexandria Cole."

Lauren said, "I remember a little about the case. We had agents working it."

"There wasn't a joint task force working this murder."

"We didn't work the murder. We were working a drug connection with DEA before the murder."

"What connection?"

"Let's talk in my office."

"I don't have time to hike around this building. Who was your connection?"

"His name was Jonathan Russo."

"Jonathan Russo was Alexandria Cole's manager. I knew the DEA was watching him. But I didn't know the FBI was involved."

"Let's talk."

THIRTY-EIGHT

Lauren Miles led O'Brien through the maze of halls, passing glass offices and conference rooms. He couldn't help but notice the difference between his old office in homicide and what federal money bought in furnishings and equipment.

When they got to the offices in her division she said, "Let's go through here. We can talk at my desk, or I'll stake out a vacant conference room."

They walked around a dozen large cubicles, agents working the phones in hushed tones, faces glued to computer screens. She said, "Many of the agents in this immediate area work counterintelligence, fraud, and organized crime."

A tall man with gray hair, dressed in a dark pin-striped suit, approached Lauren. He said, "I need the information on the Dade Federal hit. A second one was in Vero. The MO is similar. Stick 'em up and then shoot 'em up."

"Mike, this is Sean O'Brien. Sean worked Miami PD homicide for a number of years. Sean, this is Mike Chambers. Mike's our bureau chief."

"Are you no longer with Miami-Dade?" asked Chambers.

"Retired," said O'Brien.

Chambers started to ask a question, but said, "Pleasure." He turned to Lauren and said, "I'll need that report on my desk first thing in the morning."

"First thing," she said, nodding. Chambers walked away, his wing tips loud across the tile floor.

Lauren's cubical was austere. Everything in place. No pictures of friends or family. O'Brien said, "I guess it's hard to find your feng shui in a cubicle."

"Yeah, but I can find everything else. Okay, Sean, I'm all ears."

He told her the details since Father Callahan's call and the history of his investigation into Alexandria's murder. When O'Brien finished, Lauren sat very still, looked at a spot on her desk, composed her thoughts, and said, "I got the picture you e-mailed. The message left behind by the priest is chilling. Six-six-six . . . the Greek letter omega, something that looked like a kid trying to draw the Man in the Moon, and the letters P-A-T . . . we can give it a go. Run it from every angle through some supercomputers in Quantico. Can't promise you anything . . . code breaking isn't easy."

"Father Callahan didn't leave a code, he left a lead, and maybe an ID."

"But it might as well be in code because it doesn't make sense."

"Makes about as much sense to me right now as hearing the FBI was investigating one of my original suspects at the time Alexandria Cole was murdered. Any reason that information wasn't passed on to Miami PD?"

"Let me see what I can pull up." Lauren began punching in passwords on her computer. Her brow furrowed. She pushed a strand of dark hair behind her right ear and said, "Got to go deep in the archives for this. Not a ton of stuff here, but from what I see, the only reason we became involved is because DEA asked for assistance. Todd Jefferies was the Miami DEA chief at the time. They were investigating cocaine trafficking into Miami via a South Beach club allegedly connected to Miami and New York crime families. They believed Russo was responsible for bringing in a lot of product from Colombia. His day job was managing a few B-list celebs, promoting boy bands and Alexandria Cole's career, and producing bad movies that went straight to DVD. Apparently, we caught Russo with only a fraction of the goods. He did seventeen months in a country-club facility. And that's all I have. Mike Chambers worked on that with Christian Manerou. I haven't seen Christian all day. His office is farther down the hall. I'll call him."

"Maybe I can speak with the guy I just met, Chambers."

Lauren shook her head as she punched the speakerphone. She said, "Mike's in one of his 'General Mike' military moods, I call them. You don't really speak as much as listen."

"Okay, I'd like to listen after I ask him a question."

A voice came through the phone speaker. "Manerou."

"Christian, an old friend of mine from Miami PD is in my office. He's investigating a case that you and Mike worked on—it had a circuitous path to us as well. Maybe you can help. Got a minute? Thanks." She hung up and turned to O'Brien. "Christian has an excellent memory. Very detail-oriented."

O'Brien stood when Christian Manerou approached. He was in good shape for a man in his midfifties: dark complexion and eyes, smooth skin, full head of salt-and-pepper-colored hair, and his sleeves were rolled up. Lauren made the introductions. O'Brien said, "I appreciate your time."

"No problem. Lauren said you're from Miami-Dade. What division?"

"Used to be homicide. Now I'm on my own."

"Private?"

"By default. A friend of mind was just murdered. I believe it's tied to a homicide investigation I conducted a little more than ten years ago. At that time, I was looking into the death of Alexandria Cole. She was a supermodel found stabbed to death."

"I remember the case," said Manerou.

Lauren said, "I was telling Sean that we were working with DEA, per Todd Jefferies's request, at the same time the victim was killed. And we happened to be investigating Jonathan Russo, Alexandria Cole's manager."

Manerou nodded. "Absolutely, he's the kind of person you don't easily forget. Russo's day job might have been working as a manager for supermodels, but he made his real money from distribution of cocaine, racketeering, money laundering. We sent in a mule wearing a wire when we nailed Russo. But he didn't admit enough for us to bury him. He lawyered up with the defense attorneys who fly their own Learjets. By the time it came to trial, they'd cut a deal. Russo did seventeen months."

"Where's he now?" O'Brien asked.

"Back here in Miami. South Beach. Managed to keep the club. He reopened it under a new name with a few million dollars' worth of restoration and high-tech gear. We figured he'd stashed enough drug profits in offshore depositories. I'd bet the club is still nothing but a front for money laundering, probably dealing to high rollers, too. I heard he was managing a few local rock bands."

O'Brien said, "The man arrested and charged with Cole's murder didn't do it."

"What do you mean?" Manerou asked.

"All the forensics pointed to Alexandria's former boyfriend—a farm kid from North Carolina. Now, on the eve of his execution, an inmate who saw the murder, or at least saw the killer dump the weapon, confessed to a priest." O'Brien explained the events and said, "The priest, a close friend of mine, was murdered shortly thereafter. He got a written confession from the inmate. But we can't find it."

"What do you think happened to it?" Lauren asked.

"I believe the perp stole it from the priest, or a DOC guard did— who may also be dead. He's been reported missing." O'Brien held up the file folder. "The sheet of paper under the second page is here. Sam

Spelling bore down fairly hard when he wrote the confession on the top sheet. I'm hoping your lab can read whatever might be on here. It could reveal the killer's name." O'Brien handed the folder to Lauren.

"How much time do you have?" Manerou asked.

"Before the execution?"

"Yes."

O'Brien looked at his watch. "A little less than fifty-nine hours."

THIRTY-NINE

auren folded her arms across her breasts. She looked at a calendar hanging above her computer. She said, "It happens Friday morning."

"What can we do to help?" Manerou asked.

"Can you remember anything about Russo, anything at all, that might provide a lead? Something that might indicate he was involved in her death?"

"Except the fact that he was rich, arrogant, narcissistic . . . all personality traits. I wish I could add something he might have said." Manerou paused, lowered his voice, and said, "There may be something. . . . We'd tapped his phones. He'd left a message with a guy . . . believe his name was like Conti—"

"Sergio Conti?" asked O'Brien.

"That's the name. And Russo's alibi was so rehearsed I remember a little of it."

The bureau chief, Mike Chambers, walked by, and Manerou waved him over. He said, "Mike, remember the time we co-opted with Todd

Jefferies at DEA on the Jonathan Russo case—the South Beach club owner busted for trafficking coke?"

"What about him?"

"Remember how well he'd rehearsed that alibi, the one I heard on the phone tap?"

"Wasn't it something about stone crabs?"

"That's the one. Russo had coached his pal to say they'd eaten a few pounds of stone crabs because they were in season. Ate them from his penthouse balcony and tossed the shells down to the beach below them. Called it 'raining crabs.' It was so bizarre that when I see stone crabs on a restaurant menu, I remember it."

O'Brien said, "That would have been very helpful, had we known about it."

"DEA knew," Chambers said, folding his arms. "What's the issue?"

"An innocent man is on the verge of getting a lethal injection at Starke for allegedly killing his girlfriend, Alexandria Cole, eleven years ago. Now I'm finding out that your agency was running a cocaine investigation on Jonathan Russo, Alexandria's manager at the time."

Lauren started to say something when Chambers said, "What are you suggesting, Mr. O'Brien?"

"Why weren't we informed the feds were in the same ball field?"

Chambers said, "Maybe your department was, but it didn't trickle down to you."

O'Brien said nothing, his eyes locked on Chambers.

Manerou shrugged. "Unfortunately, when two agencies—or three, including the DEA—are investigating the same suspect for two separate things, and neither is aware of the other's investigation, sometimes a few items can fall between the cracks. We'd assumed Russo was referring to the off-loading of about ten tons of cocaine we were tracking as a container ship was bringing the drugs into the Port of Miami. As we were about to drop the hammer on a big bust, it looks, in retrospect, like his alibi may have been a fabrication, so he could have killed the girl the same night."

Chambers said, "I'd say it puts him deep in your suspect pool."

O'Brien said, "Right now he's the only one swimming in that pool."

Chambers almost smiled, his jaw rigid. He tilted forward on his dark wing-tip shoes and said, "Sometimes the best of communications doesn't work. Sorry we couldn't have added something about Russo in the original investigation. Good meeting you, O'Brien. I have an on-line videoconference with the director. Excuse me." He turned and left.

"Looks like General Mike's in a rather reflective mood," Lauren said.

"He has good recall," Manerou said before turning to O'Brien and asking, "How'd you know Conti's name?"

"That was the name—the alibi—Russo had given us."

"Did you question Conti?"

"I did, and he corroborated Russo's story."

"Too bad we didn't know the wiretap information was related to an alibi for murder. Between the DEA, FBI, FDLE, and Miami-Dade PD, I guess we were like silent ships running and passing each other in the dark. It's very unfortunate."

"Do you have a tape of that wiretap somewhere?" O'Brien asked.

"Not after the sentencing. We had hours on analog tape. Between this case and hundreds more, it was taking up a lot of space. Now everything is stored digitally."

"What's the name of Russo's South Beach club?"

"It's called Oz, Club Oz, why?"

"Because, based on what you and Mike just told me, now it's time I followed the road to the Land of Oz. Let's see what's behind the curtain."

FORTY

O'Brien was leaving the federal building parking garage when his cell phone rang. It was Detective Dan Grant. He said, "A state trooper says he pulled over a truck matching Lyle Johnson's last night. Says Johnson ran a stop sign at the crossing of Highway 15 and 44. Trooper gave Johnson a warning, and he said Johnson seemed nervous, much more so than anxiety from getting a ticket."

"Did you question Johnson's wife again?"

"Sean, that lady's a sad case."

"How's that?"

"Battered."

"Domestic?"

"I'd say the guy who guards inmates beats his wife . . . and does or did it regularly."

"What'd she say?"

"It's more what she didn't say. Her nails are chewed to the flesh. She was nervous. Said her husband last spoke to her around ten in the evening Monday. Told her he was meeting some guy, didn't say who. He said a deal was dropped in his lap and had to come down that night. He told her if he wasn't home by one in the morning to go on and take their kid to her mother's house and to leave early."

"Did she have any idea where Johnson was going to meet this guy?"

"No."

"If he's smart, it would have been a bar. Someplace public."

O'BRIEN LOOKED AT HIS watch.

Fifty-eight hours. He called information and asked to be connected to Club Oz.

"Oz," said a sultry woman's voice.

"Jonathan Russo."

"Who's calling?"

"Sergio Conti."

"Hold, please."

O'Brien drove another block toward the Denny's restaurant, listening to the on-hold music and promos coming though the phone: "Party at Oz this Friday with world-famous deejay Philippe Cayman."

"Mr. Conti?"

"Yes?"

"Mr. Russo has been out of town the last few days. He's expected back tonight. May I give him a message?"

"No thanks, I'll call him later."

DETECTIVE RON HAMILTON WAS waiting for O'Brien at a table in the corner of Denny's restaurant. O'Brien approached the table with a *Miami Herald* newspaper in his hand. He was surprised to see his old partner had gained weight. He had a bulbous nose, dark eyes, bushy eyebrows, and thinning hair. Hamilton, less than five feet eight, looked to be pushing two hundred pounds. He wore a brown sports coat in need of dry cleaning. His tie was down to the first button. He sipped black coffee.

"Thanks for meeting me, Ron."

"No problem. Wish I could say retirement looks good on you. Have you slept?"

"Not much. I feel so damn responsible for what happened to Charlie Williams, and to people like Father Callahan who were at the wrong place at the wrong time."

"Sean, don't beat yourself up. You don't even have to be involved in this. But you chose to try to do something. That says a helluva lot. And knowing how fast you can work, you might be the only guy who can find the evidence that will stop the ticking clock for Charlie Williams. How'd it go with the perpetually tanned DA, Rosen?"

"Not good. He seems more worried about public opinion than he does about saving a life."

"That's why he sits where he sits."

"Rosen has a fair grasp of my black-eye history with the department—the IA investigations. Sort of tossed that in my face as one excuse for not reopening an investigation into Alexandria Cole's murder."

"The guy doesn't forget much, especially celebrity cases. He'd like to have had O. J. slip up here in Miami, like he did in Vegas. When I called Rosen, it took him about two seconds to remember you, Sean. He asked if you were the same O'Brien who—and I'm quoting here—'had IA following him like a shadow.' I told him you were the best detective I'd ever known."

"Maybe your endorsement penetrated his preconceived opinion of me."

"Don't take it personally. Rosen is one of those prosecutors who only go to trial to win. For him, there's no such thing as breaking even."

"The only score that counts right now is keeping Charlie Williams alive. Did you bring a copy of the case file?"

"Yep. Right here . . . on top of the package you sent me." Hamilton lifted the thick file off the chair next to him and placed it in front of O'Brien. "Don't forget it. Took me awhile to copy that."

"Thanks, Ron. This is boiling down to a pool of hours for Charlie Williams."

"You can't get some court to grant a stay?"

"Governor's out of the country. Williams's attorney has had all of his petitions denied or ignored. I have nothing but gut speculation to file with any judge or court that might hear it. Since lethal injection isn't considered by the high court to be cruel and unusual punishment, the executioner is lining them up."

Hamilton sipped his coffee and said, "There are many on death row that deserve to be exactly where they are and meeting the fate they're facing."

"But Charlie Williams isn't one of them. I just came from Lauren Miles's office at the federal building. They'd worked a coke bust with DEA about the time of Charlie Williams's trial. Feds had been investigating Alexandria Cole's manager, Jonathan Russo, the same time I was questioning him in her death." O'Brien looked at the case file on the table. He gestured to the file. "In there, I wrote that Russo was having dinner with a business associate, guy named Sergio Conti, the night Alexandria was killed. Now I know that his alibi was a lie. So where was he?"

"Russo's no deacon in his local church. We know his club launders dirty money. But proving it is another thing."

O'Brien looked out the restaurant window and watched the lights from the traffic on the Rickenbacker Causeway bridge. "Ron, I'm going to have to play on the edge to get some answers from Russo. He's cruel and a narcissist, a guy who believes he's impervious to real trouble. If I had more time, I'd investigate this differently, play it by the book and document every move. But I don't, and I can't. I'm starting from scratch here, and I have to take the fastest course to try and save Charlie's life. I don't like this kind of investigation or interrogation. So, if you can, cover me, old friend. Maybe between the two of us we can save Charlie. If you can't cover me, I understand."

Ron stirred more sugar in his coffee. "I'll do what I can. Miami's gotten even meaner since you left. A guy like Russo takes no prisoners. If you blink or make a mistake, Sean, we won't ever find your body."

FORTY-ONE

The college-aged front desk clerk asked, "Are you staying with us only one night?"

O'Brien finished the registration and said, "Yes, one night only."

The clerk read the card. "Mr. Snyder, would you like to leave a credit card imprint for incidentals?"

"No thanks."

"There's a minibar in your room."

"I won't need it."

"Yessir. You'll need to prepay for the one night, though."

O'Brien opened his wallet and counted the money. "How do I get to the room?"

"Go back out front and follow the drive around to the right. Top of the steps. Room twenty-nine. Mr. Snyder, do you need assistance with your luggage?"

"No thanks. Packed light."

The clerk nodded and dropped the registration card on the stack next to his half-eaten peanut butter and jelly sandwich.

. . .

O'BRIEN PARKED ON THE opposite side of the building from his room. He picked up the case file and walked to a 7-Eleven next to the hotel. He bought a prepackaged ham sandwich, large coffee, and a Snickers bar to take to his room. During the short walk back to the hotel, he scanned the parking lot, the shadows in the alcoves, and the license plate of a new car that wasn't there when he had left for the store. Ron Hamilton had gone home for the night. O'Brien hoped Ron would never have to admit or deny that he knew what was about to happen.

He unlocked the room door and flipped on the lights. The odor was like opening the trunk of a car with old clothes in it. The smell had the faint trace of bleach. O'Brien locked the door, placed the Glock on a nightstand next to the bed, and sat at a small table to eat while he read the case file.

As he read his own words written eleven years ago, the visuals of Alexandria's death came back in graphic detail. He remembered the interrogation he had conducted with Judy Neilson, Alexandria's roommate. He recalled questioning her at the crime scene. The sobbing, the blotches of red on her neck and face. The incoherent, disconnected sentences, the shock of finding her best friend dead from knife wounds to the chest.

It was the second time he questioned Judy Neilson that her demeanor had changed. She was controlled, unwavering in the facts as she knew them surrounding Alexandria's life and her death. And she had the hard edge of retribution in eyes that could cry no more. The sheer horror of it had deeply affected her. O'Brien read Judy's words and remembered her sitting in the MPD interview room, her blond hair pulled back, striking face, no makeup, manicured hands folded in her lap, shoulders straight back. Her tone was resolute, her expression was one of controlled restraint and yet compassion for a friend who was murdered. "Alex was one of the most loving, gracious people

138

I've ever known. I think she still loved Charlie, but she felt it wasn't going to work. His ego was in the dumps. He kept coming around like a cat that finds its way back to your doorstep at night. It was because of Alex's big heart that she always took him in. They'd fight and make up. Eventually, he stopped coming back.

"After he was gone for most of the summer, when she had time to compare him to some of the creeps that came around, I guess Charlie was looking better. She told me she'd always have a place in her heart for Charlie. . . . She just needed time to figure it all out. That possessive manager of hers, Jonathan Russo, he was over at the condo more than I wanted to see him. Alex swore there was nothing between them, but you could tell, he kept her on a short leash. She hated going to his club, but Alex did have her weaknesses—she was only human. She liked the celebrity scene and all the fame she was getting. Russo got her hooked on cocaine . . . and that's when she started depending on him in a sick kind of way. Charlie got wind of it. Came back from North Carolina and had words with Russo. Alex told me Russo threatened to kill Charlie if he ever came in his club again. I know Charlie hated to see Alex spiraling down. Charlie did have a drinking problem, but in my heart of hearts, I find it hard to believe he went off the deep end like that. I know Russo had people watching the condo. Sometimes I'd see one of his goons sitting in a car and just watching. Used to give me the creeps."

O'BRIEN BIT INTO his ham sandwich and washed down the taste with coffee. He flipped through to the transcript of Jonathan Russo's interrogation. He remembered Russo's demeanor well, the slouch in the chair, the peaks of anger tapered by feigned boredom mixed with arrogance. He remembered the tanned face with a spiderweb-thin scar etched on the bridge of his nose. Thick lips. Dark hair pulled back in a ponytail. A diamond stud winking in his right ear. He wore a thousand-dollar olive green Armani suit and kept a five-hundred-dollar-an-hour legal beagle at his side.

"Why would I kill Lexie, huh? She was one of my top-billing talents. Besides, I was over at my friend Sergio Conti's condo when you said the coroner estimated her time of death. We picked up a jug of chardonnay, a few pounds of stone crabs from the marina, ate them and tossed the shells off the balcony onto the sand below—it was raining friggin' crabs. Threw the shells and a little crabmeat down to the beach for the birds to enjoy in the morning. I've learned to recycle those natural things best I can. Crabs are always washin' up on the beach anyway. Scavengers."

O'Brien lifted the case folder and turned to a photograph of Alexandria Cole. He remembered the crime scene photographer using a stepladder to get a higher angle over the bed. The image was of a young woman lying on her back with seven stab wounds in her naked chest. Breasts pierced with deep holes. The killer brought the blade down so hard he split her sternum. Blood had soaked into the sheets and dried like dark shadows below her outstretched arms, giving the body an illusion of scarlet angel wings.

O'Brien looked at the photo and said, "I'm sorry, Alexandria. I'm sorry you suffered like this and the man who did it is living his life. Although I'm eleven years late, I'll do my best to make up for lost time . . . for you and for Charlie Williams."

O'Brien closed the folder, picked up his Glock, wedged it under his belt, and walked out the door into the night.

FORTY-TWO

As O'Brien drove down Ocean Drive in South Beach, he watched the moon rise over the Atlantic. It looked like a big goose egg above the horizon, the reflection casting a long ribbon of light over the water. A small dark cloud moved across the base of the moon, creating a diffused edge around the lower third. He rolled down the windows in the rental Jeep to hear the sound of the breakers.

O'Brien drove slowly, watching people meander across the street, heading into the trendy restaurants and upscale coffee and wine bars. He spotted a man and a trophy blond model get out of a red Ferrari in front of a nightclub called the Opium Garden. O'Brien could hear the pulse of music, smell the grilled fish and garlic mix with the salty scent of the ocean. He missed some things about Miami, mainly the food, but not the fast-paced, instant-gratification, pseudolifestyle of the see-and-be-seen on South Beach.

He stopped at a traffic light and looked through the palm trees to the moon over the water. The cloud was rising like someone sitting up in a bed with a sheet over his head, an armless shadow in the center of the moon. Like a figure morphing in a lava lamp, it transformed into a dark image resembling the profile of a person dressed in a shawl. O'Brien smiled. The Man in the Moon was now the Woman in the Moon.

O'Brien's heart jumped. He had seen it before.

But where?

The driver in the car behind him honked. O'Brien drove, craning his neck to see the moon through the tall royal palms that lined South Beach.

He stared at the image—the figure. Where had he seen it?

"What are you doing? Dumb ass!" screamed a man riding a bike on the shoulder of the road. O'Brien swerved, just missing the man.

The likeness. Where did it come from? Think. Book. Magazine. A painting? Where? Maybe a museum. Maybe in an art class in college.

And on the floor of St. Francis Church!

An image in blood drawn by Father John Callahan.

O'Brien pulled onto the sidewalk, his car blocking two teenage skateboarders. He jumped out of his car and snapped a picture of the moon with his cell phone.

One teenager said, "It's just the moon, man. Like you've never seen it before."

O'Brien hit Dave Collins's number on his cell.

"Sean, I see it's you, and I'm not even wearing my glasses."

"Go find them. I'll send you a lunar image."

"A what?"

"An image. Just took it of the moon."

"Is there an eclipse tonight?"

"No, I want you to look at it carefully. Tell me what it looks like."

"Where the hell are you?" Collins's voice was deep, thick with rum and fatigue.

O'Brien said, "South Beach. How's Max?"

"Nick came by a few hours ago and said it was his turn to watch her. He took her down to the tiki bar for dinner. He said her presence helps him pick up women."

O'Brien had a mental picture of his little dachshund sitting on a bar stool next to Nick Cronus. "Dave, try to get her back on your boat before it gets too late. There's a reason Nick never had kids. He'd forget where he put them."

"Kim, our lovely bartender, won't let Max out of her sight, believe me on that one. The woman would like to score a few points with you, too. I'll make sure Max is tucked away tonight. Sean, you're my dear friend and you're overdue for some feminine companionship. Since your wife died of cancer and the lady cop . . . what was her name?"

"Leslie, listen—"

"Since she was shot you haven't begun to live again. I think—"

"Dave, please!"

"What?"

"Please, just listen a moment. I'll e-mail an image to you. Look at it closely. See if you can figure out who painted something similar. I know I've seen it in an art history class or somewhere."

"Why?"

"Because it reminds me of the likeness Father Callahan scrawled on the floor of the sanctuary. Maybe, when he was dying, he saw the moon through one of those big windows. I don't know. Could have reminded him of something—something that would get us closer to figuring out his message if we could match that painting or the artist who painted it. Maybe it's connected to the name Pat. There's a chance the artist has a direct clue in the painting that will reveal the killer or his location."

Collins was silent for a beat. O'Brien could hear him stirring ice in his drink. Finally he said, "Sean, I've always liked the way your mind works . . . but you're down there in South Beach howling at the moon. . . . Everything you just told me is the reason they call lunatics crazy, if one is to believe in the lunar influence. However, if the Man in the Moon, our celestial companion, second to our sun in brilliance, can affect a woman's menstrual cycle, what little hope do we mortal men have?"

"You'll have a clearer picture in the morning. Good night, Dave." As O'Brien hung up, he thought about Max. "Next time, I get Max a real dog sitter," he mumbled as he got in the Jeep and drove off the sidewalk, back to the road.

O'Brien pulled onto Washington Avenue and headed north. He passed by Club Oz and saw a line already forming at the door. He knew that later in the night the line would be much longer. Valet runners were hopping as they parked Mercedes, Jags, and BMWs. All the beautiful people were converging under a techno cathedral built on a foundation of narcissism. The house built by Jonathan Russo, a man as synthetic as the music. Follow the yellow brick road to Oz and get lost in the poppy fields.

O'Brien knew that inside Oz it would be so loud that none of the glitzy patrons would even notice the pop of a pistol. And if they did, it would blend into the pop of Dom Pérignon and Krug, flowing like fountains in VIP corners.

O'Brien didn't come here to kill Russo however, he came here to convince him to talk, and often a silent pistol barrel pressed to a forehead speaks volumes. Before he entered Oz, he would pay a visit to Sergio Conti. As O'Brien drove north on Washington, he passed the legendary restaurant Joe's Stone Crab and an upscale strip club called Club Paradise. And then he had a new plan.

FORTY-THREE

The posh Waverly high-rise condos overlooked Biscayne Bay and twinkling lights from million-dollar yachts tied to berths that rented for the price of a monthly mortgage on a luxury home.

O'Brien parked in the Palm Bay Marina next to the Waverly, pulled a Panama hat over his head, and walked toward the condo. He maneuvered through the thick canary palms and terraces of bougainvillea, carrying a small toolbox as he walked the length of the building toward the beach. O'Brien glanced up at the power lines feeding the remote left quadrant of the building. He could see where the cable television connection came in and joined a junction box to feed the cable system to each unit. As he walked, he casually removed a folding knife from the toolbox and sliced through the main feed in less time than it would take a good gardener to cut a rose. O'Brien continued moving toward the pool at the rear of the building, closer to the ocean.

Now, he thought, wait. Probably five to ten minutes before the night manager was inundated with calls. O'Brien pulled up a chaise longue near the spa, sat down, looked at his watch, and pulled down the brim of his hat. Ten minutes and he would go through the front door. Ten minutes—a year in Charlie Williams's remaining life.

O'Brien got up and stepped over to a privacy wall that separated the pool area from people on the beach. He looked through the wrought-iron bars on the door that led a few steps down to the sand. The moon was now high over the ocean, its light spilling a soft hue across the white sand. Through the bars he saw two lovers, hand in hand, walking by the surf. O'Brien imagined what Charlie Williams saw through his steel bars.

He looked up at the high-rise balconies with the million-dollar views and remembered where he had questioned Sergio Conti. The top left penthouse. The light was on, and O'Brien was coming up.

"SECURITY," SAID A VOICE with a Hispanic accent.

"Miami Cable. Got a call that your system is out."

"Yeah, even right here in the office. I was watching Brazil beating Mexico and it went to snow. How come you're not dressed in a cable shirt and stuff?"

"The regular guy on this shift had to go to the hospital with his wife. It's their first baby. Office called me because I don't live too far."

"Cool, man. Just get us a picture quick. Phone's going nuts."

"You bet. I'll look at the connections. Checked the outside already. Couldn't trace the problem. Could be something on the inside—salt air can corrode the connectors. I can check near the roof where the lines are distributed." O'Brien glanced at the directory under glass and he read: CONTI, S–1795. He said, "Box feeds from the roof down. You got any vacancies on the seventeenth floor? I'll check one of those TVs and then see if it's coming from outside."

"Sure, guy. The people in seventeen-two are in Europe. I'll get you the key."

O'BRIEN RODE THE GLASS elevator up to the penthouse floor. The elevator opened to a large atrium that looked all the way down to the imported Italian marble floors and fountains in the entrance. He walked down the posh hall decorated with pods of soft lighting revealing imported artwork and small Romanesque statues. He stopped at the door that read 1795, opened the toolbox, and removed his Glock. O'Brien pressed the red RECORD button on the tiny tape recorder in his shirt pocket and tapped on the door.

"Who is it?" The man's voice was gruff.

"Maintenance, sir. Lightning hit the system and fried a lot of cable receptors."

FORTY-FOUR

The man unlocked the door and opened it. "Yeah, my fuckin' set went off right in the middle of them opening an Egyptian tomb on the Discovery Channel." Sergio Conti stood there. Bald, shirtless, three-day growth of white beard on his fat jowls, gut hanging over boxer shorts.

O'Brien shoved the gun barrel right into Conti's wide nose and entered the room. He closed the door. "If you don't tell me want I want, they'll be closing your tomb."

Conti raised both hands and backed up. O'Brien said, "Let me get something straight real fast. Don't think about lying to me or they'll find your body seventeen floors below on the sand with crabs chewing your ears. As I remember, you like stone crabs anyway."

"Who the fuck are you?"

"I might be the last human you'll see in this world."

"I remember you . . . the fuckin' detective. I ain't sayin' shit till I call my lawyer."

"Oh, you will say 'shit' and a lot more. I'm not a detective. This mission is for someone else. He couldn't be here personally because he's locked up."

"Who sent you? Whatever you're getting, I'll double it."

"It's a long way down. And they won't find a bullet because you got so drunk, so damn depressed that you jumped. The good thing is it'll open up another condo for sale. I hear there's still a demand for high-priced cages like this."

"You're fuckin' crazy."

O'Brien said nothing.

"What do you want?" Blood trickled out of Conti's left nostril and ran into the corner of his mouth.

"In questioning, you told me that Jonathan Russo had dinner with you, on your balcony, the night of Alexandria Cole's murder."

"That's a long fuckin' time ago, so what?"

"Did he?"

"If I said it, sure." Conti shrugged.

"Russo's never had dinner on your balcony."

"What difference does it make, huh? You got the boyfriend. He killed her."

"No, he didn't."

"Sounds like your beef's with Russo. Not me, pal."

"Where was Russo the night Alexandria was killed? Was he with her?"

"Why don't you go ask him?"

"He used you as an alibi, but he didn't come here. You lied to me during the initial investigation. That means you're an accomplice to murder."

"Fuck you! I'm callin' my lawyer and then the real cops."

O'Brien slowly pulled the barrel of the Glock away from Conti's nose. Conti smiled, wiped the blood with the back of a thick hand. "Now you're comin' to your senses."

"Walk out to the balcony."

"What? I'm not sailing off the fuckin' balcony!"

"I said walk!"

"What's this really about, huh? Bitch is long dead anyway."

O'Brien backhanded Conti and shoved the pistol barrel under his blubbery chin. "Did you have dinner with Russo on your balcony the night Alexandria Cole was killed? Tell me, you sick son of a bitch!"

"No! He wasn't here!"

"Where was he that night?"

"I don't fuckin' know!"

"Was he with Alexandria when she was killed?"

"Honest to God, I don't know. He liked the younger girls, you know, the ones who wanted to get into the modeling biz—the younger teens. He paid me to find 'em for him. Still does. His wife, ex-wife now, found him with one of them, and she threatened to file for divorce. Russo was scared shitless she'd wipe him out. So he used me for an alibi . . . lots of times."

"Did Russo kill Alexandria?"

"I don't know! God as my witness, that's the fuckin' truth!"

O'Brien lowered the gun and pulled out his knife.

"What are you gonna do?" asked Conti, trying to crawl backward.

O'Brien opened the toolbox, cut a piece of rope, and pushed a high-back chair toward Conti. "Sit down and put your hands behind your back. Do it!" Conti exhaled like a bull and did as ordered. O'Brien tied Conti's hands to the back of the chair and then he cut the phone cord, dropped Conti's cell phone to the marble floor, and smashed it with his heel.

"You're fuckin' crazy!" yelled Conti. "I could die, my ass tied up here before anybody finds me. The maid doesn't come until Saturday."

O'Brien leaned down and said in a voice above a whisper, "If you somehow manage to free yourself, if you call Russo and warn him, I'll come back here. If I do, they'll find you lying on the sand in the morning with the gulls picking food out of your bleached teeth. Now you stay real quiet, like a good boy, and I'll call maintenance in the morning and tell them I heard noises coming from seventeen ninety-five. They'll run up, find you, and cut you loose. Otherwise, it's waiting for the maid. You could be stinking by then."

"I'll hunt you down for this, motherfucker. I swear to God I will!"

"No you won't." O'Brien ripped off a piece of duct tape from a roll in the toolbox, pressed it to Conti's mouth, and said, "I'll lock the door on my way out."

FORTY-FIVE

Driving back down Collins Avenue, O'Brien called Lauren Miles's cell. It took her half a dozen rings to answer. There was background noise that O'Brien could tell was coming from a bar or restaurant. He said, "Thanks again for your time this afternoon."

"No problem. Are you calling to meet me for a drink? That would be nice . . . maybe for old times' sake. I'm at Friday's with a few girlfriends."

"Wish I could. I've got another stop to make. I'd be really late."

"No problem. Do you need a place to stay? When's the last time you had a sleepover, Sean?"

O'Brien could hear the slur in her voice, the sexual attraction in her delivery. "I have a room, thanks. When do you think the lab will examine the paper I left you?"

She was quiet a moment and said, "You dropped it off at the end of the day. Everyone in the lab had left. I'm getting a tech in tomorrow. He owes me a favor."

"Every hour cuts into what's left of Charlie Williams's time."

"What if we can't pick up enough from the paper to make an ID?"

"Let's see what the paper reveals."

She sighed, hiccuped, and said, "Okay. Are you doing anything in the meantime?"

"I have to make a few stops. One is to question Jonathan Russo."

"You need backup?" She made another slight hiccup.

"I'm fine, thanks. Please let me know when you can get the lab results, bye." O'Brien disconnected and called information. "Connect me to Joe's Stone Crab restaurant."

Three rings later a male voice said, "Joe's Stone Crab."

"You offer takeout?"

"Yes, sir. What'll it be?"

"Got any live crabs?"

"They're all live till they hit the pot."

"Good. I want to order the largest one you have. But don't cook it."

"No problem. But most people want us to cook it for 'em."

"Not tonight."

The man paused. "Okay, you're in luck. Got a bunch off the boat earlier today, and I saw one of 'em as big around as a dinner plate."

"Good. Keep that one for me."

"What's the name?"

"Ralph Jones."

O'Brien drove another few blocks and pulled into a Walgreens store. He bought the largest woman's purse he could find and then drove toward Club Paradise.

THE STRIP CLUB CATERED to high rollers, sports figures, and celebrities passing through South Beach. O'Brien took a seat at a table in the corner and watched a nude dancer on the stage. She was a statuesque brunette, exceptional body, and high cheekbones that looked sculpted.

A dozen women worked the floor. A waitress approached his table. "Hi," she said. "I'm Liz. What can I get for you?"

153

"Coffee, thanks. Would you ask the girl on stage to drop by after she finishes?"

"No problem, handsome." The waitress smiled and moved on to another table.

O'Brien looked around the room. There were dozens of businessmen, ties down, alcohol causing them to lose their inhibitions and money. Two tables away from him a shapely blonde climbed on the lap of an NBA player O'Brien recognized from the Miami Heat. She gyrated, looking like a toy balancing on his leg, her feet not touching the floor.

"Hi, I hear you requested me."

The woman who was nude on the stage a few minutes ago now stood next to O'Brien's table in a cocktail dress. She had long raven hair, eyes like emeralds, and flawless skin. He smiled and said, "I did. Thanks for coming over."

"Liz is right, you're cute."

"Thanks."

"I'm Barbie. What's your name?"

"Ken."

"Really? Is your name really Ken?"

"Is yours Barbie?"

"I like my name. Most people think it's fake. Most people think my boobs are fake, too. But they're real."

"I saw that."

"Want to see some more?"

"No, thanks."

She looked disappointed. "I thought you wanted a dance."

"What I wanted was to see you. Please, sit down." She sat and O'Brien said, "Tell me about you."

"What do you mean?"

"Your dreams. What you want to do with your life."

"Are you a producer or something?"

"No, just curious."

"I just started college . . . Miami-Dade Community College. I do this job to help pay the expenses. And I'd eventually like to teach third grade."

"Why third grade?"

"My favorite teacher, Miss Stafford, taught third grade. But most importantly, I really love kids. I think I can make a positive difference in their lives. That might sound like hot air coming from someone like me, a nobody, a stripper, but it's true."

O'Brien smiled. "I believe you, and I believe you'll get there, if you want to bad enough. Look, Barbie, have you ever been to Club Oz?"

"No, and I hear it's thirty dollars just to get in the door."

"How'd you like to go?"

"Are you, like, for real?"

"It's a long story. You can help get me to the front of the line and in the door."

"I don't know. What if—"

"When do you get out of here?"

"My shift ends in an hour?"

"Can you go now? I'm not some nut. I need to see a man in Club Oz."

"Who, the wizard?" She laughed at her joke. Perfect smile and teeth.

"I'll pay you three hundred dollars just to go in the place. From there, stay if you want, or you can call a cab."

"Well, as you saw, I do like to dance. What are you going to do?"

"Visit with an old acquaintance."

"I don't have anything to wear."

"Trust me—the dress you're wearing is fine."

"Okay, I guess. But I still have an hour on my shift."

"Tell them you're sick."

"I can tell them I started my period early. That way I can say I'll

155

take the dress and dry-clean it. But I don't want them to see me leaving with you. They'll think I'm doing freelance hooking. That's where I draw the line."

"I'll meet you outside. I'm driving a Jeep."

"I'll be right out, but I'm gonna call my girlfriend, give her a description of you, and tell her where I'm going. I'll tell her if I don't call by midnight to call the police."

"Good idea," O'Brien said with a smile.

Outside, O'Brien unlocked his Jeep and made sure his Glock was where he'd left it. He started the engine and pulled to the front entrance to Club Paradise. Barbie had brushed her long, dark hair, applied lip gloss and a little makeup. O'Brien watched her walk like a runway model. She was a stunning woman, hourglass figure zipped into the red dress with a slit all the way up the right leg to her brown thigh. The low-cut dress accentuated her ample cleavage. Her breasts bounced as she walked on her platform high heels. She stepped right past him a good forty yards, turned a corner, and disappeared.

"Smart kid," mumbled O'Brien.

He drove in the direction he last saw her, slowly turning the corner, and then he saw her standing in the shadows of a thick palm tree. He stopped the Jeep. She looked around quickly, climbed in, and said, "I've never ridden in a Jeep before. Can we put the top down? I like to go topless."

O'Brien laughed, his own laughter sounding oddly foreign. He'd forgotten what it felt like. "Sure, we can put the top down." He unzipped the top and rolled it back.

They drove down Ocean Drive, the wind whipping Barbie's hair, her breasts threatening to bounce out of the dress.

"I like it!" she said. "Kinda crazy date, but I like it!"

"And the night's just begun," O'Brien said as he headed toward Joe's Stone Crab.

FORTY-SIX

The parking lot at Joe's Stone Crab was almost filled, even late on a Tuesday night. O'Brien pulled off Washington Avenue and parked.

Barbie used both hands to push her hair out of her face. She said, "What a wild ride. I love stone crabs! I can smell the garlic out here. And I'm starvin'."

"I'm getting takeout," said O'Brien. "Wait here. I called in the order."

O'Brien walked to the carryout window and said, "I ordered a single live crab."

A perspiring cashier wiped his hands on a towel. "What's the name?

"Ralph Jones."

"I'll get it for you, Mr. Jones."

"Do you have a box, maybe something like plastic foam for me to carry it?"

"Sure." The assistant manager returned with a foam box, a picture of a red stone crab on the side. O'Brien lifted the top. "The claws are banded."

"Yeah, most people like it that way. A stone crab can take a finger off. It's got the most powerful claws of any crab in this part of the world. Almost two thousand pounds of pressure per square inch."

"Good, could you cut the bands off?"

"Sure." The man got a pair of scissors and cut the rubber bands off the two massive front claws. "Don't leave him in the box too long, he'll cut right through."

"Thanks." O'Brien paid and walked back to the Jeep.

Barbie watched O'Brien approach and asked, "Did you get anything to drink, maybe a Coke or something?"

"Barbie, do you like sushi?"

She wrinkled her nose. "No way am I eating any raw fish."

"Then you wouldn't like raw crab." O'Brien set the box between the seats.

"How raw do they serve it?" she asked, picking up the box.

"If you open that, I'll call you Pandora."

"That's a pretty name," she said, lifting the top off. "Ohmygod! That's a live crab! He's huge!" She slammed the top back on the box. O'Brien started the engine.

She said, "Why do you have a crab in a box?"

"It's going into a purse next."

She looked at her small purse, shook her head. "No way! That ugly thing is not going in my purse."

"Not yours, the one in back. Would you mind getting it? Should be on the floorboard."

She turned and reached in the back. "This is heavy. What do you have in here?"

"Open it," said O'Brien.

"I'm almost afraid to. Do you have a snake in this one?" Barbie slowly opened the purse and looked inside. "Are you some kind of sick person? What are these handcuffs and this tape recorder doing in a purse?"

"Storage," said O'Brien. He took the purse from her lap, opened it, lifted the top off the foam box, slid the crab in the purse, and fastened it.

"What on earth are you doing? Why are you putting that poor crab in the purse?"

"When you travel to Oz, get a grip and hold on tight."

O'BRIEN MANAGED TO FIND a parking spot two blocks down from Oz on Washington Avenue. He said, "Okay, it's showtime."

Barbie said, "Are you forgetting something?"

"What?"

"I know this is a really weird date thingy, but you said you'd pay me. Can I get it before we go in? It's not that I don't like trust you. You seem like a very good man, too."

O'Brien smiled. "You're right." He opened his wallet and counted out the money. She folded it, dropping the cash in her purse.

"I need you to carry this purse, too," O'Brien said.

"What if that crab jumps out? Besides, don't you think it would look weird for a girl to carry two purses?"

"Barbie, no one's going to be looking at your purse or purses. Now, here's the plan. The line is too long for us to wait. So I want you to walk to the front of it—I'll be right behind you—and tell that muscular fellow in black that you really need to go to the ladies' room. Weak bladder and all of that. When he agrees, tell him your boyfriend is an old friend of Sergio Conti's, and Sergio wanted him to see the club but he couldn't call personally because he got tied up."

"What's the guy's name again?"

"Sergio Conti."

She whispered it, closed her eyes a second, and said, "Okay, let's go."

As O'Brien walked with Barbie down Washington Avenue, two Hispanic men in a convertible Lexus rode by, reggae music loud, and one yelled, "What a fuckin' ass!"

159

The line to get into Oz stretched far beyond the velvet ropes held by shiny gold-colored stanchion hooks. O'Brien followed Barbie as they walked by the tanned bodies that had spent much of the day on the beach, now freshly showered and dressed in whites and colors of the Caribbean. O'Brien smelled the perfumes mixed with a hint of marijuana.

"Can't believe we're doing this," said Barbie. "It's the best club on South Beach."

"Just keep walking."

"Everybody's staring at us."

"They're staring at you. Nobody sees me."

"The crab is moving in the purse. I can feel it. So help me, Ken—if that's your real name—if this thing sticks one of its claws out and pinches my butt, I'm going to scream loud enough for them to hear me in the Port of Miami."

"Just keep smiling and walking," said O'Brien.

As they approached the head of the line, Barbie smiled, waved a perfectly manicured finger to the doorman, and stepped to him. He looked at her swelling breasts. Barbie worked everything she had in the dress to subtle perfection. The doorman nodded, looked behind her to O'Brien, who smiled, and he waved them through the door.

As they entered the corridor of lights, it opened to a massive room filled with hundreds of gyrating people on the dance floor and others tucked away in nearby smoked-glass VIP rooms. Barbie turned to O'Brien and said, "So this is Oz."

FORTY-SEVEN

The deejay shouted into the sound system, "You're not in Kansas anymore, people! It's time to party like you're in Oz!" The deejay stood behind an elevated platform, spinning his body like an orchestra maestro conducting the last seconds leading into a crescendo.

O'Brien and Barbie walked past a waterfall lit with blue lights. They followed a winding yellow acrylic floor that disappeared around a huge artificial tree. From where O'Brien stood, he counted six bars. The light system sent a rainbow palette of colors over the entire cavernous club in a wave pattern. Stylized images of a lion, scarecrow, tin man, and dueling witches, dressed in black and white, morphed behind a fifty-foot curved Plexiglas screen near the ceiling.

On the second level, O'Brien could see a dozen or more VIP rooms looking down on the dance floor. Silhouetted figures moved behind the smoke-colored glass, resembling shadows on the blinds.

A fashion model moonlighting as a cocktail hostess walked by with a tray of drinks. O'Brien asked, "How do we get up there?" He pointed to the VIP rooms.

"See the hostess over there in the black dress." The waitress pointed

161

to a woman standing behind a lime green podium near a bubble-glass elevator.

As O'Brien and Barbie approached the podium, he stepped on a tiger-striped woven rug near the base of the dais. The woman in the short black dress wore a wireless earpiece and gray microphone. O'Brien said, "We'd like a VIP suite."

"The name, sir."

"Conti."

Barbie looked at O'Brien and smiled.

"Would you like to leave a credit card imprint to reserve it?" asked the hostess.

"It's early. I bet you have a few available. Matter of fact, I'm tall enough to see one that is vacant up there." O'Brien pointed to a dark suite.

"That's reserved for one o'clock."

O'Brien slipped her a twenty and said, "We'll be gone by then. In the meantime, we'll enjoy some of your best champagne in that booth."

The hostess smiled. She spoke into her microphone. "Sheila, we'll be having guests coming up the lift. Please show them to the Opium Den."

The glass elevator, shaped like a hot-air balloon, moved very slowly, giving O'Brien time to canvas the club as the glass orb rose above the packed dance floor.

Beyond the lights, thought O'Brien, behind the façade of Oz, was the real wicked wizard. Somewhere one of the dark alcoves led to the spot where an evil wizard hid behind a curtain pulling human strings. Somewhere in the building was Jonathan Russo's office. The key was to find it. As O'Brien stepped from the elevator to the second floor, he saw a curtain being drawn in a VIP suite.

Now he had a better plan.

FORTY-EIGHT

Barbie sat on the leather couch and said, "We sure don't have any sofas like this at the club where I work. Look at this place! Real fur. All these pillows. Soft lighting. Plants and a little fountain flowing over there in the corner. It's even got curtains. This is nicer than my apartment. Let's dance, Ken."

There was a tap at the door.

"Come on in," said Barbie.

A woman wearing a short white toga dress stepped into the suite. Her dark skin was in contrast to the white fabric. More high cheekbones. No tan lines. She had a regal elegance to her movement. She sat on the couch near them, crossed her legs, and said, "I'm Nikki. Welcome to Oz and your suite—the Opium Den. I'll be your server. I have a staff to assist me, too. We can get you anything you desire. Award-winning food and drink or even a back rub."

"That sounds nice," said Barbie.

O'Brien was silent.

Nikki said, "Here are the menus. Our specialty is gourmet tapas foods. May I start you out with a drink or a bottle, perhaps?"

"Do you carry Krug champagne?" asked O'Brien.

"Of course. What year would you like?"

"You pick."

Nikki smiled. "The nineteen eighty-seven is excellent."

O'Brien looked at the wine list. The Krug 1987 was priced at fifteen hundred dollars a bottle.

"Sounds like a good year," he said with a smile.

Barbie said, "I'm really hungry. Can I go on and order?"

"Of course," said Nikki.

"I'll take the chicken . . . how do you say it, cotee—"

"Chicken Côte d'Azur," said Nikki. She stood to leave.

"Nikki," said O'Brien.

"Yes."

"Please tell Jonathan that Mr. Sergio Conti is here and waiting for him in the Opium Den." O'Brien glanced at Barbie. "Tell Jonathan I brought him a gift . . . a gift younger than the champagne, and I hope he'll share with us."

Nikki smiled, glanced at Barbie, and said, "I'll convey your message."

As Nikki closed the door, Barbie asked, "Did you just do what I think you did?"

"What?"

"Pimp me out?"

"No, Barbie, listen closely. A very bad man will be coming in here in a few minutes. Just play along with me. I'm going to ask you to do one thing and then you can go dance the night away."

"What's that one thing?"

"I want you to cuff him when I tell you to."

"I knew it. You're a cop, aren't you?"

"Sort of."

"What does that mean?"

"It means I'm unofficially investigating a crime."

"What kind of crime?"

"Murder."

"Murder!"

"She wasn't much older than you when she was killed."

"Is this guy you just invited in here . . . this Jonathan dude, did he kill her?"

"I don't know."

"What are you gonna do? What if he has a gun?"

O'Brien stood and closed the curtains. He pulled the Glock from under his shirt and said nothing.

Barbie looked at the gun and blurted, "Ohmygod! You're gonna kill him!"

"Calm down, okay? I'm here to see if a shoe fits."

"You're one of those bounty hunters, aren't you?"

"My only bounty is to try to correct a bad mistake."

"What mistake?"

"An innocent man, Barbie, is in prison. He's on death row. The guy walking in here might know something that could free this innocent man."

"I know I'm the one askin' questions, but you don't have to tell me if you feel I ought not to know."

"I believe you'll make a good witness if I need one. You're an honest woman."

There was a tap on the door.

O'Brien slipped the Glock under his shirt. He nodded to Barbie. She said, "Come in."

Nikki entered with another woman dressed in a short toga. Blond and shapely. Dimples when she smiled. Nikki sat the bottle of champagne and glasses down. She started to open it and said, "This is Shana. She's here to assist you in whatever you may need, too." Shana set the small tray of Chicken Côte d'Azur on the glass coffee table.

"What a delightful menagerie," said O'Brien. "I hope Jonathan can join us before the champagne is gone."

"Mr. Russo will drop in soon. May we offer either of you anything else?"

"No, thanks," said O'Brien.

The women left. Barbie said, "I can't believe I'm hungry." She scooped up one of the flat tapas bites. It looked like pieces of chicken on a slice of baked pita bread. "This is sooo good," she said, pouring a glass of champagne. She sipped. "Wow! Kinda sweet and dry, too. Love the tiny bubbles. Aren't you eating?"

"I've eaten."

"Ken, cop or no cop, I think you're a good person. And this is the best, kinkiest sort of date I've ever been on." She finished the glass of champagne just as the door opened.

Jonathan Russo stepped into the room.

FORTY-NINE

Jonathan Russo wore a dark suit with a black T-shirt under the jacket. His salt-and-pepper hair was pulled back in a ponytail. Wide shoulders. Flat stomach. A bodybuilder's pronounced way of moving. A gym rat in a tight-fitting Armani jacket.

"You're not Sergio Conti," said Russo.

"And you're not the Wizard of Oz," said O'Brien. "Sit down."

"Fuck you!"

O'Brien grabbed Russo and threw him into the couch. His eyebrows arched, like they were painted on his forehead. As he tried to sit up, O'Brien used the palm of his hand to shove him back into the couch. Russo's mouth opened, a protest stopped in his throat as O'Brien backhanded him and pulled out his Glock.

Barbie jumped up, spilling the food on the floor.

"You're a dead man!" shouted Russo. "Who the fuck are you? Where's Serg?"

"He's been silenced."

"What!"

O'Brien pointed the Glock directly between Russo's eyes. He said, "I should have arrested you eleven years ago."

"What? Fuck you, pal."

O'Brien locked the door, turned the recorder on, and slid it across the glass table. He said, "You killed Alexandria Cole eleven years ago. You killed Sam Spelling and you killed a friend of mine, a priest, Father John Callahan."

"Wait a minute!" said Russo, holding up his hands. "I remember you. You're the cop, the detective, who came around when they found Lexie's body. You busted her redneck boyfriend on that one."

"But it was my mistake. And I'm done with letting my mistake make more mistakes. You're going to trade places with Charlie Williams."

"You're fuckin' insane! I told you back then, I didn't kill her. She was my meal ticket. Lexie was one of the reasons I had enough dough to partner in on this club. We've expanded to three locations on South Beach. I wasn't happy to see what that stupid fuck from Podunk Carolina did to her."

"Stand up!"

"What?"

"Stand up!" O'Brien stepped closer to Russo.

"I'll have your ass on a platter for coming in here and—"

"Shut up! If I shoot you, the music is so loud I could set a bomb off and no one would hear it."

Russo stood. He was breathing hard. His heart beat fast, causing a gold pendant to vibrate on his chest.

O'Brien said, "Put both of your hands by the door handle."

Russo slowly did as ordered. O'Brien gestured to Barbie with a quick jerk of the head. "Barbie, cuff him to the door handle."

"What do you want?" asked Russo.

"The truth. And I have very little time to get it or an innocent man dies."

Barbie picked up the handcuffs and clamped one on Russo's left wrist, ran the other through the door handle and secured the cuff to his right wrist.

O'Brien held the Glock less than two feet from Russo's face. "Since you have a hard time remembering the night you killed Alexandria Cole, let's start more recently. Where were you the last three days?"

"Out of town . . . on business."

"Where!"

"I was in Detroit on Saturday and Sunday. Orlando on Monday and up until the time I flew back to Miami late this afternoon."

"Who were you with?"

"Investors."

"Give me names!"

"Uh, Robert Kohn and Ted Jacobs in Detroit. They're with Michigan Enterprises. In Orlando, I met with, uh, Morgan Coldwell and a business attorney, his name is . . . uh, Rice, Jim Rice."

"It's all about the alibis, isn't it, Russo? You're good with calling favors, having people vouch for you—no, lie for you. Eleven years ago it was Sergio Conti. You told Conti to tell me and the other investigators that you spent the night at his place, eating stone crabs and tossing their shells over the balcony."

Russo was silent.

"Didn't anybody ever tell you that your lies can come back to bite you one day?"

FIFTY

Russo squirmed, sweat popping on his forehead. "I didn't lie."

"Sure you did," said O'Brien. "You told me you were dining on stone crabs the night Alexandria Cole was stabbed seven times. That was a lie, Russo. Your pal Conti admitted that to me earlier tonight. Said you weren't around. He tells me, right here on tape, that you— you pervert—were banging an underage girl. But I differ with him. I believe you were killing Alexandria Cole because she was firing you. She didn't need your slime around her anymore. You tried to keep her addicted to pills and coke. But she finally had enough. You couldn't stand to lose the dollar signs, the connections she represented. You knew she was making up with her boyfriend. He'd even had sex with her the night you killed her in a rage."

"You're fuckin' crazy."

"Not only could you have killed her, you had no alibi and you did have a motive. You knew enough about her boyfriend to plant Alexandria's blood in his truck. What did you do, carry some out in a Ziploc bag and spread it on his clothes and car seat when he was passed out drunk?"

Russo was quiet. He licked his dry lips. "You're making a big mistake."

O'Brien said, "You made a big mistake when you also carried out the murder weapon and tossed it, because someone in the complex saw you. He blackmailed you. He knew a big-shot supermodel manager and nightclub mogul was good for the money. All was quiet for years because he was behind bars on drug charges, but the closer he came to getting out, the more he wanted to dip back into your till. And when Sam Spelling was transported from his cell to testify in an unrelated drug trial, you shot him, or you had someone shoot him. You knew if you killed him, the cops would think it was a hit the defendant in the trial had ordered. But all along, it was to silence an old nemesis that caught you in a murder."

"I never heard of this Sam Spelling fuck."

"Sure you have. You killed him. And after you killed him, you murdered one of the finest men I've ever known, Father John Callahan."

"I'm fuckin' Catholic! You think I'd whack a priest, huh?"

"I think you'd kill anyone who got in your way, including a prison guard reported missing by his wife. The same guard that overheard Spelling talking with Father Callahan. I'm betting he got greedy, just like Sam Spelling. Called you and you gave him the same payback you gave Spelling."

Russo tried to pull the door handle off with the handcuffs. His watchband broke, the watch landing on the carpeted floor. O'Brien picked up the watch. He said, "An Omega. I bet you were wearing this the night you shot Father Callahan. I'm going to ask you one last time, why did you kill Alexandria Cole?"

"I didn't kill her."

"Your alibi is a lie! Sergio Conti admits you weren't eating stone crabs at his condo the night she was killed. Where were you?"

Russo licked his lips. Sweat soaked his T-shirt around the collar. He said, "Look, man. I was with somebody I shouldn't have been with, okay?"

"Who?"

"A girl."

"What girl?"

"I don't even know her name. I bought her from a pimp for a few hours. I have a little problem." He paused and looked at Barbie. "I find myself drawn to girls . . . you know, the young ones. Said her name was Lucy, but who the hell knows. They all lie."

"The tough life of a pedophile," said O'Brien. "So many kids, so little time."

"I haven't ever stalked a girl. I'm surrounded by so many people—women, lots of adult bitches. It's nice to do it with someone I can teach, somebody that won't talk back. So, now you know my secret."

"Where is this girl? Where's this pimp?"

"I don't know, man, it's been eleven years. She's probably grown with kids. He's probably dead."

"She's probably warped for life after you taught her something, something evil."

Russo shrugged. "This has been goin' on since Roman times."

"Shut up! You disgust me! I believe your little story, you sick narcissist bastard. But I don't believe it happened the night Alexandria was killed. You stabbed her in an emotional rage."

"You got some fantasy thing happening, Detective."

O'Brien leaned in closer to Russo, looking for any hint of deception in Russo's eyes or body language. "Look at me! What did you do with the letter Spelling wrote to Father Callahan?"

Russo smiled and said, "What fuckin' letter?"

O'Brien stared at Russo and finally said, "Barbie, hand the purse to me."

"Since we're being recorded," she said, "the purse isn't technically mine."

"Hand it to me."

She gave O'Brien the purse. He lifted the stone crab out, holding it by the back of the shell. The two large claws opened wide, snapping, the crab's eyes as dark as small black pearls.

"Hey! C'mon, man! What the fuck you doin'?" Russo's voice was higher, pleading.

O'Brien said, "A stone crab this size can generate almost two thousand pounds of pressure in its claw when it clamps down."

Russo's eyes darted from the crab to O'Brien. "You're insane."

FIFTY-ONE

W ait a fuckin' minute!" shouted Russo.

O'Brien said, "This is the kind of crab you told me you ate at Sergio Conti's, then tossed the shells over the balcony. Their claws are amazing—almost too large for their bodies. They use them to crush clams and mollusks. Imagine what this claw could do to your nose."

"You're a dead man, O'Brien."

O'Brien stepped closer with the crab, the claws opening like traps.

"Name your price!" said Russo. "Look, I'll give you anything you want. A hundred grand and you and big tits here can go away to some fuckin' island."

"All I want is the truth."

"I'm telling you the truth!" Russo looked down at the large crab.

O'Brien said, "If this crab can shatter a clam, it could split your little finger like a chicken bone."

"O'Brien . . . please . . ."

Barbie held her hand to her mouth. "Now I've really lost my appetite."

"A hundred thousand bucks! I'll give it to you in cash. And you walk outta here. No questions asked. We do a deal and all this is history."

"Where's Spelling's letter?" shouted O'Brien, the crab's claws snapping air.

"You got the wrong guy! Look up your own tree—" Russo's face twisted like the skin was going to peel off. The veins in his neck expanded. He turned crimson and then lost all color.

"My chest!" he yelled. "I can't breathe! My heart!"

"I won't cheat the state out of its right to lock you away, Russo, so I'll dial nine-one-one, but before I do . . . tell me, why did you kill Alexandria Cole? The truth!"

"All right!" screamed Russo. "All right! I killed the bitch! That what you wanted to hear? I fuckin' stabbed her!"

He stopped talking. His arms and hands shook. He slumped to his knees. Saliva dripping out of his open mouth.

"Ken!" shouted Barbie. "Do something! He's dying!"

O'Brien said, "There's a house phone on the table to the left of the couch. Tell them Jonathan Russo is in the Opium Den having a heart attack." O'Brien unlocked the handcuffs and Russo dropped facedown on the floor like a broken doll. As Barbie made the call, O'Brien set the crab back in the purse, picked up the tape recorder and handcuffs.

"I'm scared, Ken!"

"Don't be."

"What if he dies?"

There was a pounding at the door. O'Brien opened it. Two large bouncers, dressed in black, entered. "What the hell happened?" one of them asked.

"Jonathan got a little too excited," said O'Brien. "Barbie has a way of heightening the excitement level more than the snow Jonathan snorted. Poor guy just collapsed."

One bouncer knelt down and held a finger to Russo's neck. He said, "I can barely feel a pulse. EMTs ought to be here soon. We called them as soon as the girl called down."

Another man in black entered. Nikki and a half dozen cocktail waitresses stood outside the suite. One of the bouncers said to another, "Johnny, help me get Mr. Russo to the couch." The bouncers gently lifted Russo and positioned him on the couch.

O'Brien said, "Barbie, let's go."

The bouncer, kneeling by Russo, looked up and saw the pistol beneath O'Brien's shirt. He said, "You two are staying."

"Don't think so," said O'Brien.

The bouncer grabbed O'Brien's shoulder with two hands, trying to throw him off balance. O'Brien twisted, pulling one of the man's arms behind his back. He hit him solidly in the jaw, the blow sounding like a hammer hitting Sheetrock.

A second bouncer stepped in and threw a punch at O'Brien's head. He sidestepped, grabbed the bouncer by the T-shirt, pushing him hard against the glass wall. The impact shattered the wall, glass raining down in a thousand pieces.

A third man started to enter, this one lifting a pistol from beneath his black sports coat. O'Brien's Glock was in the man's face in a split second. "Freeze!" shouted O'Brien. "Arms high! Now!" As he raised his arms, O'Brien lifted the pistol out of the man's belt. O'Brien could see the man had no fear in his eyes. He had the thick, scarred hands of a fighter. Neatly trimmed black beard. Shoulders solid with muscle. His lips were thin and his eyes looked like wet lava rock.

He looked at Barbie and said, "Almost didn't recognize you with your clothes on. Kinda out of your league over here, aren't you, Barbs? Mr. Russo has a fine business relationship with your joint. Wouldn't want to jeopardize that . . . now would you, girl?"

"Shut up and sit down!" ordered O'Brien, motioning with the Glock.

The man sneered, his eyes mocking O'Brien. He pursed his lips, popped callused knuckles that looked like barnacles, and sat in a black leather chair.

O'Brien grabbed Barbie by the hand and stepped out of the suite. Dozens of people crept out of their VIP suites. As O'Brien passed Nikki he said, "Mr. Russo is picking up the tab for the Krug. You're right. It was a good year."

Barbie took off her high heels and ran to keep up with O'Brien as he descended the acrylic steps, weaved through the crowd, and stepped into the warm Miami Beach air.

They stood for a moment in front of Oz as the wail of police and ambulance sirens drew closer. O'Brien signaled a cab. He looked at Barbie, holding her shoes and both purses. He said, "Here's some money. Take the cab home."

"Can I go with you?"

"It would be too risky for you. Police will have my description. If Russo lives, he'll come after me. How'd you know that guy, the one who recognized you?"

"I've seen him at the club. He was there about a week ago. Creepy guy. He's been around for a few weeks. One of the girls said he's an enforcer for some of the drug dudes. He's probably just a high-paid errand boy for people like Russo."

"Remember his name?"

"Carlos Salazar. I remember 'cause one of the girls said he was beyond kinky."

"Barbie, I have a feeling that Salazar is more than an errand boy for Russo. Since he recognized you, be very careful. Lay low. Don't go places alone."

"You're scaring me, Ken." The sounds of the sirens were closer. "You're doing the right thing . . . speaking for that poor dead girl and those others."

The sirens were less than two blocks away.

"Barbie, I have to go. Give me the big purse."

She smiled. "You do look weird carrying a purse. But here, nobody will bat an eye. What are you gonna do with the crab?"

"Let him go. Crab's earned its freedom."

Barbie paused. She leaned in and kissed O'Brien on his cheek. "You're a good man, Ken. Take care of yourself."

O'Brien smiled. "You do the same."

He took the purse and started walking toward his Jeep. As Barbie opened the taxi door, she turned to watch O'Brien in the distance. In a whisper she said, "Thanks for the date, handsome. Too bad we never got to dance."

FIFTY-TWO

As O'Brien started his Jeep, two ambulances and a half dozen police cruisers flew past him, screaming like a posse racing to Club Oz. O'Brien pulled onto Washington Avenue, cut over to Ocean Drive, and headed north toward North Shore State Recreation Area. He didn't know if Russo was dead or alive. He also didn't know what the state attorney would say about the confession on tape. O'Brien thought it might be tossed out, acquired as it was under duress, but at least it was an admission of guilt. God, he thought, please let it buy Charlie Williams some time.

The prime question, the one Russo hadn't had time to rehearse answers to, was what happened to Sam Spelling's letter? Why hadn't he shown the slightest sign of deception when he was asked about the letter?

Something in O'Brien's gut was rumbling—something unsettling about Russo. The information Father Callahan left in blood—how did it connect to Russo? Omega, did it refer to the watch Russo was wearing? Doubtful. The image Father Callahan had drawn . . . was it something from Club Oz? A witch flying across the moon? Or was it something else? The 666? P-A-T? What did it all mean?

Russo would do or say anything to survive. The cockroach in him was indestructible. The psychosis in him was a personality trait that kept his lawyers deep in six-figure retainers. Russo's attorneys would argue that the confession was acquired under physical threat of violence. O'Brien wasn't an officer of the law. There were no Miranda rights. Nothing but a confession on tape. But it might give the state attorney a card to deal—something to get a federal judge to sign an order for a stay of execution. If the FBI crime lab could find that Sam Spelling left a sufficient handwriting impression, maybe it would point to the location of the murder weapon. That would give O'Brien time to find physical evidence.

Russo may have left a print somewhere on the knife—an object he was so sure would be buried under tons of garbage in the dump. Yet he didn't know that Sam Spelling was watching him that night.

So close, O'Brien thought. Something was coalescing in O'Brien's gut. Russo, the subhuman that he was, seemed credible under the stress of an intense interrogation and the threat of a crab snapping his appendages. If he didn't kill Father Callahan, maybe it was someone Russo had sent.

O'Brien parked under a tall royal palm. He could hear the breakers and smell the sea salt. He took off his boat shoes, lifted the lethargic crab out of the purse, and walked toward the surf. He said, "Hold on, pal. You're almost home."

He stood in the rolling waves and gently set the crab in the water. The salt water rinsed the exhaustion from the animal. The crab scurried a few inches. Then it was lifted by the pull of a swell, vanishing into the dark sea.

O'Brien stepped back to dry sand, up to the line of royal palms. He sat under one palm tree, drained, resting his back against its trunk. The ocean breeze felt good on his face. He closed his burning eyes for a moment and simply listened to the sound of the waves. He could feel the fatigue rising in his mind, a fog drifting through layers of consciousness. He leaned back and looked at the moon shining down between branches of the tall palm. What was the image he'd seen earlier? The one he captured on his cell phone? He lifted the phone from his belt and retrieved the image. A woman in the moon? Where had he seen it? He was so tired, the concentration was getting difficult.

O'Brien stared through the palm fronds at the moon directly above him. He could see the profile of a roosting bird, an osprey, sitting on one of the branches.

He remembered seeing a bird in the same painting with the moon—a hawk or an eagle—but the other details in the picture were obscure. He glanced back at the photograph on his cell phone screen. His eyes blurred. The image now looked like his dead wife, Sherri, but the picture was murky. He shook his head. She was still there. Shadowy. He snapped the phone closed.

O'Brien stared toward the breakers. He remembered the day he emptied Sherri's ashes into the ocean, pouring them slowly from the bowsprit of their sailboat. Yet he couldn't remember the details of her face—of the wondrous smile she had. God, he missed her. He watched the crashing surf, the flowing white water and pieces of sea foam scattering by the breeze and tumbling like cotton balls onto the sand. He remembered first meeting Sherri in Miami Beach years ago. The way she played in the surf caught his eye. The way she played in life caught his heart.

O'Brien shook the ghosts out of his head and walked to his Jeep. He lifted a garbage can lid and tossed the purse inside. The odor of dead catfish, pizza, and coconut oil crawled from the garbage.

On the drive to the hotel, he thought about the image he'd seen in the moon, the image captured on his cell. He thought about the osprey sitting atop a royal palm, and he thought about Sherri. If he could get some sleep, maybe in his dreams he could travel to some point in time, someplace in his subconscious where the painting was more than abstract art. If he could hold the subliminal up to the light, what would he see? Where in the frame of grainy film—his memory—did the painting make an impression? Where in the archives of his mind did the painting hang? A life depended on finding it.

He just couldn't remember. *Think!* He closed his eyes, but now he couldn't even remember the details of his wife's face. He wished she were there.

To talk.

To listen.

O'Brien looked at his watch. It was two o'clock.

What is it?

Where is it?

The pressure made it feel as if his brain were being cooked in his skull.

When he got back to the hotel, he would allow himself only four hours to sleep. He hoped sometime in those four hours of sleep that the Dream Weaver would visit and help tie the loose ends together.

FIFTY-THREE

O'Brien set his internal alarm clock for 6:30 A.M. He stretched out on the hard mattress in his motel room and listened to the air conditioner shift gears. The old machine blew alternately warm and cold air across the room, the air smelling as if it had been filtered through a used vacuum cleaner bag.

He watched the pulse of the motel's lavender neon VACANCY light spill through a long horizontal strip where a piece of Venetian blind was missing. Between the deep noises from passing semi trucks and the rattle of the air conditioner, he drifted off to sleep.

In his dreams, O'Brien was in a medieval setting, a cathedral. It was in a remote area—fields of dark flowers at the edge of an ancient forest, trees and trunks all the color of dark green olives. The massive wooden door on the front of the cathedral opened slowly. It made no sound. O'Brien didn't walk into the cathedral, he floated— his body settling on a pew carved from stone. No one was there. Then O'Brien saw something scurry between the pews.

He knelt down, the floor cool and damp on his hands and knees. O'Brien looked beneath a stone row and saw a large rat. The animal stared at O'Brien, its eyes the size and shape of marbles, but the color of fire. Then the rat morphed into an elfish figure, a small gnomelike man with a face as old as time. The little man snarled at O'Brien and darted out into the fields of black flowers.

The interior of the cathedral turned from gray to a shade of lemon yellow. O'Brien looked toward the front of the church and saw something descend from an open window. He slowly walked toward it. The figure was that of a young woman with delicate features. She had wings that folded behind her back when she reached the floor. The angelic figure smiled, closed her eyes demurely, and floated toward the pulpit.

From the open doors, a hawk flew in and landed on the back of a stone pew. O'Brien turned around and watched the bird move its head, following the floating motion of the woman.

In the next instant, O'Brien was on a high bank overlooking a harbor with ships in the bay. The water was the shade of tea. It was late in the evening and a dark cloud was dropping, revealing the moon. O'Brien could see the image of the woman floating out of the moon; this time he could see her face, the face of the Virgin Mary.

"Who are you?" O'Brien heard himself say. "Where am I?"

He reached out to touch the figure and touched wet paint on a canvas. He looked at his fingers, the tips dripping in flesh tones, and he looked back at the woman in the painting. Her face was smeared.

O'Brien sat up in bed. His heart hammered in his chest, sweat rolling down his sides, over his rib area, and into the sheets.

He looked at his watch: 6:30 A.M. Somehow the inner timepiece always went off when set. It always managed to stir him from the dark.

O'Brien showered, changed into a fresh shirt and jeans, then headed for the Jeep. He drove a few miles until he came to a 7-Eleven on Arthur Godfrey Road, where he parked to use a pay phone. He called the Waverly Condos to report loud noises coming from 1795.

Soon he crossed MacArthur Causeway, turned south, and pulled in next to the Corner Café for breakfast. It had the feel of a wannabe

Irish pub and restaurant—a dozen green and white booths and as many tables. The tired bar had a single customer and an older bartender with the name tag JESSE held in place with a single clip. The place smelled of bacon, beer, and cigarettes.

A fortysomething waitress with a smoker's hack picked up a menu, yellowed under the scratched plastic, and led O'Brien past the bar to a corner booth. A television over the bar was tuned to a channel broadcasting the *Today* show.

"Need a few minutes or do you know what you want?" asked the waitress.

"Eggs, scrambled. Wheat toast, potatoes, and black coffee."

"Be right back with your coffee, darlin'."

O'Brien handed her the greasy menu, and after she walked away, he picked up his cell and began typing an e-mail to Dave Collins. He attached the image of the moon and the cloud he shot.

> Dave, attached is the moon image you may remember
> me mentioning last night. Do you think it resembles what
> Fr. Callahan drew? I've seen it—or something like it
> somewhere. A painting. Very old, I think. Probably
> Renaissance or before. Could have a bird of prey in it.
> Maybe you can do a little research . . . see what you can
> find, OK? Thanks. How's Max?

The waitress brought O'Brien coffee. "Order will be up in just a minute."

O'Brien nodded and sipped his coffee. He opened the case file to read. When he got to the transcript notes from Judy Neilson, Alexandria Cole's roommate, he read something he'd forgotten. Responding to a question about how often Jonathan Russo came around their apartment, Judy said, "Too much. And then he stopped coming over. I don't know why. Alex didn't want to talk about it. I think she thought I'd tell Charlie. Anyway, then Alex started getting calls and she'd have to go. She hated going. Said the guy was creeping her out. She'd come back from meeting him, in a motel, I guess, and take long showers. One day, when I heard her crying in the shower, I sat her down and we talked. Said she'd thought about suicide. I told her if her life had gotten that bad, it was time to do something else. Cut your losses and run. She was killed three days later."

O'Brien reread the statement. He sipped his coffee and thought about what Judy had said. Something wasn't coming together. Why would Russo meet Alexandria at a hotel? He had a private office in his club, a Mediterranean-style house on the bay. When Alexandria was killed, she was twenty-four years old, not a prime age for a pedophile.

O'Brien's cell rang.

"Where the hell are you?" asked Detective Ron Hamilton.

"Breakfast. Ron, I have Russo's confession on tape."

"And we have a warrant for you. Russo's attorney swore out the warrant."

"What charges?"

"For starters, aggravated assault, battery, destruction of property, and grand theft."

FIFTY-FOUR

Through a side window in the Corner Café, O'Brien watched a police cruiser pull across the restaurant parking lot and stop in front of a Waffle House next door.

"Grand theft?" asked O'Brien.

"Russo says you stole a bottle of champagne worth fifteen hundred. He says you pulled a gun and assaulted him with a deadly weapon."

"A crab?"

"A what? You threatened him with a crab?"

"Not just any crab. A stone crab."

"Sean, you're in some serious shit. The assault charges include battery on three of his employees and destruction of property. Says you did five grand in damages, knocked apart a private VIP soundproof booth. Russo's in Jackson Memorial's coronary care unit."

"He's trying to cover his ass because he knows I have him on tape admitting to killing Alexandria Cole."

"He swears he was coerced, and he only offered the admission under threat of physical violence."

"I had a witness."

"Who?"

"A woman."

"Who?"

"Girl's name is Barbie. Works at Club Paradise."

"How'd a stripper become your witness? Maybe I don't want to know."

"I took her there because I knew she could get us in the club without waiting three hours. Charlie Williams can't spare three hours. Russo came to the VIP booth because he thought his pimp, Sergio Conti, had delivered an underage girl to share with him."

"So where'd the damn crab come in?"

"Remember his alibi about eating stone crab claws with his over-fiftysomething pedophile buddy the night Alexandria was murdered?"

"I read it, but I didn't remember it from when you originally worked the case."

O'Brien said nothing.

"Sean, you there?"

"Yeah, Ron, I'm here. You were my partner, and you don't remember that when it was brought up during the investigation."

"You know how many homicides I've worked? You think I can re—"

"Of course not," said O'Brien. "When I drove by Joe's Stone Crab, I had the idea for the crab. Figured it'd scare Russo so much he couldn't remember how to lie, and I'd get it straight. Look, I got it on tape. I asked him if he killed Alexandria Cole and he responds, quote, 'I killed the bitch.' Ron, take the tape to the DA. Maybe Stanley Rosen can get a court order for a stay to give us time to get an innocent man off."

Hamilton sighed and said, "The fiftysomething pedophile, as you call him, Sergio Conti, is filing charges, too. Conti says you assaulted him with a deadly weapon."

"The back of my hand. Ron, these freaks lied to the FBI and DEA and me."

"It's not what I think. It'll be messy, going to Stan Rosen, because of how you got the admission. And now there's a half dozen felony charges filed against you."

"You know better than anyone, there is no time to go through the system and keep Charlie Williams alive."

"I'm on your side. But you have to get the state attorney to hear the tape."

O'Brien was silent.

Hamilton said, "If I get the recording from you, the DA will know where it came from and want to know why I didn't take you into custody. I don't want you to think I'm abandoning you, but there's not much I can do. I'm sorry."

"A man's life is at stake."

"I have to go by the book. Get me something I can sink a big physical hook into, and I'll reel it in. But right now, you're fishing with dull hooks, and you're the one getting caught."

"If I hold a news conference, somebody will hear the asshole's confession."

"You already got more exposure than one man needs."

O'Brien looked up at the bar as the *Today* show broke for local stations to insert their newsbreaks.

A young, petite news anchor said, "Miami Beach Police are combing the area for a man and a woman who allegedly tried to kill one of the owners of Club Oz, a nightclub on South Beach. Security cameras caught the couple on tape, and they've been identified as Sean O'Brien, a former Miami homicide detective, and Elizabeth 'Barbie' Beckman, a stripper employed by Club Paradise. The pair made their getaway after allegedly pulling a gun on owner Jonathan Russo and destroying thousands of dollars in club property. Russo was admitted to Jackson Memorial, where he's listed in fair condition."

O'Brien stood and looked around the restaurant at the dozen customers buried in newspaper or conversation. He saw his picture with Barbie on the front of *The Miami Herald*, the man reading the paper making his way through the sports section.

O'Brien walked toward the door as the news anchor continued, "Police believe an earlier break-in was related to the shooting in Club Oz. O'Brien allegedly broke into the posh condo owned by film and music producer Sergio Conti, threatened Conti, and tied him up. Conti and Russo were known business associates. Sean O'Brien is said to have abruptly quit a thirteen-year career with the Miami Police Department less than two years ago."

As O'Brien walked by the bar, the only customer was an older man wearing a Jim Beam baseball cap and nursing a sweating bottle of Budweiser at 9:00 A.M. He glanced up as O'Brien stepped down the length of the bar and exited. The man said, "I'll be damned. That feller on TV just walked out the door. Call the law, Jesse."

The waitress who'd served O'Brien approached. She watched O'Brien get in his car. "He's a good tipper. Don't call the po'lese. . . . But maybe there's a big reward."

As O'Brien's car pulled away from the lot, she said, "Hand me the portable, Jesse."

FIFTY-FIVE

O'Brien glanced up in his rearview mirror when he pulled his car onto Highway A1A. The police cruiser remained parked in the Waffle House lot as O'Brien rounded a curve. He dialed Special Agent Lauren Miles's cell number. "Things have intensified a little. Did you get your lab tech to come in this morning?"

"Sean, I almost spit my orange juice out when I saw your picture in *The Herald*. Who was that woman—that *girl*? And yes, the tech is in as a favor."

"It's a story longer than I have time to tell. As the lab tech works on Spelling's letter, can someone edit an audio tape for me?"

"What do you mean, edit?"

"Shorten it. I've got a confession from Jonathan Russo on tape."

"Did you have to bust up part of his club to get it?"

"Don't believe everything you read in the news. Russo admits to killing Alexandria. I want to get the tape to the DA, Stanley Rosen. If he hears it, he could ask a judge to issue a stay until an appellate court can consider it."

"Rosen will only go to bat if he's sure you can deliver a point in his win column. Makes no sense for him to pinch-hit for a public defender."

"But to execute an innocent man, especially if that man's innocence might be proven after the state executes him, doesn't look good for Rosen. My way, he comes out smelling like a hero and preserves the judicial use of the death penalty at the same time. It puts two wins in his column."

"Eric, the lab tech, is also good with electronics. It's fairly easy to edit the audio down and run a duplicate for you."

"While he's at it, make a couple of dubs."

"Where are you?"

"About twenty minutes from the FBI office."

"I'll meet you in the parking lot."

O'Brien said nothing.

"Sean, let's meet in the parking lot, okay? About twenty minutes?"

"I really appreciate what you're doing. But right now I have to keep a fairly low profile. Let's meet at South Pointe Park off Washington."

"Shall I bring a snack for a little picnic?"

"I just had a breakfast that I'll taste all day."

"Sean, be careful."

O'Brien looked at his watch.

Forty-five hours remaining.

AS HE PULLED OFF A1A and began driving the secondary roads, O'Brien scanned the intersections as he approached them. His eyes took in the periphery, looking for police cruisers and unmarked cars. It was a surreal feeling to be watching for police. He drove just below the posted speed limits, checking his mirrors, ready to turn into a side road, an alley, or a fast-food drive-through if he had to.

His cell rang. O'Brien recognized Detective Dan Grant's number. "Sean, we found Lyle Johnson's truck."

"Where's Johnson?"

"Don't know. FHP clocked two teenage boys doing a hundred in a forty-five zone off State Road 27. Said they found the truck with the keys in the ignition. Decided to take it for a joyride. Got a couple of glum faces when they were booked on grand theft auto."

"Where'd they find it?"

"A place called Pioneer Village. Said they found the truck pulled off a dirt road, parked under a tree. The village is one of those living history things. It's a remote spot on the west side of Volusia County, not too far from the river. County has a few old turn-of-the-century buildings, houses, barns, and whatnot set up there. Schools take kids out to the place for field trips. We have deputies combing the area."

"Thanks, Dan. Go back to the hospital security room. See if they have video of Lyle Johnson in the hospital using a cell phone during the time Sam Spelling was in recovery. Pull his phone records. See if he made a call to Miami Beach."

"Where're you?"

"Miami Beach. Meeting with the FBI. We might have enough to get a stay for Charlie Williams."

"Make any more sense out of that scrawling the priest left in blood?"

"Not yet."

Dan sighed. "Hope we can come up with an answer to the riddle soon. TruTV wants to do a whole damn exposé, calling it the 'satanic ritual murder.' The woman on CNN, the prosecutor turned TV moderator—I forget her name—anyway, she interviewed the chief on live TV and asked him if the priest was believed to have been killed by a cult, some sort of sacrifice. How's this shit get started, huh?"

"I wish I knew."

"People are driving by the church at all hours. They've had to hire security. When are you back in town?"

"Look at what we're facing: Sam Spelling killed in his bed, Father Callahan killed in his church, and now you might find Lyle Johnson's body. A possible third homicide in less than *six* hours."

"We got us a killer doing some serious overtime."

"Russo has admitted to killing Alexandria Cole, but after questioning him this time, I don't believe he's that good—three hits in six hours. It's the mark of a pro."

"You saying Russo brought in a hired gun?"

"Yeah, and I might know who it is."

FIFTY-SIX

Deputy Sheriff Ray Boyd recognized the flies. He remembered them coming out of the woodwork when his grandfather killed hogs on the farm in Valdosta, Georgia. *Grandpa called them blowflies and sucker flies.* The blowflies had large red eyes and green bodies. The sucker flies had red eyes, yellow-gray striped bodies. Both drank blood. The horseflies drank blood, too, but they got it from biting live animals. These flies drank the blood from dead animals.

Deputy Boyd left his patrol car at the entrance to Pioneer Village as he walked along the perimeter, following the split-rail wooden fence as it looped around the edge of the property. He'd first spotted one of the flies sitting on the fence rail.

Then there were more.

Something was dead. Maybe a petting goat or one of the chickens he saw pecking in the small barnyard.

In his eight months with the sheriff's department, he'd never come in contact with a dead body. He stepped from the path and cut across toward the back of an old general store. He walked by the Burma-Shave sign painted on the whitewashed cypress side. It wasn't yet noon, and the hot Florida sun licked the back of his neck like a flame.

A black crow called out and flew from a tall pine to the top rung on a tower supporting the windmill blade. The wind picked up and turned the blade a few times, the clatter not spooking the crow.

Deputy Boyd could smell an odor. It wasn't like any from the hog carcasses. He walked around the front of the store, toward the porch. He reached for his gun and his mouth at the same time. *Don't vomit*, he told himself.

The body was sitting in a rocking chair. Head slumped on a shoulder, like the neck was broken. Eyes and mouth open. Flies were darting in and out of the mouth, biting into the bluish, swollen tongue. More flies worked at a gaping wound in the head.

The crow's call sounded like a mocking laugh as it flew from the windmill.

Deputy Boyd spun around, his gun pointing at darting butterflies and late-morning shadows between the barn and the old church. He turned back to face the body. His hands shook as he reached for the radio on his belt. Under the rocking chair, fluids pooled like dark oil. Boyd stepped back. He stepped away from the porch. Stepped away from the smell of death.

He keyed the radio and said, "I got a ten fifty-six . . . and it's a bad one!"

FIFTY-SEVEN

O'Brien parked two blocks away from the beach. He walked toward South Pointe Park. Two women on Rollerblades, wearing nothing but string bikinis, whipped around him, laughing and skating north on Washington Avenue.

He could see Lauren Miles sitting alone on one of the benches. O'Brien approached her and said, "I really appreciate you coming here."

"No problem. Got here just a few minutes ago. I was watching that photo shoot on the beach. Probably be on the cover of some magazine next month." She looked toward the beach where a photographer with long white hair, open white shirt, and white cotton pants hunched over a camera, composing a shot of a model dressed in a pink bikini bottom. She had her arms folded over her bare breasts.

O'Brien sat beside Lauren. "Here's the tape. I've cued to his confession—to the question I asked, and to his answer." He played the tape.

Lauren said, "The whole thing is less thirty seconds. No problem to get a couple of dubs for you. I just hope it's something you can post in Rosen's win column. It's obvious to me that Russo sounded stressed. Maybe his life was threatened."

"Only his pinkie finger, the one with the diamond ring. When he made that statement, there was no gun visible. I had him handcuffed to the door. He's an admitted pedophile who didn't want me squeezing him. After our chat, he admitted what he did."

Lauren gazed at O'Brien a beat, looked at a spot on the bench, and said, "What's wrong, Sean?"

"What do you mean?"

"You're not happy with the confession. You know it. Might be enough to temporarily stop an execution, but not enough to get a conviction, right?"

"Russo could have called in a pro, a hired gun to kill Spelling and Father Callahan. The hit man may have taken out a prison guard whom we believe overheard Spelling's confession. The guard, Lyle Johnson, could have called Russo, tried to blackmail him and was eliminated. Last night I saw a guy who looked like he may be the man who impersonated a priest and killed Sam Spelling. I'd seen a black-and-white security camera tape image of the impostor priest who walked into Spelling's room. He was the last person to see Spelling alive. He has a beard, similar build. If he's the same guy, he's working for Russo. He was in Club Oz. Tried to draw down on me. I managed to be a little faster. Can you run his name through NAIS? It's Carlos Salazar."

As Lauren wrote down the name O'Brien said, "Put another name on the list. It's Judy Neilson. She was a high-fashion model here in Miami at the time of Alexandria Cole's murder. She was Cole's roommate."

"Something suspect about her after all these years?"

"No, but in rereading her interviews, she mentioned that Alexandria was sometimes called out, presumably to have sex with Russo. But now I know Alexandria would have been way beyond his age limit. I want to question Judy again."

"You have to remember all this was eleven years ago, Sean. People forget."

"Some things you never forget. I'd like to know if she's still here in Miami."

"I'll see if anything turns up." Lauren paused, looked out toward the ocean, and watched a sailboat. "Didn't you have a sailboat once?"

"A long time ago. Sold it."

"Why'd you get rid of it?"

"It became a ship of ghosts for me. On my last sail, I emptied my wife's ashes."

"I'm sorry."

"Thanks . . . now I've moved from sailing to a powerboat—a stinky old diesel. Thirty-eight feet long. I bought it in an auction for ten cents on the dollar at a county sale of confiscated drug boats. I've been fixing it up with the intent of learning the charter boat business. I have a great teacher. He's Greek and has salt water in his blood." O'Brien smiled.

Lauren pushed a strand of hair behind her ear and turned back toward O'Brien.

"Does the boat have a kitchen?"

"Yes, it's called a galley."

"When this ends," said Lauren, searching for the right words. "When it's over, maybe we could spend some time on your stinky old boat, as you call it. Go fishing or something. I'm pretty good at cooking seafood." She smiled and then bit her lower lip.

"I'd like that," said O'Brien.

Lauren smiled wide and looked above O'Brien's shoulder to watch three brown pelicans sail over the tops of palm trees. She said, "I got to know you some during the hunt for Santana. Maybe now we can get to know each other a little more."

"If we can save Charlie Williams, we'll celebrate together." O'Brien handed her the recorder. "Here's the tape. How long before we might have something from Spelling's letter?"

"Give us until six o'clock."

"Okay, I'll call your cell then. One other thing . . . do you know where the DA lives? . . . Where's Stanley Rosen's house?"

"Are you just going to drop by unannounced, at his home?"

"I am."

FIFTY-EIGHT

Barbie Beckman heard the phone ringing in her dreams. Finally, she surrendered to the incessant noise, rolled over in her bed, and picked up the receiver. "Haallo . . ."

"Barbie?"

"Yeah . . ."

"It's Sue. Baby, you sound different. Have you seen the paper?"

"Huh?"

"The newspaper, sweetie, as in *Miami Herald*?"

"No, why?"

"Because your beautiful face is plastered on the front page."

"Ohmygod!"

"And you're running with some cute guy . . . looks like the actor Clive Owen. The paper says his name is Sean O'Brien."

"So he really isn't Ken."

"What?"

"Oh, nothing."

"Barbie, you gonna turn yourself in, or grab that guy and run like Bonnie and Clyde? I like it . . . Barbie and Clyde."

"What do you mean . . . turn myself in?"

"Baby, you're my favorite first cousin. I want to see you get famous, okay? Like in *Playboy* or a Miami Heat cheerleader or something, but sending a man to the hospital, wreckin' a club. Wow!"

"What?"

"The TV news said y'all run off with a two-thousand-dollar bottle of champagne, too. You know that expensive brand the hip-hop singers drink in the clubs? Hey, did you and cutie pass the bottle to each other in the back of the cab makin' your getaway?"

"Sue, look, I just woke up. I'll call you back. Has Mama seen any of this?"

"Don't know. Want me to call her for you . . . sort of ease her into it?"

"No! No, I'll talk to her. Bye."

Barbie pulled the sheet over her body and sat at the edge of her bed to think.

The phone rang again.

Barbie looked at the caller ID. Club Paradise. She picked up the phone. "Hi."

"Barbie, it's Jude. Had two cops in the club and a detective asking me questions about you. I've seen that shit on the news that you pulled in Club Oz with that ex-cop. What the fuck were you thinkin', huh?"

"Jude, look, I didn't do anything. The whole thing at Oz was kinda like a date, that's all. I was just there."

"You and ex-cop picked the wrong club to start crashin' and the wrong guy to be bashin'. Russo's got connections. Lots of people owe him lots of favors, you know what I'm sayin'? Do you, huh, stupid—"

"Yeah, I know."

"Take a couple of days off to let the heat die down some. Come back then."

"I need the money. I have rent and—"

"But I don't need this kind of headache, not to mention the unwanted publicity."

He hung up.

Barbie pulled on a pair of jeans, T-shirt, and flip-flops. She ran her fingers through her hair and stepped out her apartment door, leaving the door unlocked. She walked downstairs to the first floor and bought a paper out of the machine. Looking at her picture with O'Brien made her blush. She read a few lines and held the paper to her breasts, glancing around before walking up the steps to her apartment.

Barbie entered, locked the door, and sat on the couch to read the story. She pulled her feet up under her. After a few minutes she mumbled, "This is bullshit. . . . That's not how it happened—"

There was a sound. The creak of the simulated-wood floor. Barbie stood. Listening. She sat the paper on the couch, picked up a knife from her kitchen, and slowly walked down the hall toward her bedroom. She wished her roommate were home, but she knew Jan was still at work. Barbie gently pushed opened Jan's bedroom door, her heart racing. Nothing. Only an unmade bed and a pair of Jan's jeans draped over a chair.

There was a knock at the door.

Barbie lowered the knife to her side and tiptoed into the living room. She raised one blind a quarter inch and looked out the front window.

The police. An officer and a man in a shirt and tie. Probably a detective.

They knocked again. Louder. "Miss Beckman," said one of them through the door. "This is Miami Beach Police. Please open up the door. We need to talk with you."

Silence.

Barbie tried to control her breathing. She thought her heart was going to leap out of her chest. Her mouth was dry, and she couldn't swallow.

"Okay, Miss Beckman, next time we come, it'll be with a search warrant and a warrant for your arrest. Rather than talk in your apartment, we'll take you downtown for questioning."

She waited a full minute before tiptoeing to the door. She looked through the peephole. Gone. Barbie let out a pent-up chestful of air and turned to enter her bedroom.

She placed the kitchen knife on the bathroom counter, slipped out of her clothes, and got under a hot shower, letting the water run over her head a long while before opening her eyes. When she did open her eyes, she turned to reach for the soap.

The shower door was open. Barbie screamed.

A man stood there—watching—holding the butcher knife. His eyes absorbing her naked body like a cat watches a bird in a cage. The eyes were primal. His thin lips bright red and wet from licking them. His jaw muscles popped, causing his short beard to move like something crawling under a rug.

"Hello, Barbie," said Carlos Salazar. "My, what a sharp knife you have."

FIFTY-NINE

FBI lab technician Eric Weinberg pushed his glasses back up on the bridge of his nose and looked at the computer screen for a half minute in silence. He punched the keyboard and enlarged the image. He turned to Lauren Miles and said, "I can get a reading on some of it, but the rest is less distinct, like the writer was growing weaker the farther along he wrote."

"Let's see what you have," said Lauren.

"I'll route what I have on the high-def monitor." He hit a few of the keys and Sam Spelling's handwriting appeared on the screen.

To Father John and God–

My name is Sam Spelling. I am real sorry for my sins. I wish to ask God for forgiveness . . . and I know now I done some bad things in my life. I hope to make amends. On the night of June 18th, 1999, I was working a deal, trying to score some cocaine at the Mystic Islands condos in Miami. I was supposed to meet a dealer there. It was the same night Alexandria Cole was stabbed to death. I was sitting in a car in the condo lot, waiting for the dealer to show when I seen a man come out of Miss Cole's condo. But before I go any further in this letter, I want to say right now where the knife can be found in case I get too tired to finish this letter. It's in the town of St

Lauren stared at the screen and said, "Looks like Spelling was writing the 'town of S - t . . . something . . . maybe St. Petersburg?"

"Could be," said Eric.

"Run a search on all Florida cities and towns beginning with S - T."

Eric keyed in the information. Within seconds he read, "Starke, Stuart, St. Augustine, St. Petersburg, St. Cloud, Steinhatchee, and St. George Island."

"Maybe Spelling has or had family in one of those. See what you can find."

Eric nodded. "Are you going to send the letter to headquarters?"

"Yes, counter-to-counter."

He handed Lauren the letter. She carefully placed it in a folder. "Thanks, Eric. I appreciate you staying late to help with this."

LAUREN CAUGHT THE ELEVATOR down to her floor. She entered the office and saw someone walking into the break room. She followed.

Christian Manerou poured himself a cup of coffee as Lauren stepped into the break room. She said, "Oh, Christian, it's you. I thought everyone had gone home."

"Yeah, I forgot the Dade Federal folder." Manerou looked at the file Lauren carried. "What's keeping you here?"

"Trying to offer some assistance to Sean O'Brien."

"Yes, according to *The Herald*, his old employer, MPD, would like to find him."

"Sean has always operated on the edge, but when he was a detective, his conviction record was unparalleled. He knows he's up against the clock in this Charlie Williams execution, which will be a deathwatch soon. Sean's squeezing Russo."

"It wasn't easy for the DEA to get a drug conviction pinned on Russo. I imagine O'Brien will have his hands full, especially since it didn't go so well the first time. And now Russo has had a lot of time to separate himself from Alexandria Cole."

"Could work against him. Too much time and he forgets which lies he told."

"Lauren, I know you put a lot of stock in Sean O'Brien. You worked with him on the Santana murders. Any way that I can help, let me know. My caseload isn't so heavy now that I can't offer some assistance if it's needed. I'd have to get the okay through Mike. I remember Russo pretty well. He's a first-class son of a bitch. Let me know if I can help."

"It might be a stretch to get Mike's permission—he seemed preoccupied. Maybe even a little territorial about the Russo–Alexandria Cole investigations. That's kind of odd for him. But you can ask him."

"Mike's under a lot of pressure. Maybe you'll get something on that page O'Brien left."

"Just did. Eric helped me."

"What'd he find?"

Lauren's cell rang. It was O'Brien. She answered it quickly. "We have a little something more. Where do you want me to meet you?"

"Miami Beach Marina, off Alton Road. Thanks, Lauren. Please hurry."

FIFTEEN MINUTES LATER, Lauren Miles drove slowly through the Miami Beach Marina parking lot. She saw O'Brien approach in a Jeep. He pulled up and lowered the window. "Thanks for coming. What do you have?"

"We managed to read some of Spelling's letter. The first sentence or two he says he's sorry for his life, makes amends, and says he was in the condo parking lot that night to score some cocaine. We lost the best imprint as he was identifying where he hid the knife. A Florida city that has the first two letters beginning with an S and a T."

"St. Petersburg would be the largest."

"But there are six others, including his old home, Florida State Prison in Starke. I have a list for you." She handed O'Brien the slip of paper. "Here is your recorder, too, and dubs of the Russo confession. Spelling's letter is in this package. I'm going to the airport to send it to Quantico. We'll see if they can get a better read."

"Lauren, I really appreciate what you're doing." He touched her shoulder.

O'Brien's cell rang. It was Detective Dan Grant. "Dan, do you have anything?"

"One of our deputies found Lyle Johnson's body. Pretty nasty, Sean. It's the best attempt to make it look like a suicide that I've ever seen. There is GSR on Johnson's hand. The perp nailed Johnson in the right temple. Probably reloaded with a round after he'd killed Johnson. I'm betting he held Johnson's hand to the pistol grip as he fired off a shot. If it weren't for the circumstances, Johnson's connection to Spelling, this would be written off as a suicide, considering Johnson's marital strife and debt load. How are we going to catch somebody this good in the time Charlie Williams has left?"

"Begin by seeing who Lyle Johnson spoke with before he was killed. See if he placed a call to Jonathan Russo."

SIXTY

It was around seven o'clock when district attorney Stanley Rosen finished a tenth lap in his backyard pool. He climbed out, toweled off, and stood by his terra-cotta tile wet bar to mix a vodka and tonic. As he squeezed a fresh lime in the drink, he saw something move to his far left.

"Hello, Counselor," O'Brien said, opening the screened pool door and stepping onto the Mexican-tiled patio.

"What are you doing here, O'Brien?" Rosen sipped his drink.

"I have an audio tape of Jonathan Russo admitting to stabbing Alexandria Cole eleven years ago."

"Did you have to assault Russo to get it?"

"Those media reports aren't accurate."

O'Brien pressed the PLAY button on the small tape recorder. His voice came through the speaker: "I won't cheat the state out of its right to lock you away, Russo, so I'll dial nine-one-one, but before I do . . . tell me, why did you kill Alexandria Cole? The truth!"

"All right!" screamed Russo. "All right! I killed the bitch! That what you wanted to hear? I fuckin' stabbed her!"

Rosen said, "What did you mean, 'right to lock you away'?"

"I wanted Russo to admit his guilt in the Alexandria Cole killing."

Rosen sipped the drink. "First, we have to indict Russo. If he's found guilty—"

"You can use his admission to request a stay. Buy me some time, Rosen."

"Why? Doesn't mean I'd get one. Besides, like I told you in my office, a place where we ought to be having this discussion, I'm not going in front of a jury to reopen the Cole case unless I have solid proof—real evidence—that I feel will result in a conviction. This screaming match between you and Russo won't stand up."

"Maybe not, but a stay will give me time to find what you need."

"Find what?"

"The murder weapon for starters. FBI's running tests on a piece of paper that was directly beneath the page that Sam Spelling used to write the confession. We couldn't find Spelling's letter on Father Callahan's body, but we believe we can find the knife in a matter of days."

"Even if you find it, O'Brien, you don't know if there's anything on it. Could have been wiped clean."

"Maybe, but we don't know until we run tests."

"You won't know that until you find it. Until then, I'd appreciate it if you leave my property. And the next time, make an appointment." Rosen turned and walked over to a chaise longue and sat down.

O'Brien said, "Alexandria Cole was murdered. In the last two days, three people who knew the ID of the killer are dead. The last one was a prison guard who overheard Spelling's confession to Father Callahan. They just found his body. Shot in the head. Close range. I think Russo's hired a pro. And now Charlie Williams has thirty-five hours to live. They'll remove him from his cell and take him to a deathwatch cage less than fifty feet from the death chamber. You have a chance to postpone it for a few days. If I can't find evidence, at least you tried to save a man's life."

"Twelve people agreed Williams killed his girlfriend in a fit of jealous rage. You helped convict him, remember? And nothing you've said to me or have shown me changes that. If you aren't gone in ten seconds, I'll have you locked up."

"I can admit my mistake. You won't even consider the fact you're making one. But consider this, Counselor: You'll be just as guilty as Russo if Williams dies. If I find the proof after Williams is dead, you can tell the media why you did nothing to stop it."

O'Brien walked to his car, parked on the side of the palm-tree-lined street.

Rosen knocked back the rest of his vodka and picked up the cell phone by his chair, dialed a number, and said, "This is district attorney Stan Rosen. I understand there's an APB out for Sean O'Brien." He paused. "O'Brien just left my house, on Monroe Terrace. Looks like he's in a green Jeep and heading south toward Collins."

SIXTY-ONE

The female police dispatcher sat in front of a darkened console at police headquarters, looked at the LED grid map of Miami Beach, and keyed her radio microphone. "Airborne, unit three."

"Unit three."

"Need the bird for an aerial recon in the vicinity of Flamingo Park and Collins."

"Ten-four."

"Subject vehicle is a green Jeep. Two ground units are in the area. Subject is considered armed and dangerous. ID Sean O'Brien, forty-three-year-old W.M. Knows the area well. Formerly with Miami-Dade homicide."

"Be airborne in three minutes."

As the two helicopter pilots suited up and left the building, one said to the other, "Let's go round up Dirty Harry."

O'BRIEN LOOKED IN HIS rearview mirror driving east on Eleventh Street. He assumed that Rosen had made a call to MPD. O'Brien cut off of Eleventh onto a side street and drove slowly down the street until he saw a house with a FOR SALE sign in the front yard. The grass was in need of mowing and the curtains were gone from the windows. O'Brien pulled in the driveway, shut off the motor, and sat. He lowered the windows and listened. He heard the ticking of the cooling engine, the chant of a mockingbird in the tree, a tennis racket serving a ball, and the howl of sirens. O'Brien lowered the window a little more. The unmistakable sound of a helicopter was coming his way. He started the Jeep and pulled farther up the driveway, under the cover of a massive banyan tree.

A minute later the helicopter flew directly over him, the prop wash causing a few leaves to spiral down off the tree and land on the Jeep's hood and windshield.

He opened his laptop, found a signal, and keyed in a name: Tucker Houston, defense attorney, Miami, Florida. He scanned a biography. Houston retired nine years ago. Lived in Coconut Grove. O'Brien set the GPS for the address, backed the Jeep out of the driveway, and headed in the opposite direction from where the posse was going.

In less than five minutes, O'Brien was approaching MacArthur Causeway. A traffic accident blocked an intersection, causing O'Brien's Jeep to become part of a parade going nowhere. He couldn't back up, go right or left. Stuck.

They were just pulling the sheet over the biker's face as O'Brien came into the intersection. He purposely avoided looking directly at the officer who was waving cars around the scene. As O'Brien passed, he glanced up in his rearview mirror. The officer had stopped the cars behind him and turned to look at O'Brien's Jeep. He tilted his head toward his left shoulder, keyed the mike, and began speaking.

"All units, APB subject's Jeep just drove around signal seventeen at Euclid and Eighth. Looks like he's heading for the Mac Causeway."

O'Brien knew he'd been made. He pulled off Euclid, cutting through a 7-Eleven lot and onto Poinciana Boulevard, heading north.

He pushed the Jeep to ninety as he weaved through traffic. He heard sirens. Dozens of cars. He knew the Taser and SWAT sniper squad would be among them.

O'Brien slammed on his brakes and cut down a street lined with banyan trees. He drove north on Collins, cutting through the parking lot of the Haulover Golf Course. He pulled into a strip mall parking lot. A grocery stock boy was ending his shift. The teenager walked through the lot and opened the door to his green Jeep, turned on the air conditioning, and called his girlfriend on his cell as he waited for the Jeep to cool.

O'Brien drove on through the lot, the sound of sirens in the distance. He whipped into a Mobil gas station and headed behind the building to a covered automatic car wash. O'Brien shoved eight quarters in the slots and drove his Jeep inside the car wash, stopping when a red light flashed. In seconds, the wash began. Even with the sound of water all around him, O'Brien could hear the MPD helicopter circling nearby.

THE SWAT TEAM surrounded the green Jeep in the parking lot. The teenager sat in his Jeep, rocking to his loud music and talking to his girlfriend on the phone.

"Put your hands on the wheel! Do it now!" shouted the police command over the bullhorn.

The teenager swallowed nervously and said to his girlfriend, "Shit! I'm surrounded by cops! They're pointing guns at me! Call my mom!"

O'BRIEN LEFT THE CAR wash and tore out of the lot toward Collins Avenue. His cell rang. It was Detective Ron Hamilton. "Sean, I've heard all the noise on the radio. You have to turn yourself in! It can all be explained."

"You know as well as I do that it can't be explained quickly. I'd be held, then go for a bond hearing. In the meantime, a good chunk of time that Charlie Williams has left on the planet is gone. For his sake, I can't afford to come in."

"You can't afford not to!"

"Volusia SO found a body, the prison guard. Name's Lyle Johnson. He was assigned to watch Sam Spelling. Whoever killed Spelling and Callahan killed Johnson."

"You think it's Russo?"

"I think it's one of his hired guns."

"We found that girl you were with at Club Oz."

"Is she okay?" O'Brien almost knew what Ron was about to tell him.

"One of our detectives went over to Barbie Beckman's house. First time, she wouldn't come to the door. Second time, we entered with a warrant. Found her on the bathroom floor."

"Is she alive?"

"Barely. She's at Jackson Memorial. And she's in bad shape."

SIXTY-TWO

Within two blocks of Jackson Memorial Hospital, O'Brien saw a medical supply store. He pulled in the parking lot and entered the store. He picked up a black stethoscope for a hundred fifty dollars and blue scrubs—the top and pants. He paid the bill, got back in his Jeep, and for less than two hundred dollars, O'Brien had a temporary license to practice medicine.

He maneuvered the Jeep around double-parked cars at Jackson Memorial Hospital, found a place at the farthest end of an employee parking lot to park, changed clothes, and headed for the doctor's entrance.

ON THE SECOND FLOOR, O'Brien got out of the hospital elevator and headed in the direction in which he saw a lone guard sitting outside a room. The guard, a Miami-Dade police officer, was reading the sports section of the newspaper as O'Brien approached. "Think the Dolphins new draft pick will make a difference on offense?" O'Brien asked.

"Hi, Doctor . . . um . . . I don't know, he was in the running for the Heisman. He put points on the board in college."

"We could use him. Season starts soon. How's Miss Beckman?"

"I haven't been inside the room, but from out here, she looks bad."

"I'll take a look." O'Brien smiled and entered Barbie's room.

The name on the door said Elizabeth Barbie Beckman, but the woman in the bed looked like a mummy. Her face had been so badly beaten the swelling had forced her eyes closed. The lumps were the color and shape of dark plums. A knot on her head was the size of a lemon. IVs ran into both arms. One arm was in a cast. He saw dried blood in her left ear canal.

O'Brien stepped to the bed. The woman's breathing was quick and shallow. He looked at the monitors. Her heart rate was fast, even in her sleep. She made small whimpering sounds, like a puppy might utter. Her body jerked as if she was trying to shake out of a bad dream. O'Brien leaned down, his lips near one of her ears. He said, "Barbie, this is Sean O'Brien. Can you hear me?"

There was no movement. No flutter of the eyes. Nothing. O'Brien thought she might be in a coma. He said, "Barbie, this is Ken, how are you feeling?"

A soft moan, the words trying to rise to the surface. She managed to open her right eye. The entire white of her eye was dark red, the look of a moldy strawberry.

"Ken," she mumbled. "You're here. . . ."

"Barbie, who did this to you?"

"He hurt me so bad," she whispered. Her eyes filled with water, the tears spilling out of the swollen corners and soaking into the gauze.

"Who did it?"

"They'll kill you. . . ."

"Barbie, who hurt you?"

She sobbed and said in a raspy whisper, "Carlos Salazar."

"Russo's guy—"

216

"Please, don't . . . they're part of the mob . . . soldiers. . . . Life means nothing to them."

O'Brien held one of her hands, careful not to touch the IV. He said, "Listen to me, no man has the right to do this to you. Do you understand?"

"I'm so scared. . . . He hurt me so . . ."

O'Brien used his thumb to wipe away the tears from her right eye. He leaned down and kissed her forehead. "I'm going to help you."

She tried to smile. Butterfly stitches in her swollen lips prevented it. She managed to say, "In my English lit class I read about poetic justice . . . you know, like some Shakespearean play where good beats evil."

O'Brien smiled.

Barbie continued, "Kind of poetic justice that I'm in the same hospital where they brought Jonathan Russo. I read in the paper that they brought him here. You sort of put him in the hospital. And one of his guys did the same to me. I don't understand it, though—if good beats evil, why am I here?"

"It's not over yet."

SIXTY-THREE

As O'Brien left Barbie's room, he picked up a clipboard on the nightstand. When the elevator doors opened to the eleventh floor, O'Brien stepped out. He casually looked right and left. He could see a man dressed in a tropical shirt near the end of the hall. O'Brien walked in that direction. He paused at every other door, glanced at the clipboard, and pretended to look at the patient's name on the door.

A few feet from room 1103, the man in the tropical shirt looked out a window at the parking lot. O'Brien approached him and said, "Is Mr. Russo resting comfortably?"

Tropical shirt's face was so bloated his eyes squinted. His breathing sounded labored. O'Brien could smell the stink of dried sweat, beer, and cigarette smoke on the man's clothes. He looked at O'Brien suspiciously and said, "He'd be better if you people would let him sleep. What kind of doctor are you?"

"Head doctor."

"Shrink?"

O'Brien smiled, looked down at the clipboard for a second, and said, "No, I aim for the head." He hit the man squarely in the jaw, knocking him out cold. O'Brien dragged the man into a janitor's closet. Then he opened the door to Russo's room.

"O'Brien! How'd you get in here?"

"Your hall monitor is resting comfortably next to a mop. Probably wake up with a nasty headache, though."

Russo reached for the nurse's call button. O'Brien was faster, grabbing the remote control and pulling it off the wall.

Russo tried to sit up in bed. The heart monitor raced. "What do you want?"

"Why'd you sic your dogs on Barbie?"

"That fuckin' whore, who gives a shit." His voice was thick with disgust.

O'Brien lifted his Glock, holding it by the barrel, the butt of the gun pointed toward Russo's face. "I give a shit. This is where your goon hit Barbie. It's where I'll begin with you. And guess what, Russo, if she slips into a coma or dies . . . you do too."

Russo pushed himself as far back in the bed as he could get, the electrodes popping off his chest. "Please, O'Brien . . . I'm a sick man."

"Why'd you have the girl beaten?"

"Wanted to make sure she knew not to show up as a witness when we took your ass to trial. Figured we could get you five to seven and it'd send a clear signal to others—cops, PIs, and anyone who thought they could shake us down or was thinkin' they could come in our place, trash it up, and threaten us."

"Who's us?'

"Me and Sergio Conti."

"I believe you hired Carlos Salazar to hurt the girl, maybe kill her. Just like you hired him to kill three people—you wanted to make damn sure Spelling's letter was kept out of circulation. You wanted to make sure Charlie Williams takes a hot needle. And if you put me out of the picture, that pretty much guaranteed it. So now you beat up Barbie because she was with me in your club, maybe send me a message, maybe scare me."

Russo's eyes looked toward the door for less than a half second. It was long enough for O'Brien to know someone had entered the room.

O'Brien dropped to the floor, rolled, and came up with his Glock pointed in the man's face. "Drop it!"

The man, his jaw swollen, his right eye watering, held his pistol in front of him. It was at least fifteen degrees to the right of O'Brien.

"Thought you'd sleep longer," said O'Brien. "You've got a choice . . . you can take a chance and try to point that squarely at me and get off a shot before I do. Or you can set the gun down on the floor, kick it to me, and walk to the back of the room."

"Shoot him!" ordered Russo.

The man looked at Russo and then looked at O'Brien without turning his head. He said, "He's got the drop on me!"

"You fuckin' pussy!"

The man slowly lowered the pistol to the floor.

"Kick it this way!" O'Brien ordered.

The man kicked the gun. O'Brien picked it up. "I bet that if I have a ballistics test run on this, I'm wagering that this gun, or one very close to it, killed Father Callahan. What I don't know is who fired the killing bullet—you . . . or Carlos Salazar."

"Wasn't me! Tell him, Mr. Russo!"

"I don't know, pal," said O'Brien. "You were so very eager to take a shot at me. You could very well be the hit man responsible for three murders in the last three days. The priest was a close personal friend of mine." O'Brien stepped closer.

"I didn't shoot no priest! Tell him, Mr. Russo! Fucker's crazy . . . gonna kill me!"

"Shut up!" snapped Russo.

The sounds of sirens could be heard close to the hospital. O'Brien stepped to the window and looked out. More than a dozen squad cars were half circling the main entrance. He turned to Russo. "Here's the plan. Russo, you're going to call Detective Ron Hamilton. You're going to tell him that you and Sergio are dropping all charges against me. The second thing: You're going to pay for Barbie Beckman's medical expenses. After she's healed, you're going to subsidize her college education."

"And if I don't."

"I walked into your club, and I got to you. I got to you in your hospital room. I'll get to you wherever you are. Now the last item. Where's Carlos Salazar?"

"He calls us from time to time. He checks in when he wants to. I don't have his number. Sometimes he drops by the club."

O'Brien pointed the gun at the man in the corner. "Where's Salazar?"

"Spends a lot of time at the Sixth Street Gym. Likes to shoot pool at a joint called Sticks, in Little Havana, and likes to buy pussy at the high-end clubs. Take your pick."

O'Brien placed both pistols under his belt, hiding them under his shirt. As he opened the door to leave, he turned back to Russo. "Your time's up. Call Hamilton."

When the door closed behind O'Brien, Russo said to his bodyguard, "Get Salazar on the fuckin' phone. Now!"

SIXTY-FOUR

O'Brien walked down the hospital corridor, following the signs to an operating room. He ducked into a stockroom and found a supply of trash bags. O'Brien wrapped the two pistols in linens and stuffed everything into a trash bag, tied it, and walked down the hall to a service elevator. He rode the service elevator to the first floor.

Sitting alone in a wheelchair near the patient discharge area was an elderly woman with a suitcase by her side. O'Brien approached her, smiled, and said, "Ma'am, are you ready to be taken to where someone can pick you up?"

She smiled and said, "Yes I am. My husband went to get the car."

"Hospital policy is we take you to the curb, the patient pick-up areas, and see that you get in your transportation safely."

She smiled and nodded. O'Brien picked up her suitcase, tied the plastic bag to one of the wheelchair handles, and began pushing her through the corridor toward the patient pick-up section of the building. Three police officers rushed by him, hands on their holstered pistols as they ran. O'Brien could see more officers at the front entrance.

"What's all the excitement?" the woman asked O'Brien.

"I can't say for sure."

"Maybe they have a crazy person doing something, you think?"

"Maybe."

O'Brien pushed the wheelchair toward the double glass doors that opened automatically. Other patients, all in wheelchairs, holding flowers and overnight bags, waited to be driven away.

The woman pointed toward a Buick and said, "There's Harold. He's pulling up."

Harold, a slender man in his seventies, thin white mustache, neatly parted white hair, moved spryly as he got out of the car. He smiled, popped the trunk, and waited for his wife to be wheeled to the car. Harold said, "Let's get Carolyn into the front seat."

"No problem, sir," said O'Brien.

They stood on either side of the wheelchair and carefully lifted Carolyn up to her feet. She walked three steps with O'Brien and her husband on either side. She eased into the front seat and said, "Take me home. I'm ready to see my roses."

O'Brien shut the car door. "Sir, let me get your wife's suitcase into the trunk."

"I appreciate your help," said Harold.

O'Brien started to close the trunk and said, "I just got off work. My friend's car is over in lot L. He works here, in ER. We carpool, but the lead asked him to pull a double. I'll catch a cab home, but may I impose on you for a lift to the car? I left some of my things in it. I wouldn't ask, but it's been a long day in the operating room."

"No imposition at all," Harold said, smiling.

"Great. I'll just toss my bag in and we'll be on our way." O'Brien put the bag in the backseat and pushed the wheelchair to the sidewalk under the alcove.

Two police officers were walking under the porte cochere, coming toward O'Brien. He turned his back to them, knelt beside a young girl in a wheelchair holding a teddy bear, and said, "Take care of that bear, okay?"

She smiled and looked up at her mother, who said, "They're both feeling better."

O'Brien smiled and climbed into the backseat of the Buick. "Thank you."

"Glad to help," Harold said. "Now where's lot L?"

"On the other side of the hospital. You can go out of here, take a left, and follow the drive around to the back."

As Harold got closer to lot L, O'Brien scanned the parking lot, looking for people sitting in unmarked cars—people talking into police radios.

"It's the Jeep by the tree," said O'Brien. "I won't be but a few seconds."

"Take your time," said Carolyn.

O'Brien unlocked the Jeep and leaned across the seat to get his laptop and tape recorder. He looked through the rear windshield and saw it.

A wink. A small reflection of light. The setting sun coming off a handheld lens. It was from the roof of a doctor's office building next to the hospital. O'Brien didn't know if the reflection came from a rifle scope or binoculars.

He got the laptop and recorder, tossed the Jeep keys on the floorboard, and maneuvered around to keep the Jeep between himself and the reflection on the roof.

O'Brien darted as he returned to the car. He said, "You can get into traffic by going through that alley—it opens onto Tenth Avenue."

"You sure know your roads around the hospital," said Harold.

"You learn it."

The old man pulled out of the lot and started down the alley.

. . .

THE POLICE SNIPER KEYED his radio. "Subject just got out and back into a dark blue Buick. Heading toward Tenth and Newman."

"All available units move!" barked a command from the radio.

WHEN HAROLD PULLED OUT onto the corner of Tenth, O'Brien said, "This is fine. I'll get out at the light. You both have been so kind. I can get transportation from here."

"Sure we can't take you any farther?" asked Carolyn.

"No, ma'am. This is good. You go home and take care of those roses."

"Be careful," said Harold as O'Brien got out of the car. O'Brien jogged across the street, where a city bus was about to pull away. He banged on the door. The driver slowed, opened the door, and O'Brien got in. He paid and walked past a dozen staring faces. He took a seat in the back of the bus, next to an elderly Hispanic woman holding a paper bag filled with plantains.

As the bus pulled away and headed north down Seventh Avenue, O'Brien glanced out the back window. A pack of squad cards was going the opposite direction. Sirens screaming—cops ready to catch one of their own who they were convinced had crossed the line.

SIXTY-FIVE

wo miles from the hospital, O'Brien got off the bus, walked into a convenience store restroom, and changed back into his clothes. He tossed the hospital clothing into a garbage can on the outside of the building and flagged a passing cab.

"Where you need to go, sir?" asked the driver, his accent heavy Cuban.

"One thirty-eight Hibiscus Court, Coconut Grove."

"Twenty minutes, no problem."

The driver pulled into traffic as O'Brien looked at his watch.

Thirty-four hours remaining.

He picked up his cell and called Lauren Miles. "Did you come up with anything on Judy Neilson or Carlos Salazar?" he asked.

"Just about to call you. Neilson first. After Alexandria Cole's murder and Charlie Williams's trial, Judy Neilson left Miami and moved to New York City. She worked as a model, but the bright lights and big city seemed to fade. She moved back to Florida, married, and divorced. Now sells real estate near Orlando. Salazar is bad news."

"How bad?"

"Extortion, racketeering, five cases of aggravated battery. And try this one on for starters . . . we believe Salazar was recruited by the Aryan Brotherhood."

"He seems to have a little different ethnicity than what they look for."

"Florida has more hate groups than any other state. As a matter of fact, omega, one of the symbols the priest drew before he died, is tied to a Far Right extremist group based in Tampa called the Omega Order. One of the many things they preach is that violence is a means to an end and justified to achieve their goals. Sort of a jihadist creed. People with Salazar's skills can freelance. These groups don't recruit him to join them. They hire him to train them."

"Train them in what?"

"Plain and simple—killing."

"Wouldn't imagine they need that much coaching."

"They don't, Sean. What they needed was someone who could teach them the art of traceless killing."

"Traceless?"

"They call it 'dusting without leaving any dust behind.'"

"Like he did with Spelling and Father Callahan. There's another to add."

"Who?"

"The DOC guard assigned to Spelling. Volusia SO found his body in a rural area. Perp shot him at close range. Made it look like suicide. Traceless, if you will."

"You think it's Salazar?"

"Him, or someone connected to him and Russo. Whoever did it was extremely precise, calculating, and very fast. In a few hours, he killed the three people that could tie Russo to a murder eleven years ago. I know that Russo sent Salazar to intimidate and beat Barbie Beckman."

"How do you know?"

"She's at Jackson Memorial, a few floors down from Russo's room."

"I gather that you've paid them both a hospital visit."

O'Brien said nothing.

"Sean, we know Russo uses his club as a front for drugs. These people get so deep in the cartel that they have dozens of shell companies. They're in bed with some of the Miami mob families with extended business dealings with their New York and Chicago cousins. One of Russo's eccentricities is he likes to dabble in the model, music, and movie scene. Club Oz gives him the stage. Salazar's one of the dozen or so pros he has at his disposal. You can't effectively function as a one-man army. It's suicide."

"With the hours running out in Charlie Williams's life, I don't have a choice."

"You get ready to go in . . . call me, okay? Bye, Sean."

From the window of the cab, O'Brien watched a high-speed powerboat zip over the glasslike surface of Biscayne Bay. He called Ron Hamilton. "You'll probably get a call from Russo dropping charges against me."

"Why would he do that?"

"Because he knows it's in his best interest. But I'm betting the call won't come until I neutralize Carlos Salazar."

"Where is Salazar?"

"I'm beginning at the Sixth Street Gym and then going to Sticks Billiards in Little Havana. If he's not at either place, maybe somebody will know where I can find him."

"What are you going to do? For Christ sakes, Sean, you can't even arrest him. What proof have you found to tie him to the murders of the priest, Spelling, or the guard?"

"None, yet. But he almost killed Barbie. You could hold him on that."

"So you want me there. . . . The question is, do you want me as backup or as someone for you to hand Salazar to?"

"You'd have to come alone. Anyone else in the department would try to take me down. You hold Salazar before he skips. I'll find the nail to hold him for good."

"I'd bet the pool hall would be a good possibility first."

O'Brien smiled and said, "I bet you're right. Also, I'd bet that Russo's tipped off Salazar. Be careful on your approach."

"When?"

"I have one stop I have to make. See you in one hour. And Ron . . ."

"Yeah?"

"Thanks."

SIXTY-SIX

It was sunset when O'Brien got out of the cab in front of a small house tucked away behind old banyan trees and terraces of blooming bougainvillea. The house was built in the late fifties. Mediterranean. Beige stucco exterior veiled behind banana trees. Rose-bushes were in need of pruning. As O'Brien walked up the river-stone footpath, he could smell the fresh-cut grass, roses, sweet bananas, and mimosa flowers.

Knocking on the door, he watched a bumblebee hover above a flowering yellow periwinkle. The door opened and a man in his late sixties looked over the rims of his reading glasses at O'Brien. The man didn't seem surprised. His eyebrows were as wild as his rosebushes, kind blue eyes, uncombed white hair, forearms scarred from the sun. He wore chlorine-faded swimming trunks and a Miami Dolphins T-shirt.

"I recognize you," said Tucker Houston. "How you been, Sean?"

"Better. It's been a long time, Tucker. May I speak with you?"

"Come in."

O'Brien followed Tucker Houston through the house to a screened-in patio by a small pool. "Sit down, Sean. Excuse the look of the place.

Everything is sort of under control of the forces of nature. Wherever I leave a magazine or book, it seems gravity won't release its grasp, hence, I don't pick up too much since Margaret passed. Want something to drink?"

"No thanks. I'm sorry to hear about Margaret. After Sherri died, I sort of got out of touch."

"And you got out of Miami. Then I retired. So I guess we both clocked out, but reading *The Herald*, looks like you clocked in, and everybody in the city knows it."

"I'm here to ask you a favor." O'Brien stared at the blue pool water before looking at Tucker. "When I was a cop, I used to think about you."

"Oh, how so?"

"You made me a better cop. Because one of the first things I thought about was how the defense would work the case—how Tucker Houston would work the case. You grilled me enough times on the witness stand that I knew you did your homework. And you forced me to do mine."

Tucker Houston listened without interruption as O'Brien played the audio tape recording, told him the story of Alexandria Cole and the events that had transpired during the last three days.

"I see your dilemma," Tucker said, sitting back in a deck chair. "I'm not sure I can help you. I've been out of the legal loop awhile now."

"While a lot of defense attorneys troll for scum to turn a dollar, the misfits that they plea out and collect a toll from, the junkies they re-cycle, the snitches they use . . . you seemed above reproach on that. I wanted to tell you that one time. The scales of justice on the Charlie Williams case are beyond out of balance . . . eleven years' worth of extra weight added to Williams's side, plus the execution pending. Can you get a federal judge to issue a stay for at least thirty days?"

Tucker was silent, the circulating blue of pool water reflecting from his eyes. "If I could catch old circuit court judge Samuel David-son tomorrow, I might have a chance to get his ear."

O'Brien smiled and said, "Thank you." He looked at his watch and stood. "I need to call a cab. I have to make a couple of stops down-town."

"Tell you what. I've got two cars in the driveway—one more than I need. Couldn't bear to part with Margaret's black Thunderbird after she died. She loved that car. We used to enjoy putting the top down and heading to Key Largo on weekends. The car is one of the last Ford made before ending production in oh five. She only put three thousand miles on it. Car's in need of driving. Take it. Drop it off when you're done."

O'BRIEN CROSSED THE MacArthur Causeway, keeping the little T-Bird humming just below the speed limit. His cell rang. It was Dave Collins. "I may have come up with a lead on the picture of the moon you e-mailed me. I compared it with a cropped close-up from the image Father Callahan drew, the one you had Detective Grant e-mail to me. I believe it may date to a fifteenth-century painter, a man many people thought was deranged. But, with Father Callahan's art history background, it makes sense."

"Why?"

"Because the painter used the omega sign. A lot of his work was about good and evil, heaven and hell. . . . That might explain the six-six-six."

O'Brien thought about the night he found Father Callahan dead—open eyes locked on the stained glass.

"Sean, you need to see this."

SIXTY-SEVEN

It was dark and a light rain fell as O'Brien drove slowly by the Sixth Street Gym. It was a two-story art deco, rehabbed and painted a shade lighter than a slice of ripe honeydew melon. A canvas awning with a red neon sign hanging beneath the marquee read:

SIXTH STREET GYM
BOXING, JU JITSU, AND TAI CHI TRAINING
WORLD'S BEST AEROBICS AND WEIGHT TRAINING

O'Brien read the marquee as he drove past the gym, circled around, and parked a block away on Seventy-first Street. He walked in the rain, watching the bounce of headlights reflecting off dark, wet streets, the neon like red lava flowing into dark puddles.

O'Brien saw a woman get out of a parked car on the opposite side of the street. She used the palms of both hands to smooth down her miniskirt, stood under an awning to light a cigarette, blew the first drag of smoke over her shoulder, and started walking. Her heels were like taps against the wet sidewalk.

A man in the car pulled away from the curb, driving fast down the rain-slick street, the red taillights leaving a reflective trail as he hit brakes, turned left, and was gone.

O'Brien approached the front door of the Sixth Street Gym. A Cadillac Escalade, a white Chevy pickup truck, and a yellow Ferrari were parked near the curb. The black writing on the melon-colored door had the style of Japanese characters that were painted to look like small samurai swords. They read:

BOXING—KICKBOXING—KARATE—
HEAVY BAG TRAINING—PERSONAL TRAINERS
WORLD'S BEST EXERCISE
FOR THE MIND AND SPIRIT

Enter the house of dragons, thought O'Brien as he opened the door to loud music and the smell of gym sweat. He walked down a hall that resembled a hall of fame. Pictures of boxers and celebrity boxers framed and placed on both walls. Kid Gavilan. Sugar Ramos. Kid Chocolate. Stallone. Ali. Mickey Rourke. Foreman. Sugar Ray. Angelo Dundee. Among them stood an old black-and-white photograph of Ernest Hemingway in the ring with a smaller man. The caption read: PONCHO AND PAPA.

O'Brien could hear the pounding on the heavy bags, the rattle of the speed bags, the clank of metal on metal, the buzz of machines, and the rock 'n' roll from the loud speakers. When he turned the corner and entered the gym, he wondered whether he would see Carlos Salazar lifting weights, punching a heavy bag, or ready to take his head off.

He stepped into the main part of the massive gym. No one was at the reception desk. A large American flag hung at the far end of the gym. There were dozens of people training on machines, lifting weights, and riding stationary bikes, while half a dozen others worked the heavy bags. They wore wireless headphones and pounded leather on leather to soundtracks only they heard.

There were two separate rings. Inside both rings, personal trainers barked encouragement, threw jabs and taunted the boxers. The trainers used hand-boards, the boxers smacking the boards with lightweight gloves.

O'Brien stood near a heavy bag that was not being used. He scanned as many faces as he could. Mostly men. Mostly white. Lots of ink on the bare chests and backs. Testosterone as heavy in the air as the smell of sweat.

A twentysomething Hispanic woman, dark skin, hourglass figure, tight black shorts, using pink boxing gloves, sparred with a male trainer.

O'Brien walked through the gym, trying not to seem like he was looking for something or someone. Less than ten feet to his right, a man began doing arm curls with a thirty-pound weight. He had an Irish shamrock tattooed on his shoulder, the interconnecting cloverleafs forming a 666. His left earring was a black onyx shaped like an eye.

O'Brien glanced at the man's face. Ruddy. Irish-American. Big boned. Shoulders like a buffalo. The man said, "Do I remind you of somebody, pal?" His accent was brogue Irish.

"No, just passing through," said O'Brien.

The man said nothing, his eyes suspicious and the tendons in his neck taut like piano strings as he lifted the weight.

O'Brien moved on toward the center ring. A trainer was finishing a light sparring round with a man who looked as if he had a military background. Shaved head. An American flag was tattooed above a Special Forces insignia on his right upper arm. The left arm had a small map of Iraq with the dates 2006–2007. The man removed his gloves, toweled off his face, and climbed out of the opposite side of the ring.

The trainer stepped down near O'Brien and said, "Can I help you?" He wore a sweat-stained tank top. He had a square, angular face. One eye looked more to the left than the other eye, a white scar between the left nostril and lip. Biceps and forearms like hammered iron. He used his teeth to pull on the drawstring to his left glove.

"I like your place. What does personal training cost?"

"Depends. Nothing better than working with a trainer on the heavy bag. Great for the cardio and upper body. You'll build stamina and add muscle to your legs."

"How about training in the ring?"

"The best. It builds mind and body. Why sit on a stationary bike and watch some clown on TV when you can go one-on-one in the ring?"

"I see you offer training in the martial arts?"

"Absolutely. Got some of Miami's best trainers."

"Would Carlos Salazar be one?"

He turned his head slightly, looked at O'Brien a beat through his left eye, cocked his head like a lizard before attacking an insect. "Never heard of the guy."

"Rather than train people in martial arts, maybe he just comes here as a customer—big guy, like you. Wears a beard short—"

"Don't recognize the dude. Got another client waiting."

"Here's how you can recognize the dude. He'll look like a coward because he beats women and priests. If you see Salazar, tell him Sean O'Brien sends his best."

The trainer used the back of his knuckle-scarred hand to wipe a drop of sweat from his chin. He stepped around O'Brien, grazing his left shoulder against O'Brien's shirtsleeve and leaving a dark stain of perspiration.

O'Brien walked to a remote corner of the gym and called Ron Hamilton. "I'm at the Sixth Street Gym. Spoke with one of the trainers. He knows Salazar. Wouldn't admit it, but definitely knows him."

"I'm at Sticks Billiards now. Just drove around the place. Checked the parking lot for Salazar's car. Not here."

"What's he drive?"

"We checked DMV's database. The world of contraband and selective elimination must pay well. There's a 2009 Ferrari registered in the name Carlos Salazar."

"He's here. Get here quick as you can."

As O'Brien ended his call, he saw a reflection off the dark cell phone screen. A slight movement. Someone behind him. No time to duck.

Time stopped in the bright flash of white light and faded to black.

SIXTY-EIGHT

He was hit in the face with a pail of cold water. O'Brien opened his eyes. Dizzy. His head aching. He was sprawled on his back, lying on hard canvas. O'Brien reached behind his back for his Glock. It was gone. Someone had taken it. He squinted under the bright light directly above the ring. He leaned to one side, slowly sat up, and tried to stand. His legs felt like they had gone to sleep—the circulation beginning to push blood through the calves and feet.

Where was he? How long had he been out?

"I hope you like the ring!"

O'Brien turned around. Carlos Salazar walked into a pocket of light near the ring. He was dressed in boxer shorts. No shirt. His lean body hard and sculpted. Muscles moving under the skin like waves. Thick, hairless chest. In the center of his chest was an image of the Virgin Mary. Below it, in Spanish were the words *La Virgen*.

Salazar climbed in the ring, held his arms high above his head, and slowly turned around. On his back was a red and blue tattoo of a muscular winged demonlike figure, hooves for feet, serpent's tail. In Spanish the word below the tattoo spelled *el Satanás*. Salazar stepped closer to O'Brien. "You like the art, no? The finest artist in Bogotá did this. You know what it takes for great art to be better?"

O'Brien said nothing.

"I'll tell you," said Salazar. "Great art becomes more valuable after the artist dies. When he can no longer produce because of his death, whatever is left is, shall we say, limited quantity. After the master finished with me, I turned to the old man and gave him a mushroom to chew. He said he enjoyed the feeling, the illusions—the paintings that came alive on my body. When he looked at the art, I said to him, 'Old man, you have a choice in life. Like the Virgin, you can choose to be good, or like Lucifer, you can choose to be bad. You are a good artist. I, though, am a bad person. I'll make you a great artist by ending your life before your talent fades. It ensures your place in art immortality—and it confirms my place in hell.'"

O'Brien shook his head. Must be a dream—a nightmare. He heard a muffled sound. Then there were the collective sounds. The drone of whispers. People shuffling. Just beyond the curtain of light— shoes, pants, the soft, dark roundness of people sitting. A crowd watching—watching him in the ring with Salazar.

"Know what I did, Mr. Detective O'Brien? I cut the old man's throat." He took his index finger, moving it swiftly from ear to ear, smiled, and continued. "The old man, he looked down at the blood turning his shirt red, touched it with the tip of his finger, and placed a drop on my chest—the Virgin's mouth, he gave red color to the Virgin's lips. Then he smiled and whispered 'masterpiece' and he went to sleep . . . forever."

"What do you want?" O'Brien asked. His voice sounded like he crawled in a drainage pipe to speak.

"What do I want? Isn't it what you want? You want me, no? Isn't that what you told Russo, and you come in here and tell that to Michael, yes? You want me. Now, ex-cop, you got me. Or maybe I got you . . . because these are the once-a-month fights that we do here. We conduct them for invited guests only. It is not a fight for a few rounds.

239

It is a fight for life." He laughed and said, "But, since you asked, I'll tell you what I want. I want to make you my masterpiece. Maybe the canvas below your feet will be my work of art. With only one color, the color of your blood, sweat, and finally . . . your tears. Because in the end, you will be on your knees in your blood and piss, crying."

Salazar walked to the ropes and said, "Because they—turn up the lights—they like to see art in motion, the physical and psychological process of creativity."

The ring was surrounded by about thirty people. All men. Some Japanese. Some Hispanic. Businessmen. Others looking as if they might be attending a function at their country club. They sat, whispered, and placed bets.

Salazar slipped on a pair of fingered, black leather gloves. The leather cut off at the center joint in each finger. He said, "See there, O'Brien?" He pointed to a camera in the ceiling, one on a tripod at one side of the ring, and another camera on the other side. "The art will be captured on video, packaged for international sale on DVD and on a password-protected Internet site." He turned to speak to a man that O'Brien didn't see when he entered the Sixth Street Gym. Salazar said, "My face."

The man tossed a rubber mask into the ring. Salazar pulled the mask over his head. It was a Japanese Noh mask—pale white, depicting the face of an elder Japanese man, goatee, white hair, red lips. Salazar said, "Let the fight begin."

The house lights dimmed. A single light illuminated the ring. O'Brien saw the small red lights now glowing from the three video cameras. He hoped there were microphones recording the sound. Maybe he could get Salazar to incriminate himself.

O'Brien said, "Russo's laughing at you. Calls you his horse. Says you're a little smarter than a mule he uses to haul his coke, but you don't have much horse sense."

"I got you in the ring, dude. Who's the dumb ass, huh?"

"You are, Carlos, you are because Russo's going to put you through a tree shredder and chum for fish off the back of his yacht with your body parts."

"Fuck you, cop! That's bullshit. You got nothing."

"Really? FBI has sixty-seven hours of digital conversations on one of their secure hard drives. It's amazing how the bright boys at NSA work so well with the FBI. This Patriot Act has given them a license to stick a chip in you while you're sleeping. They know where you eat. They stake it out. Pay off the right people—people in the finest South Beach restaurants. They slip a little 'medicine' in your Caesar salad, you can't taste it. Delayed effect, until you get home. Usually kicks in three hours after ingesting. You drift into a heavy sleep. Then, about 4:00 A.M., the pros silence your home alarm, pop the locks, and walk into your bedroom. Takes them less than three minutes to insert the microchip just under the scalp. It's equipped with both GPS and an Internet broadcast of up to fifty miles. You wake up. Don't feel a thing. Maybe an itch now and then, but your think it's dry scalp. The feds tell me for the first week, when Russo scratched his scalp, it sounded like a cat in a trash can."

There was a collective murmur from the crowd.

O'Brien said, "I'll spare you the details about some of what the feds are getting ready to hang on Russo, but chances are they won't go to the grand jury until you're out of the picture. Russo has a contract out on you, Carlos. Sorry, pal."

"You're full of shit!"

"Bet the name Vincent Pitts might mean something to you."

"Never heard of him."

"Maybe you've heard his professional name: Pit Bull. They say Pitts got that name because, just like a pit bull, he goes for the throat. Likes to use a garrote. Prefers rope to piano wire because rope takes a little longer to kill."

"Shut up! 'Cause you're sayin' this shit, I'm gonna take a little longer with you before I kill you."

O'Brien could see the tiny red camera lights glowing. He said, "Is that what you told Father Callahan before you killed him? Russo says he told you to tell Sam Spelling 'because he was'—and I'm quoting here—'because he was a greedy fucker and this was his last bedtime story.' So did you follow Russo's orders and tell Spelling it was his last bedtime story?"

Salazar grinned, danced in the ring, threw an air punch at O'Brien, and said, "Russo doesn't tell me what to do. When I take somebody out, I say what I want to say! This Spelling dude. You want to hear what he heard, huh? It'll be right before I hit you with the final blow—the death punch."

SIXTY-NINE

R on Hamilton sat in stationary traffic. The wipers did little to clear the rain off the windshield. He watched a cluster of flashing blue lights at an intersection. He tried Sean O'Brien's cell phone. No answer. Hamilton was stuck in a three-car pileup on rain-sliced Dixie Highway. Hamilton could move the single blue light from his dash, stick it on the car roof, and try to maneuver and bump stalled traffic out of the way. But he was still fifty yards from the intersection. There was no turning around.

He tried O'Brien's phone again. It went to voice mail.

SALAZAR CAME AT O'BRIEN and danced around him. Jabbing. Faking. Weaving. The dark eyes laughing behind the mask.

O'Brien turned. He was still groggy from the earlier hit to the head. He countered Salazar's every move, the wind from Salazar's punches fanning O'Brien's face. Salazar connected with a glancing blow to O'Brien's forehead, cutting him above the eye.

Blood splattered on the mat. Salazar danced to the ropes and said to the crowd, "I give you the first stroke of the brush!" The crowd cheered. Salazar pranced around the ring like a rock star. Then he ran straight for O'Brien. He stopped abruptly, spun around, and kickboxed, landing his foot in the center of O'Brien's chest. Nausea rose from O'Brien's stomach into his esophagus. The blood ran into his left eye. He shook his head, causing a stream of dark blood to splatter across the mat.

Salazar shouted, "Art in its purest form!" Applause and laughs from the crowd. Salazar dropped into a forward stance and then did a flying kick, his heel grazing the tip of O'Brien's nose. O'Brien jerked backward as Salazar followed with a second spinning kick, connecting again with O'Brien's chest. His mouth filled with blood. He spit it out and wiped the stinging sweat from his good eye.

"The painting grows, my friends!" shouted Salazar. There was applause and a few jeers directed toward O'Brien. Salazar looked up at the ceiling camera and said, "Capture the canvas. I will call this painting 'Dance of the Butterfly'!" There was a burst of applause and laughter as Salazar did a backflip and crouched low, arms extended, eyes following O'Brien.

Salazar moved in a slow circle around O'Brien. "Don't run out of paint just yet, there is still much canvas to cover."

Salazar charged, throwing a full roundhouse kick. His right foot missing O'Brien by an inch. O'Brien hit Salazar hard in the ribs. The crowed yelled for more.

Salazar trotted around the ring twice. He stopped and moved like a cat, low, sizing up his prey. He sprang toward O'Brien with a triple butterfly kick, his left heel catching O'Brien in the chest.

O'Brien saw nothing but white for a second. He closed one eye to stop the double vision. Blood poured from his mouth.

"This may be my best painting yet!" Salazar raised a clinched fist. He turned his back to O'Brien, the crowd now on its feet. The cheering was louder, mocking.

O'Brien focused on the blue and red tattoo on Salazar's back. He concentrated on the image of the muscular winged beast with hoofed feet, the scaly tail of a snake. He stepped forward. Closer. O'Brien drew back, ready to plant his fist right between the horns—right in the center of Salazar's spine.

Salazar spun around, his left connecting with O'Brien's lower abdomen. The contact knocked O'Brien to the ropes. Salazar laughed. He jabbed. He danced and heckled O'Brien. Then Salazar made the mistake of looking toward one of the cameras.

Focus. O'Brien shut out the noise of the crowd. He heard only his own breathing. He saw only one spot—Salazar's chin. When Salazar started to turn, O'Brien plowed a powerful right into the chin. The impact spun Salazar in a circle. As he turned, O'Brien waited for the exact second when the mask would face him again. Then slammed a hard left into the rubber lips. Even through the mask, O'Brien knew he'd taken out some of Salazar's front teeth. Blood flowed from below the mask. Salazar stumbled. The audience yelled for more.

Salazar shook his head, regained his footing, and landed a blow in O'Brien's stomach. O'Brien slammed his forearm into the center of the mask. The sound was like stepping on a foam cup. O'Brien hit Salazar with all of his strength, driving his fist deep into Salazar's solar plexus. He bent over, vomiting behind the mask. O'Brien brought his knee up hard, connecting to Salazar's chin. The strike caused Salazar to fall back as if his legs had disintegrated. He dropped to his knees.

The crowd chanted, "Kill . . . kill . . . kill . . ."

O'Brien took a few steps toward Salazar, who was still on his knees, his arms dangling powerless by his side, like a puppet with the strings severed. Blood rained from beneath the mask, dripping over the image of the Virgin Mary. O'Brien used his left hand to pull the mask from Salazar's head.

The crowd chanted louder. Salazar's eyes were rolling back. O'Brien steadied Salazar's floating head with his left hand. He tuned out the chants. Heard only the gurgling, sucking sound of Salazar trying to breathe through the blood.

Focus. No sounds. Nothing but Salazar heaving for air.

O'Brien drew back his right fist. He said, "What did you tell Sam Spelling before you killed him? What did you tell Father Callahan before you shot him? Tell me!"

Through shattered teeth, pulverized lips, and bloody gums, Salazar tried to smile, his face muscles jerking, lips trembling. He coughed and said in a raspy voice, "I beat up the girl, but those others, that's something between you and Russo, 'cause I don't know who the fuck you're talking about, cop." Then Salazar fell backward, his back flat against the mat, the demonic image pressed into the bloodied canvas. He stared up at the overhead camera, breathing heavy, the tiny red light glowing dimly like a distant planet in a universe of black.

O'Brien staggered across the mat. He steadied himself on the ropes. His right eye was swollen. He tried to climb down through the ropes, faltering on the edge and dropping against the concrete floor. Nausea rose in the pit of his stomach. He felt someone pick him up, carrying him on a set of massive shoulders.

Through his left eye, O'Brien saw a shiny black eye, an earring, attached to an earlobe. O'Brien batted weakly at it, the earring falling to the concrete. Then the room grew dark; he fought back the bile and vomit. The last thing he heard was an Irish accent. "You're one tough motherfucker, dude. Bet you killed him."

SEVENTY

O'Brien awoke to the guttural sounds of feral cats challenging each other. Their long, throaty snarls and hisses echoed off the brick walls in the alley. The shrieks reverberated, like two cats at the bottom of a well, backs arched, falsetto cries calling out in the dark. He opened his eyes. Through one eye, he could see the gang graffiti painted all over the walls. Through the other eye, the graffiti was blurred, as if he were looking through a keyhole to read an eye chart where the letters were in soft focus.

He was lying on his back in an alley, having been tossed between leaky plastic garbage cans and wet newspapers. The stench of cat litter, acrid urine, and feces came from a broken, black plastic bag near his head. His shoe and sock were soaked. He lifted his foot from a pothole filled with rainwater. A single lightbulb burned above the back entrance to a place called Laura's Lounge.

O'Brien touched his face, feeling the dried blood around his mouth, eyes, and nose. He touched a torn piece of flesh, the size of a nickel, which hung over his eyebrow. He struggled to sit. He could feel the Glock under his belt, near the small of his back. Somehow he had slept with the pistol grip pressed against his spine. He propped himself up against the wet brick wall and wondered if he had suffered brain damage. He whispered: "Name: Sean O'Brien. Birthday: December twelfth . . . mother's . . . maiden name . . . Lewis."

He looked at his watch. It was 6:01 A.M. How long had he been lying there? Where was he? Where's the car he borrowed? What happen to Ron Hamilton?

Salazar. Was he dead? 6:01. Twenty-four hours left for Charlie.

O'Brien looked at the flesh torn off two knuckles on his right hand and one knuckle on his left. He tried to stand, inching himself against the wall. He checked his pockets. His car keys and wallet were there, and so was his phone.

All the witnesses. The video cameras. If he'd beaten Salazar to death, it was self-defense. As he leaned against the wall, he could feel the rain begin to fall, the cool water rolling down his sore and bloodied face. O'Brien started to walk, slowly, his ribs on fire. His head pounded, and his body felt like it had been beaten with a mallet.

When he got to the end of the alley, he stepped out onto the sidewalk and looked for a street sign. Biscayne Street. O'Brien knew where he was. He stood more than ten blocks from the Sixth Street Gym. Somebody had dumped him there, dumped him in the garbage far enough away from the gym to keep an ex-cop out of their trash.

O'Brien went to the right. He was less than a block from the ocean. At this point, the sea would be his best friend, his best place to begin recovery. He walked through the deserted streets, an occasional car trolling by—buyers and sellers—slowing and moving on when they saw O'Brien's bloody face.

A black man, homeless, crouched near the front door of a closed print shop. He sat under a yellowed shower curtain he'd wrapped around himself to keep off the rain. As O'Brien walked slowly by, the man said, "Hey, my man. You look like somebody's walkin' bad dream. You covered in blood, dude. You need some hep. Hospital ain't close enough for you to be walkin' to it. You might bleed out."

O'Brien nodded and turned to walk. The man said, "I hate axkin' you this, seein' is how you look worse than me, but you hap'en to have a dollar, cap? I can get me a doughnut in an hour or so when the shop opens."

O'Brien's hands were sore, bloodied, and he could barely open the wallet. He pulled out a ten-dollar bill and handed it to the man, who stood up. The man said, "Thank you so much, I do appreciate your generosity."

O'Brien nodded, walked on, following the sound of the sea in the distance.

IT WAS A BLUE world—at least fifteen minutes before the sun crept over the Atlantic Ocean and the sea and sky merged in a palette of cobalt. O'Brien stood alone in the diffused morning, no wind, no people, and few cars passing. He stripped to his boxer shorts, folded his clothes neatly, covered his gun and phone, left them at the base of a tall palm tree and then he walked out into the flat ocean. When he got to where the warm water came up to his chest, he leaned back, lowering himself into the sea. He held his breath and let the salt water soak into every pore of his body. Then he floated on his back, gazing up at the sky that was beginning to lighten with the approaching dawn.

The moon hung over the South Beach skyline like a pumpkin, a perfect chamber-of-commerce poster. O'Brien looked at the face in the moon and thought about what Dave Collins had said, "You have to see this."

What was the moon going to reveal that the death match he somehow survived had not? Was Salazar lying when he was down? He admitted beating Barbie but said he'd never heard of the others. "That's something between you and Russo . . ."

O'Brien dropped back under the dark water. The warm therms in the shallows felt good. The gentle swells scrubbing the poisons, the potential infections, from his open cuts. He knew the cut above his eye would require stitches. His rib cage needed attention. He walked out of the water, back to the tree. O'Brien dressed, sat on a park bench, and used his cell to call a friend's home—a man he hadn't seen since Sherri died.

Dr. Seth Romberg answered the phone after three rings. "Dr. Romberg here."

"Seth, it's Sean O'Brien."

"Sean, how are you?"

"I've had better mornings. I need a few stitches. Maybe a tetanus shot. I would have waited a little later to call you, but I'm on a little deadline."

"Deadline? I know I spent a lot of time with you and Sherri. But you might want to try the emergency room. I don't—"

"Seth, I never would ask you this if it were not a life-and-death situation."

"Are you hurt that severely?"

"No, but someone else will be if I'm delayed. Please meet me at your office."

"Forty-five minutes, my office."

O'Brien disconnected. After he was stitched up, he would call Ron Hamilton to see if they found a body—Salazar's body. Then he would see if they were going to charge him with murder.

Now, however, he would see a Thursday morning sunrise. The horizon was building in soft strokes of orange and deep scarlet reds. The flat sea was indigo blue. A pelican flew across the purple sky, flapping its wings only twice and sailing the rest of the distance, as an ocean dressed in colors for a new day.

SEVENTY-ONE

D r. Seth Romberg was sewing up O'Brien's eyebrow when Detective Ron Hamilton entered the small office, less than two blocks from the hospital. Hamilton looked at O'Brien. "Sean, what in God's name happened? How bad are you hurt?"

The doctor answered. "He'll live, but he'll be sore for a while." The doctor, early thirties, prematurely balding, began writing a prescription. He looked over the rims of his glasses and said, "Sean, start taking these twice a day, soon as you can, to keep infections down. Put an ice pack on the eye. And this one is for pain." As he turned to leave, he said, "Sorry to hear you were mugged."

When the doctor went into another room, Hamilton said, "Mugged?"

"What am I going to tell him? Doc, I was thrown into a ring with a psycho killer who literally wanted to take my head off. I became the victim in what amounts to a human slaughterhouse. A place where international tourists go to watch one man beat another to death. If you can't catch it live, it's available on black-market DVD and Internet sites for armchair psychopaths."

"Can you walk?" Hamilton asked.

"They haven't broken my knees yet."

"Let's go outside to talk about this, okay?"

HAMILTON AND O'BRIEN got into an unmarked Miami PD car, and O'Brien tilted his head back against the headrest. His cell rang. It was Detective Dan Grant.

"Sean, we looked at Lyle Johnson's cell phone records the day he was killed. He made one call. It was to his home number—his wife."

"No calls to Miami Beach?"

"No."

"He made one. Probably stole a cell there in the hospital. See if anyone reported a phone stolen. If you find one, check those records for that day. Thanks, Dan."

O'Brien disconnected and looked over toward Hamilton. "Before I tell you how I spent my night, can I ask what happened to you? If ever I could have used backup, Ron, it was last night."

"Bad wreck, Seventh and Collins. Even with a blue light, I couldn't go anywhere for twenty minutes. By the time I got to the gym, the place looked as vacant as a church on Monday. Locked. Dark. No sign of a yellow Ferrari. Nobody. Saw a black T-Bird parked about a block away. That was about it."

"T-Bird is mine."

"Yours?"

"Borrowed it from former defense attorney, Tucker Houston."

"Wait a minute—you have Tucker Houston working for you?"

"He's doing me a favor. He's really doing Charlie Williams the favor. He's trying to get a stay of execution from a federal judge, Samuel Davidson."

"How'd you get Tucker Houston to sign on?"

"Simple. He's an honest defense lawyer. When were you at the gym?"

"After nine."

"Unless I went through some kind of time warp . . . that was about when I was getting the shit kicked out of me, literally." O'Brien spent the next ten minutes telling Hamilton everything that happened from the time he entered the gym through his waking up in an alley with piles of garbage next to him.

Hamilton leaned back in the seat and made a sound somewhere between a sigh and a grunt. He said, "Think you killed Salazar?"

"No. Wanted to. He went down, and when I stumbled out of the ring . . . he was still breathing."

"Sports betting on fights to the death—like something you'd find in Malaysia or some damn place."

"Why can't the cocaine importation capital of the world have world-class death spectator sports for its clientele?" asked O'Brien.

"Russo never called me to drop the charges against you."

"Probably because he instructed Salazar to kill me. So with all these charges pending against me—now manslaughter charges potentially on my portfolio, and Charlie Williams facing an execution in"—O'Brien looked at his watch—"in twenty-two hours."

Hamilton started to say something when his cell rang. He answered, nodded, and said, "Where exactly was the body? . . . The ME thinks it's what?" A long pause and Hamilton said, "Thanks, Jim." He hung up, exhaled a sigh. "We found Salazar's body. They said he looked like he'd been beaten with an aluminum bat. Coroner's preliminary at the site is that Salazar died from a broken neck."

"Broken neck? Someone killed him after the fight. Where'd they find the body?"

"An alley at Ninth and Jasmine. Lying behind a Dumpster. That's less than a half block from where you spent the night. You have no memory of fighting him outside, in an alley?"

"No. It didn't happen. I was dumped there. I'm betting Salazar was, too. It takes the heat off the gym and maybe off Russo if he has an interest in what goes on there. And if I'd been spotted by a prowl car in that alley before I came to, in such close proximity to Salazar's body, I'd be in a holding cell now. Let's go."

"Go where?"

"Sixth Street Gym."

SEVENTY-TWO

A dozen cars were parked on the street outside Sixth Street Gym when O'Brien and Detective Ron Hamilton arrived. Going through the front door, Hamilton said, "How you holdin' out? You look like hell."

O'Brien said, "The body's a temple. . . . Mine's just a little cracked."

They walked down the hall and entered the gym, O'Brien scanning every sweaty face to see who was there from last night. He recognized no one. He stood next to a heavy bag and looked. His eyes followed a man skipping rope near the large American flag on the far wall. There was something different.

The flag moved. Just slightly at the left corner where the man fanned the rope. Yesterday, the flag was pulled tight across the door. Now it hung there, the ends next to the floor not secured.

There was a noise that sounded like a saw. O'Brien turned toward a small windowless office, away from the speed bags. He said to Hamilton, "That guy, the one with the blender going . . . he was here last night. He's got a thick Irish accent."

They approached the man who was topping off the smoothie he

poured from the blender into a large foam cup. He said, "Good morning, gentlemen. Here for a workout?" To O'Brien he said, "Tell me I should see the other guy."

"I would, but he's dead."

The trainer sipped his drink. No reaction. Then he said, "Guess you don't need boxing lessons."

"I need a straight answer. What happened to your accent?"

"Pardon me."

"The Irish accent. You're dropping it now. Why?"

"Sorry, mate, I don't have a clue as to what you're talking about."

"Like hell you don't! You're the one who carried me out of the ring. You were the one who probably finished off Salazar."

"Ring? Salazar?"

"The fight! Salazar attacked me in front of at least three dozen cheering, betting witnesses. What'd you do, bus them in and then take them back to their hotels?"

"I think it's time you two move on."

Ron Hamilton showed his badge and said, "I say when it's time to leave. We're investigating a murder. And as far as I'm concerned, this is a crime scene. What's your name? And show me an ID."

"Michael Killen."

"Where's the ring?" asked O'Brien.

"As you can see, we have two rings."

"Not those. You have another. Intimate seating for your morbid fans."

The trainer sipped his drink and said, "I haven't a clue, pal."

"Oh, really?" said O'Brien. "I can tell you're lying. You keep your body in shape, but you can't control the pulse through the carotid artery in the side of your neck. It speaks volumes." O'Brien turned to walk toward the American flag. "Let's see what's behind door number one."

SEVENTY-THREE

The trainer and Hamilton followed him. O'Brien lifted up part of the flag from the floor. Two large gray metal doors were behind it. He started to enter. The doors were locked. "Open it!"

The trainer finished his drink. "Not without a warrant."

Hamilton said, "Don't need a search warrant at a crime scene."

"This is not a crime scene."

"Sure it is," said Hamilton. "It's a slow news day. One call and the media will be all over this place. We'll slap some crime scene tape in front of your door and this gym will carry a nasty stigma for years."

The trainer looked toward the front of the gym floor a second and said, "It's nothing but a warehouse for storage."

"Then open it," said O'Brien.

The trainer sighed, fished for a key in his pocket, and unlocked the door. They entered. There was no ring. No seating for a crowd. No video cameras. Nothing but metal chairs stacked in one corner, lots of old heavy bags and broken weights, a dismantled ring, ropes, posts, canvas, old fight posters, and risers stacked in one corner.

O'Brien would have laughed had his face not hurt so badly. "How'd you do it?"

"Do what?" asked the trainer, deadpanned face.

"How did you take this apart, store it, sweep the place up, and make it look like no one's been in here."

"Maybe it's because nobody has been in here in weeks."

"Open that canvas!"

"What?"

"Take the rolled-up mat out of the corner and unroll it on the floor."

The trainer laughed, shook his head, kicked the canvas down with one of his massive legs, and unrolled it. The mat was old and worn, but no signs of fresh stains.

"Where's the one you used last night?"

"This canvas hasn't been used since Foreman trained on it. Look, pal, all this stuff is like a graveyard of old boxing junk . . . outdated . . . not much more than a novelty. We got some stuff in here that goes back to when Ali was training over at Fifth Street with Dundee. We got stuff in here that goes back way before Ali. Look at that fight poster of the Raging Bull, the Bronx Bull, ol' Jake LaMotta. They tell me he ran a club here in Miami Beach after his retirement. But that was before me time."

O'Brien reached behind his back and pulled out the Glock, pointing it at the trainer's chest. He said, "Before me time? LaMotta was said to have a granite chin. How about you, asshole?"

"Get this crazy fucker away from me!" shouted the trainer to Hamilton.

"Sorry, he's an independent contractor. Doesn't answer to me."

The trainer's eyes bulged in disbelief. "I'll sue!"

O'Brien said, "No you won't! You carried me out of here. Tossed me out with the garbage. You, or one of your grunts, snuffed Salazar and dumped his body near me to make it look like I killed him."

"You're crazy!"

"Yes! Yes I am. Wanna see how crazy? Who're you working for?"

Hamilton's cell rang, the rings sounding far away in the warehouse. He answered it. Hamilton listened, holding a hand in the air to get O'Brien's attention. Hamilton cradled the phone between his ear and shoulder and made time-out sign with his hands. He said, "I'll need that statement in writing. Your attorney can bring an affidavit or contact the state attorney and give it to him in writing. This applies to Sergio Conti, too." Hamilton grunted and hung up. He said to O'Brien, "Sean, let's talk."

O'Brien lowered the Glock. The trainer grinned. O'Brien said, "Stay right there!"

O'Brien and Hamilton walked to the opposite side of the small warehouse. Hamilton said, "You're not gonna believe who called."

"Russo."

"How'd you know?"

"Because with Salazar dead, the last living witness to Russo's connection with Charlie Williams is gone. I become a moot point."

"Now we have another murder on our hands. This one is the death of a hit man."

"And I'd bet you a day's receipts from Russo's drug operation that the big leprechaun here in the corner is nothing more than a real con. I'm sure he works for Russo. And probably snapped Salazar's neck as soon as they tossed me in the trash."

Something caught O'Brien's eye. A reflection. A small object lying next to a stack of cardboard boxes. He stepped to the boxes, knelt down, and picked up the item. O'Brien held it to the light.

"What's that?" asked Hamilton. "Looks like an eye."

"This is a black onyx earring. Last night our Irish host was wearing it. I saw it fall off his ear when he tossed me over his shoulder."

"So much for no one in here in weeks. This place is a boxing museum in boxes, for God's sakes. Looks like we stepped into a twilight zone time warp, a place where Joe Louis and the Rock are on faded posters. A killer is dead. Somebody snapped his neck. He was breathing when you left the ring. This fight didn't exist. In the alley, you got rats, roaches, and a body found a hundred yards from you. So what?"

"What are you saying, Ron?"

"I'm saying you have less than twenty-something hours to save Charlie Williams's life. You're off the hook. We'll see if we can find something tangible to tie Steroids over there to Salazar's slip on the banana peel. You'll have a better chance to toss Williams a life ring now that Tucker Houston's on board. When's he meeting with Judge Davidson?"

O'Brien looked at his watch. "About five minutes."

"In five minutes Charlie Williams may have something to cling to."

As they walked past the trainer, O'Brien said, "You swept up well, but you missed something." O'Brien tossed the earring to him and said, "Something always slips through the cracks. I would have thought that earring was onyx, but it's only polished blarney. Gotcha, mate."

SEVENTY-FOUR

It was 11:00 A.M. and O'Brien had not heard from Tucker Houston. O'Brien put the top down on the T-Bird and pushed the car up to eighty as he crossed the Rickenbacker Causeway on his way back to Tucker's house. The bay was deep sapphire, the afternoon sun scattering diamondlike reflections from the swells kicked up by boat traffic. O'Brien watched a large sailboat raise the spinnaker as the skipper cut the motor and caught the wind toward the outlet to the sea.

Tucker Houston's car was in the drive. O'Brien parked the T-Bird and knocked on the door. When Tucker answered, he was dressed in pleated slacks and a powder blue shirt with a maroon tie loosened to the first open button. He'd kicked off his shoes and was sipping tomato juice from a clear glass mug.

"My God," said Tucker, "if I had known you were going to look like this, I'd have said a prayer for you before starting the fight." Tucker motioned for him to come in the house. They sat in the pool patio area.

"Sean, what the hell happened?"

"I managed to survive what amounted to a death match."

"What?"

261

"Back room, gym." O'Brien told Tucker what happened.

Tucker sipped his juice and said, "FBI needs to be made aware of that operation."

"What did Judge Davidson say?"

"His wife said he was in Seattle, something to do with their oldest son and a business deal he was trying to tie together."

"When's he return?"

"Not until Saturday."

"What are our options?"

"I can file with the Fifth Circuit. Because of the impending ominous hour, the court might move it up the docket, if we're lucky."

"And if they don't?"

"They could simply refuse to hear it. Period. Our options then fall considerably more narrow . . . as in the governor or the high court."

"You mean the Florida Supreme Court?"

"I mean the U.S. Supreme Court."

O'Brien was silent.

"To get Governor Owens's ear, we'll need something tangible. A pending DNA test, something like that would legitimately give reason for doubt until the tests were conclusive . . . one way or the other. The Supreme Court may simply refuse to hear it. We could ask for a stay alleging lethal injection is a cruel and unusually painful way to fulfill the mandate of the lower court. However, in this all we're saying is you can go on and kill Williams, you just need to kill him in a kinder, gentler, less painful way."

"So what are our odds in any of the scenarios?"

"Not good. I'll launch every legal red flag I can. What can you do next?"

"I'm going to look at a painting."

"What?"

"A fifteenth-century painting."

"You pick a hell of a time to visit an art museum."

"Maybe. A painting from the past may be the best thing we have right now to keep an execution for happening in the future."

"How so?"

"I'm not sure. A friend of mine has spent some time these last few days on the computer, researching and analyzing an image that Father Callahan left in blood." O'Brien paused. "I know it's going to sound weird . . ."

"Trust me, I was a defense attorney—nothing sounds weird."

"This might. The painting is somehow tied to the Greek letter omega, the last letter, and the twenty-forth letter in the Greek alphabet. If the painting can reveal the link, the connection between all of this, it might spell out the real killer's name or something that will give you that tangible evidence to take to somebody's court."

Tucker smiled and asked, "You'd mentioned the image, a cloaked figure or something silhouetted against the moon, correct?"

"I know I'd seen it somewhere before. Kind of like a scent you haven't smelled in years, and you remember a time and place you thought was forgotten a long time ago. I saw an image of clouds against the moon the other night, and I remembered a painting of the Virgin Mary, sort of descending with the moon, or maybe she was rising with the moon. Now I remember she was looking down at a man. I don't know who he was, but he was looking up at her and taking notes. Can you take me to the airport?"

"Let's go."

SEVENTY-FIVE

Max was the first to see him coming down the dock. She darted around the cockpit of Dave Collins's boat, whimpering, tail going a mile a second, pink tongue sticking out of her panting mouth. She barked. O' Brien said, "How's my little girl?"

Dave stuck his head out of the salon, grinned, and said, "I haven't seen Max this excited since I cooked shrimp over an oak grill last night."

"It's one of her favorites," said O'Brien, picking up Max. She licked his face, huffed and puffed with excitement, and looked at O'Brien with adoring brown eyes.

Dave said, "I'd surmise that she missed you."

"Surprised she doesn't run away. My face has looked better."

"I started to ask you—who in Miami Beach did you fight, the whole damn cocaine cartel?"

"Felt like it." O'Brien stepped onto *Gibraltar*. "Thanks for watching Max."

"She's a great companion. Bounced between my boat and Nick's.

I'm not sure if she was being social or simply wanted to see who had the best food at the moment."

"I think she gained a little weight. Okay, show me what you found."

"Enter into my window to the world of Renaissance art—my computer."

O'Brien carried his laptop in one hand and Max in the other.

Dave was set up at his small office desk. He typed in a few words and said, "I'm going to use the split-screen function to help illustrate this. For a moment, I'll leave the left side of the screen black. On the right side is the image you had Detective Grant send me of the drawing Father Callahan left. In a minute, I'll fill in the other side of the screen with an enhanced image that you snapped of the moon the other night and e-mailed to me." He looked up at O'Brien, over the top of his glasses. "You happened to be at the right place at the right time, have the right atmospheric conditions—"

"You mean clouds?"

"Much more than that. It's quite remarkable that you saw it and managed to capture it. A passage of seasons, planets, and time."

"What?"

"The equinox—the unique moment in the year when day and night, or black and white, if you will—are equal on earth. The moon rises at a point exactly opposite the sun. When the moon rises, coming up from the east, like it did over the ocean, you see an optical illusion. It will appear the moon is much larger at the horizon than it is at other positions in the sky. The ground effect, or in this case, the ocean relative to the moon, gives the moon an illusion, a false perspective, of being larger than it will be later that night in any other spot in the sky."

"What I saw, what I caught on the camera phone, is real."

"So here we have a nice artist's canvas, a big harvest moon, and then along comes a moving image in black—a cloud—that sort of does a freeze-frame long enough for you to capture it. It's no Mona Lisa,

265

but the image is striking. You hear people say when 'planets align'—well, you had the atmospheric conditions, the time of the year, and the moon at the right place above the ocean to give you a perfect opportunity for this. . . ."

Dave tapped the keyboard. On the left side of the screen appeared the image of the moon O'Brien had captured. Dave said, "Take a look at that. Your equinox moon and cloud, as you thought, have an uncanny resemblance to what Father Callahan drew."

O'Brien sat next to Dave and studied the two images without saying anything. Max trotted over and sat beside him. O'Brien said, "When I saw that cloud rise in front of the moon, it triggered something I'd seen at some point in my life. I didn't make the connection earlier when I found Father Callahan's body and saw the drawing he'd left, but when I saw that image in the moon, I felt the two were somehow related. In a dream I saw an image of . . . the Virgin Mary. She was coming out of the moon. It was overlooking a bay, ships, maybe one ship on fire in the harbor. A hawk flew in and out of an old cathedral. There was an elfish figure there and an angel. Then the angel was pointing toward the Virgin Mary. I saw a man in a flowing robe reading a book, maybe the Bible. I remember reaching out to touch Mary, and I touched a wet painting."

Dave nodded. "I combed the halls of every museum that has its art online, and most do. If not, the work of the masters can be found hanging on plenty of cyber walls."

"Masters?"

"Indeed, Sean. You're not dreaming schlock nightmares, my friend. You're picking up pieces of memory paint from one of the best, perhaps most overanalyzed painters in the history of Renaissance art."

"Who?"

"Today, he is just as misunderstood as he was in his day, around the late fourteen hundreds. When Columbus was discovering the New World, this artist was painting a tortured world. A place revealing a garden of earthly delights, seven deadly sins, the last judgment . . . and

I present to you, Sean O'Brien, the painting done by Hieronymus Bosch that brings together the puzzle pieces."

Dave typed in few keystrokes. Both images on the screen faded to black and then a painting appeared. It was an old painting—one depicting a man sitting on a hillside overlooking a harbor. In the harbor, a ship was burning. A hawk was sitting in the left side of the frame. The right side showed a gnomelike man tiptoeing. An angel was descending a hill in the background, pointing to an image of the sun or moon with the Virgin Mary in the center of it sitting on a crescent moon and holding an infant.

O'Brien leaned in closer to the image. "This is it! I remember seeing this as a child in a traveling exhibition in a museum in Spain."

"Bosch's painting is called *Saint John on Patmos*."

O'Brien looked at Dave and said, "Patmos. Now I know what Father Callahan was referring to with the letters P-A-T."

SEVENTY-SIX

Gibraltar moved. "We have company," said O'Brien.

Dave looked at his watch. "It's Nick. We're supposed to be heading down to the Tiki Hut about now for dinner."

Nick Cronus entered the salon. He grinned, the thick mustache rising like a cartoon drawing on his face. "Sean, what happen to you, man?"

"Long story. The short side is, to save a life of a man on death row, you have to step around or over people who don't want that life saved."

Nick snorted, popped the knuckles in his calloused hands, and said, "Man, you got to call me before you get yourself in those situations."

"Believe me, Nick. I had no idea I'd wind up in a sport boxing ring where the sport ends in death."

"What? Like hell, man. What happened?"

"I'll tell you when I have more time. Dave just showed me a picture of a very old painting. The artist was a guy named Bosch. He painted a lot of art depicting the forces of good and evil. Look at this."

Nick stepped over to the computer. O'Brien said, "This is one of his paintings. It's called *Saint John on Patmos*. What do you know about this Greek island?"

Nick studied the painting and said, "It is a holy island. A big monastery is there. Many people in Greece go there at least once in their lives. It is where Saint John was exiled. He survived with the help of God. He lived in a cave, lived there for almost two years, man. Listening to God and foretelling the Apocalypse . . . Armageddon."

"The Book of Revelation?" asked Dave.

"Yeah, man. He was chosen by God to tell it like it is, you know. You screw up . . . I mean screw up a lot and you don't enter the kingdom of God. Good triumphs over bad. The place where the saint lived, in Greece, we call it the Holy Grotto."

Dave looked at the painting. "Bosch was apparently influenced by all of this. I was trying to figure out the reason Father Callahan drew the Greek letter omega, too." Dave hit a few keys and another painting appeared. "This Bosch painting is called *The Temptation of Saint Anthony*. Let me pull up an isolated section. See right there."

O'Brien and Nick leaned in closer. "Yeah, man," said Nick. "It's there, omega."

"This," said Dave, "look carefully above the piece of cloth he painted over here, next to the fellow in the top hat. Above it you can see a shackle, a spot where a prisoner could have been chained . . . and right there is the perfect depiction of the letter omega." Dave typed in another key and another painting appeared. "This Bosch painting is called *Ship of Fools*. Some in the art world theorize the flapping sail of the mast, if you look at in a horizontal position . . ." Dave touched a key and flipped the painting into a horizontal perspective. He continued, "Now you can see the sail makes a perfect omega."

Nick chuckled. "This dude Bosch looks like he ate too much of his paint."

O'Brien said, "It looks like he left it up to the viewer's interpretation."

"Exactly," said Dave. "Bosch was an allegorical painter. He dropped all kinds of symbols, things that might depict hidden meanings, maybe not. He straddled the art border somewhere between medieval and Renaissance, and he straddled the lines between the age-old conflict of good and evil. Salvador Dalí was influenced by Bosch."

"And it appears that Father Callahan was too," said O'Brien. "But why? What is the significance of the omega sign, the Bosch painting of Saint John, and the six-six-six?"

Nick squinted at the painting. "This Bosch guy, he liked to paint a lot of naked people running all around. I'm getting a headache just trying to look at it. Let's eat!"

"I don't have time to eat," O'Brien said.

Dave said. "Take twenty minutes, tops. We want to hear what happened in Miami Beach. And I'll tell you more of what I've learned about omega."

SEVENTY-SEVEN

They took a corner table at the Tiki Hut, away from the tourists and a few charter boat captains who sat at the bar and swapped stories about how, too often, they had to teach tourists to fish once they got out to the reefs or the flats.

O'Brien tied Max's leash to a leg of his chair and looked at his watch.

Kim Davis approached the table with three menus in her hands. She said, "Sean, what happened to you?"

"My boxing career is over," he said. "Kim, I'm in a big hurry."

"No problem. Want some ice for that eye?"

"It's actually much better."

Kim smiled as the men ordered.

"First round is on me," said Dave. "Three Coronas."

"I'll bring Miss Max a little bowl of ice water."

When she left, Dave turned to O'Brien. "Okay, what happened in Miami Beach?"

"Think they'll have stone crabs here tonight?"

"Don't know, why?" asked Nick.

O'Brien began to tell them what occurred in Miami Beach. Both Nick and Dave listened without interruption until Kim brought the beers.

Dave said, "Sean, my old gray head is spinning. Let's take a breather for nourishment." They ordered food and reached for the beers.

O'Brien concluded by saying, "Tucker Houston is filing every petition he can think of to get the courts to intervene. I'm tracking down Alexandria's old roommate and trying to figure out what message Father Callahan left behind. Charlie Williams paces his cell, and I want to let him know we're close, but I couldn't bear giving him false hope. I've given him eleven years of hell. His execution, set for tomorrow morning at six."

Dave said, "Hope, false or real, is all he has right now."

Nick raised a bottle and said, "To you, Sean, for gettin' outta that ring alive."

"But right now I can't even prove I was in the ring. It's like some bizarre dream."

"Not unlike a Bosch painting," said Dave.

Kim brought the food, and they ordered a second round of beer.

Dave pulled the shell off a steaming shrimp, the flavor of garlic and Old Bay seasoning heavy. He said, "Let me try to put this in perspective. After Salazar's body was found, Russo dropped trumped-up charges against you. His pedophile cohort, Sergio Conti, did the same. Salazar, as Russo's hit man, is dead. Assuming Salazar spoke to no one about killing Spelling, Father Callahan, and Lyle Johnson—Salazar is dead and his secret goes with him to the grave. Russo knows you have nothing on him to stop or delay the execution of Charlie Williams. So Russo steps out of the radar to lay low until the state executes Williams. Am I there so far?"

"You're there," said O'Brien as he handed Max a bite of flounder.

"So," said Dave, "Lauren Miles, with the FBI, is trying to see if equipment in Quantico can reveal the name of the Florida town where Spelling's mother lives. You're trying to track down Alexandria's former roommate. You have a Miami defense attorney trying to engineer some legal way to make lethal injection illegal. In the meantime, we're trying to help you solve a riddle Father Callahan left behind that's fitting of a Herculean challenge and worthy of a sphinx trophy if solved. And you have"—he looked at his watch—"you have about eighteen hours left to do it."

"Pretty much sums it up."

Nick pushed back from the table. "Sean, I keep telling you to sell your old house on the river. Let me teach you to fish and you'd stay outta this kinda shit, man."

"I'm trying to get there, Nick." O'Brien said to Dave, "Omega, what were you going to tell us about it?"

Nick interjected, "I told you it means the end of something."

Dave grinned. "He's right. Viewing the omega letters in Bosch's paintings and the one that Father Callahan left behind, it intrigued me, so I did a little research. Omega is the Greek letter that physicists and cosmologists have taken to represent an equation that could mean the end of the world and universe or the continuation of it."

"Got to mean the end," chimed in Nick.

"Perhaps," said Dave. "There is this huge tug-of-war going on in our universe. As the planets go zipping around the center of our cosmos, the sun, there's an outside influence from other galaxies—a push and pull, sort of a yin and yang of gravity versus matter. So in the simplest terms, omega equals the push or the pull."

"Which one?" O'Brien asked.

"No one knows what the omega number—the key to the fate of the world—really is. If omega is greater than one, there is more pull than push in the universe, which could lead to the reversal of the big bang theory. It's called the big crunch—the end of life. If omega is less than one, the universe and our little Earth may go on expanding forever. But, like finding clues to solve Alexandria's murder, the challenge scientists have in hunting for omega is this: They can't measure distances in space or matter. Sean, you've got eleven years of time and space from the first killing."

Kim brought another round of beer and cleared the plates.

When Kim left, Dave said, "I believe omega, the twenty-fourth letter or the first number, is connected to whoever killed Father Callahan and the others. Not only is it found in Bosch's paintings and the horrific sketches Father Callahan left in his blood, but omega is truly symbolic of what Saint John was scribbling in his cave. Omega today is the life sustenance—the pot liquor—that combines physics and theology into one spiritual soup. If it boils over, it's the end of the world. If it simmers a billion more years, its existence is the ingredients of life and it tastes good. The hunt for omega is like the hunt for Alexandria's killer. Both very difficult to track, and time may be running out in each instance. Omega is said to be the prophecy of Armageddon, dictated to Saint John on the Isle of Patmos. Somehow the meaning of the twenty-fourth letter is inextricably tied to Father Callahan's death—and ultimately Alexandria Cole's. *And* the salvation of the innocent in all of this . . . Charlie Williams."

"Man," Nick said, "I feel like I should make the sign of the cross."

"Sean, what do you think?" Dave asked.

"I'll go back to the beginning—to the place and the time when and where Sam Spelling was shot. But before I go there, I need to go all the way back to the beginning—Alexandria Cole's murder—back to alpha. Maybe there I'll find what I missed."

SEVENTY-EIGHT

Judy Neilson lived in a remote neighborhood on the east side of St. Cloud, near Orlando. As O'Brien checked his GPS and followed the coordinates to Neilson's address, he wondered if the S – T in St. Cloud might prove to be the place that Sam Spelling hid the murder weapon.

There was one car in the drive. A late-model Lexus. Lauren Miles, and her FBI database, had scraped up enough information on Neilson to let O'Brien know that she worked in time-share sales. Probably worked weekends and had a week day off.

He parked and rang the doorbell. A woman peered from beyond a chain lock.

O'Brien smiled and said, "Judy?"

"Yes?"

"I'm Sean O'Brien. I arrested Charlie Williams in the death of Alexandria Cole."

"What do you want?"

"May I come in? . . . It's about Alexandria."

"Don't know what this has to do with me. Come in." She opened the door and led O'Brien into the living room. He could smell stale wine on her breath. She wore a long lavender robe tied at the waist. No shoes. Dark hair pinned up. O'Brien remembered her features from more than a decade ago. She had been a near supermodel in her own right. Now she was turning prematurely gray, darker skin under puffy, suspicious eyes, gauntness to her face. Fingernails chewed. Nostrils slightly red.

"Would you like a drink? Coffee or something?" she asked.

"No thanks."

"It's my day off—so I fixed me a little Bloody Mary."

O'Brien smiled. "Enjoy."

"As I recall, I told you all I knew about Alex's murder when it happened."

"Judy, there have been some things happening recently that have convinced me that Charlie Williams did not kill Alexandria."

"What things?"

"The murders of a priest and two others who knew that Williams did not kill her."

"Then who did?"

"I was hoping you might tell me."

"I've told you what I think."

"Maybe you could refresh my memory of Alex's relationship with Russo."

She grinned, stirred her drink with a stick of celery, and said, "He was an asshole. I didn't like him when he managed Alex's career. He's the reason she got so heavy into coke. But I never thought he stabbed her like that. Charlie was having awful fights with Alex, trying to take her back to North Carolina, trying to get her away from Russo. I think Charlie got so damn drunk he just went crazy and killed her." She made a sniffling sound with her nose.

"I went back and reread the old statements you gave me eleven years ago. In one of them, you said that Alex started getting phone calls at different times, and she had to drop everything and go. You said she hated going . . . said the 'guy was creeping her out.' You said she'd come back from meeting him in a motel and take long showers. You told me you heard her crying, sobbing loudly in the shower one day, and you sat her down to talk with her. Friend to friend. Alex mentioned she'd been thinking about suicide, and then she was killed three days later."

Judy stared at a spot somewhere on the coffee table. O'Brien could see her eyes moisten. She looked at a photograph on the mantel. She was standing with Alexandria near a zoo. "I remember what I said. Thought about it some since her death."

"Is there anything you didn't tell me . . . anything at all?"

"Alex said she felt so lonely—'alone' was the word she used. So damn violated. I remember she wrapped herself in a big fluffy white towel, sat on the side of the tub, and we talked. I mostly listened and she broke down and told me that her stepfather sexually abused her when she was eleven. And now this new bastard, the guy calling her, was bringing back the nightmares. She said she felt helpless, like when she was a little girl. Nowhere to run and nobody to run to. I remember just holding her there on the tub, like I was holding a child, and she just cried and cried."

Judy's fingers gripped the glass in her hand, her knuckles turning white. O'Brien said, "When you originally told me about the calls, I believed that it was Russo soliciting her. Part of his narcissist DNA. In the last few days, I've come to realize that Russo is on the same scum level as Alexandria's stepfather."

Judy walked to the wet bar and said, "How about some tea or something?"

"No thanks."

She fixed another drink and returned to her seat. "This, in a way, makes what you're telling me a little easier to stomach."

"Did Russo, at that time, have someone working for him that might have had a lot of access to Alexandria?" O'Brien asked.

Judy crossed her legs and took a sip. "Not really. Russo was a hands-on kind of manager. I remember Alex telling me in the bathroom that night, if she didn't cooperate, he'd destroy her career. Now why would Russo want to destroy a career that was making him a shitload of money? Before Alex died, she told me she was using heroin."

"Heroin?"

"She'd pointed to places between her toes and said that's where he gave her the drug. Maybe somehow Charlie knew about it and that's why he went crazy . . . trying to get her out of that nasty scene. But that's still no excuse for what he did."

"I don't remember you mentioning heroin during my original questioning."

"Between the coke, pills, and crap that came through her life, heroin was just another one to chalk up to being naïve, too trusting and too dumb to care. Alex had told me she was not gonna use it anymore, and begged me not to say anything to anybody. You had arrested Charlie for the killing, so it didn't seem to make any difference because Charlie wasn't a user and he sure wasn't giving heroin to Alex."

"Then who was?"

"I don't know. She wouldn't say, but I don't think it was Russo."

"Judy, having a girlfriend-to-girlfriend talk with Alexandria, at the moment you describe, would lead me to believe she might have opened up a little more."

"What do you mean?"

"You were her best friend. It seems like she would have confided in you and told you who she was meeting—who had her hooked on heroin."

"She was afraid. She said that if I didn't know much, I couldn't get into trouble."

"What do you think she meant by trouble?"

"I don't know. I remember her saying that sometimes you can put your trust in the wrong people . . . even those people paid to protect you. I thought she meant one of Russo's security—his bodyguards—the guys who kept the paparazzi out of her face."

O'Brien said nothing.

Judy lifted the framed photograph of her and Alexandria off the mantel. She looked at it a moment, smiled, and sipped her drink. She handed the picture to O'Brien and said, "We were at the Miami Zoo when this was taken. Alex loved going there. Loved the animals and the peace she found. She's never getting older than that picture. Alex may have been beautiful outside, but she was beautiful on the inside, too. Before she was stabbed in the heart, she was scarred there a long time ago. I hope you find this guy."

SEVENTY-NINE

Anita Johnson slept much later than she wanted. Had the postman come yet? She bolted from bed, slipped into her robe, and checked on her toddler. Ronnie was still sleeping. Probably tired from the trip back, Anita thought. Mama was right. Go on and leave Lyle. Leave his abuse and crazy get-rich-quick schemes behind.

She put on a pot of coffee, peeked through the kitchen curtains, and waited. What would Lyle send? She hadn't been home in two days since she talked with Lyle, having decided to spend time with her mother. She told her mother everything, even the last weird conversation she had with Lyle. She could leave him now. Anita had driven five hours, getting home late last night. She couldn't sleep; took the damn pills, and now it was afternoon.

She sipped her coffee, put on a touch of lipstick, tied the robe around her waist, and walked down the dirt drive to the mailbox. She listened for the sound of his rattling diesel engine. Nothing. Nothing but a mockingbird singing its fool head off.

As she reached for the mailbox, she felt her heart beat faster. Shouldn't get nervous, she told herself. Just something Lyle wasn't man enough to say in person—to say when he wasn't crazy drunk. She pulled out a stack of bills. Lights. Mortgage. Home Depot. Best Buy. New TV would be paid off when little Ronnie was six. Four envelopes with four bills. Nothing from Lyle. Where was he?

The sound. The diesel. It was coming. The postman's truck was at the Madison's house, just through the pines. She would wait.

"Come on, mister mailman," she whispered. Anita thought she heard the baby cry. She looked back at her house. Did she leave the door wide open? Come on, where are you? Government ought to get the mail carriers better trucks. Keep them from going postal. She almost smiled at her own joke.

He was coming around the bend. The postman wore a Panama hat, short-sleeve shirt, and blue shorts. He had a walrus mustache in need of a trim. "Mornin'," he said.

"More like good afternoon," said Anita. She smiled but showed no teeth.

"Yeah, I'm runnin' a little later than usual." He sorted through the mail and said, "Got only one for you. Someone even took the time to handwrite your name and address." He held the letter. "I was telling Larry, on the next route, that only about 15 percent of my mail has handwritten addresses anymore."

She grabbed the letter, nodded, and said, "Thank you." Anita turned and went back to her house.

She locked the door behind her and wondered whether she should call her mother to let her hear whatever it was that Lyle had to say. She took a deep breath and began to tear at one edge of the envelope. Her fingers trembled so much it was hard to open. Her heart pounded.

The baby cried.

"Be right there, Ronnie . . . give mommy a sec."

A mournful wail came from his room. "Coming. You probably had a bad dream." She began to read aloud her husband's handwriting as she walked toward the baby's room. "Dear Anita, if you're reading this, chances are I'm dead. I want you to know that I always loved you. If nothing else, you got a real good insurance policy to help take care of yourself and Ronnie. The first thing you need to do is call the sheriff's office. . . ."

Her hand trembled so much she had to hold the letter with both hands as she entered the baby's room. He laid in his bed and cried. Blanket creases in the side of his red, tear-streaked face. She bent down to kiss his face. "Mommy is going to give you a bath and some lunch. Just a second, sweetheart."

She continued reading. "Call them and tell them your husband has been killed. No, tell them he's been murdered. I will spell out the killer's name in print so there is no mistake as to his identity. He is the same man who killed Sam Spelling and—"

The baby screamed. Anita saw that he was looking to her right. Looking toward the door. She turned just as a man in a dark ski mask grabbed her in a strong headlock.

"Please don't!" she pleaded. "Please don't hurt me! I'll give you anything you want."

"Shhh," he whispered. "You're going for a long sleep now. Don't resist and you will feel no pain."

She fought with all her strength, clawing and pulling at the ski mask. He snapped her neck. Eyes tearing, disbelieving. Her body quivered as her heart pumped its final frantic beats. He let her body slump to the carpeted floor. Anita's dying eyes locked on her crying child.

Reaching down, he removed the letter from her clenched fist and whispered, "You are the last link. . . . The chain letter dies with you."

EIGHTY

O'Brien pulled out of the Willows in the Wind subdivision and didn't want to look back. He thought about Judy Neilson—now an alcoholic, drowning pain when it pooled in her spirit and left stains on the fabric of who she had become.

Was there something she wasn't admitting? *You can put your trust in the wrong people . . . even those people paid to protect you.* He thought about the heroin connection—Judy finding Alexandria dead with seven stab wounds. Who had been that angry with Alexandria Cole?

O'Brien drove north, toward Daytona, and called Tucker Houston. "What's the status with Judge Davidson?"

"Still in Seattle. I've got a call in to him, but he needs to sign the order in person and right now he's about three thousand miles away. In the interim, I've spoken with Charlie Williams's attorney, Robert Callaway. He's a pleasant, if somewhat defeated, fellow. He e-mailed me some of the information that I needed about the case. I'm writing the petition for a stay as we speak."

"What are you throwing at them?"

"I call it collateral attack—a habeas corpus petition. I start in state court, where I know I'll lose. Then the Fifth Circuit, where I know I'll lose. Then the Florida Supreme Court . . . where I might get the ear of Governor Owens or the Florida attorney general via the media. It could wind up on the docket of the Supreme Court in the very last hour. Call it a legal grandstand. Enough sawdust flying to start cutting through the system. It'll be up to you to add the real teeth to the saw, Sean. Until you do, I'm petitioning the court to halt the execution on the grounds that Charlie Williams wasn't adequately represented the first time. He simply did not get a fair trial in view of the transcript I've read. He contends the sex between him and Alexandria was consensual. She was not raped, as the state alleges. There were many people in and out of the condo the day she was killed. Who's to say there wasn't a previous fight? Along comes bumbling Charlie, a lovesick puppy trying to wrestle the only girl he's loved out of the grip of vice. The cocaine, pills, booze, the—"

"Heroin."

"Heroin?"

"I just spoke with Alexandria's former roommate, Judy Neilson. She told me two days before Alexandria was murdered they'd had a heart-to-heart. Came after Judy found Alexandria in the shower trying to scrub her skin to the bone because she felt dirty after having forced sex."

"With whom?"

"Says she doesn't know. Probably the same guy who got her into heroin. Toxicology report after the autopsy didn't reveal heroin in her blood, but then if she hadn't used in a while, it might not show up. When do you think you'll hear something from the courts?"

"I'm hoping by the end of the day. If national media jump on this, there could be time to have the courts consider the petition, and Charlie Williams could get a stay. But, Sean, right now neither you nor Williams can afford to assume this will get heard, and we'd all be greater fools to think that even if it is heard, the federal courts will do anything to stop it."

"Call me soon as you hear something. Thanks, Tucker."

O'Brien hung up and called Lauren Miles. "Hear anything from Quantico?"

"Yes and no."

"Lauren, I have enough riddles to solve. Just give it to me straight."

"The straight talk is that Simon Thomas, the guy who is the world's best at forensic 3-D electroscope analysis, is probably landing at Reagan about now. He was the keynote speaker at a police forensics seminar in Las Vegas. I spoke with him before he boarded the flight. He'll give it his best when he gets to the lab this afternoon."

O'Brien said nothing.

"Sean, it probably comes down to the indentation that Spelling left. Like a fingerprint, if he didn't touch it in the right way, the impression from his ballpoint pen will only leave so much. So we don't know what Thomas may or may not get from it."

"I understand, but Charlie Williams is down to hours now."

"I've got a friend in the bureau running Father Callahan's blood letters and symbols though one of our so-called supercomputers. Nothing yet."

"Tell your friend we have one part of the code solved, but we still don't know what Father Callahan was trying to tell us. One of the symbols, the moon with the image on it, I believe is connected to a fifteenth-century painting by one of the masters. The artist was Hieronymus Bosch. The painting is called *Saint John on Patmos*. I'm convinced the P-A-T Father Callahan wrote is Patmos, the Greek island. He died before he could finish the word. That leaves us with omega and six-six-six. Maybe the mark of the beast and the end of the universe. Let your supercomputer chew on that."

"We want to help you solve these murders, not the fate of mankind."

"I appreciate all you're doing, Lauren. I'm just running on empty."

"I know you could use more manpower. I was chatting with our chief, Mike Chambers, and Christian Manerou, too. Christian has a break in his caseload. Said he'd be glad to assist any way he can. Mike sighed but relented and said okay."

"Excellent. If we get anything back on the letter, maybe he can help find the murder weapon, or Sam Spelling's remaining family."

"I'll tell him."

"I know Christian and your boss, Mike Chambers, were part of the team that put Russo away for the drug charges. Was heroin part of the mix?"

"Don't think so. It's been awhile. Think it was a few kilos of coke. I'll ask Mike or Christian."

"Also, I don't know for sure, but I believe Russo has ties to a gym in South Beach called the Sixth Street Gym. In a back warehouse, behind a large American flag on the wall, they're operating bare knuckles fights. They amount to gladiator-style death matches. They tape it for black-market sales. One of the Steroids in charge is a big redheaded guy. Name's Mike Killen. Uses an Irish accent when he wants to. I bet a background check on this guy would pull a long sheet. If you can find out when they hold one of these fights, a raid would put a stop to this."

"How'd you find out about it?"

"I fought Salazar in the ring."

"What? Did you kill Salazar?"

"No. I think he was killed after they threw me in a pile of garbage in an alley. After Salazar died, Russo dropped the bogus charges he and Conti had filed against me. Salazar, as Russo's hit man, could be the last living connection that could possibly tie him to Alexandria Cole's murder."

O'Brien heard the beep for an incoming call. He looked at the number and said, "Lauren, it's Dan Grant. I'd better take it." He connected with Grant.

"Sean, it's getting worse," Grant said.

"How?"

"Anita Johnson, Lyle Johnson's wife, has been found murdered."

EIGHT-ONE

Detective Dan Grant met O'Brien at the crime scene. The Johnson drive and front yard were covered with police and emergency vehicles. The Volusia County medical examiner's car was one of the vehicles parked closest to the house.

The medical examiner was coming out of the house as O'Brien and Grant approached the front porch. The ME wore dark green suspenders holding up trousers that seemed secure around his paunch. Wire-rimmed glasses. Gray beard and hair to match. He loosened his tie and said, "She died a quick death."

"What happened?" asked Dan.

"I hope you gents can tell me that. I can tell you how she died. Broken neck. Whoever did it knew exactly what the hell he was doing. I'm assuming it's a he, 'cause it takes a strong person to break a human neck like you would yank a chicken's neck."

O'Brien said, "How long do you estimate time of death?"

"Few hours, tops. Some reddening on the neck and intracutaneous hemorrhages around the eyes. Died in her child's bedroom."

"Talk with you later, Doc," said Grant as he led O'Brien into the home. A half dozen uniform deputies and crime scene investigators moved around the house. One investigator dusted the walls for prints. O'Brien and Grant could see flashes from a camera coming from an open door down the hall. They entered the room just as the crime scene photographer was shooting the final pictures of the body.

Anita Johnson's body was on its back, hand on her chest. Eyes open.

A detective got up from squatting beside the body, jotting in a small notebook. He looked to be near retirement. White hair about two weeks beyond the need for a haircut. He had a look of resolve and pessimism over the state of mankind that the body seemed to represent to him. He stepped next to Grant and O'Brien, pursed his lips in a low whistle, and said, "Another young one. A mother. What a waste."

Dan made the introductions and said, "What do you think, Ralph?"

"No apparent sign of rape. No sign of burglary. Neighbor next door heard the kid crying and screaming. Came over to check and saw the front door open. Found the body and the little boy in that bed crying his eyes out."

"So he saw his mother die?" asked Grant.

"Looks that way. Neighbor is taking care of him until social services gets here."

"Anyone see anything? Stranger? Delivery person?"

"I questioned the neighbor. She didn't see or hear a damn thing until the kid started wailing. Not much to go on here. Maybe we'll get some prints, but I doubt it."

O'Brien looked around the room, tuning out the drone of the detective. Near the child's bed, on the floor, he saw a small piece of paper about the size of a postage stamp. O'Brien used the clip on his pen to lift the paper off the floor.

"Got something?" Grant asked.

"Don't know. Looks like it is a piece of an envelope. I can make out the top of a curved letter. Possibly an S. Maybe she'd just opened her mail, reading a letter, walked in here to quiet the child and was attacked." He handed the paper to Grant, who dropped it in a Ziploc bag. O'Brien crouched next to the body. He looked at the position on the floor. The angle of her head. Hands. He was silent for more than a minute.

"Sean," said Grant, "the guys are here with the body bag."

O'Brien said nothing.

"Come on, Sean, the place has been picked over. Photographed. Examined by the CSI team."

"Got a pair of tweezers?" asked O'Brien.

"Tweezers?"

Grant turned to an investigator standing near the door. "Hey, Jimmy," he said. "Hand me some tweezers out of your box."

The investigator dug around in a box twice the size of an average fishing tackle box and handed Grant a pair of long tweezers. Grant gave them to O'Brien.

They watched as O'Brien used the tool to lift something from a ring on Anita Johnson's left hand. Caught in a prong, barely detectable, was a dark fiber that O'Brien slowly lifted with the tweezers.

"What do you have?" asked Grant.

"Looks like a piece of wool. Probably not from something she'd wear in the summer in Florida. Doesn't match the carpet color. Maybe it's dyed black. Hand me a bag." O'Brien placed the fiber in the bag, stood, and said, "How would a piece of wool get embedded on the woman's ring?"

"Good question," Grant said.

The senior detective, Ralph, put his glasses on and leaned over the body. He said, "That was a nice catch."

"It stood out against the stone, which, at that size, looks like a nice imitation diamond. If it is wool, the fiber might have come from a ski mask." O'Brien used his pen to point. He added, "There, near the corner of her mouth . . . the lipstick goes from a horizontal application—the way she applied it—to a vertical serration."

Ralph said, "Maybe that's where she sipped her coffee."

"Maybe," said O'Brien, "but it might mean she bit the hand of the guy snapping her neck. Check her teeth for skin cells, and if the perp wore plastic gloves, see if any tiny bits of plastic might be between her teeth."

O'Brien started for the door.

"Where're you going?" asked Grant.

"To see if our only eyewitness might have seen something."

Ralph cleared his throat and said, "Who's the only eyewitness?"

"The postman." O'Brien turned and left.

EIGHTY-TWO

D an Grant followed O'Brien to his Jeep. O'Brien pulled out his cell phone. He paced the length of the Jeep for a moment, collecting his thoughts.

Dan said, "Some nice work in there. Superman's vision got nothing on you."

"Wish I'd had better vision investigating Alexandria Cole's death. If I had, we wouldn't be standing here today with all these people dead. We have a big problem."

"Tell me about it. The woman's dead."

"The problem is that the person who killed her is definitely not who I thought was behind this."

"Talk to me, Sean."

"Russo's confined to a hospital bed. The guy I thought did the hits, Carlos Salazar, is dead. Whoever killed Alexandria has murdered four people in the last three days: Spelling, Father Callahan, Johnson, and now his wife, Anita . . . and perhaps Salazar."

O'Brien pounded the fender of his Jeep with an open hand. He turned to Dan. "I've been chasing a ghost. The real killer just wiped out the last person alive who knew his name. I'm sure he destroyed any letter that Johnson may have sent to his wife."

"So the son of a bitch who's gone on this killing spree is as clueless to us now as that stuff the priest left in his own blood."

"Right now the stuff the priest left in his blood is the only thing pointing us in the right direction."

"Which direction?"

"Call your office and have someone call the post office. Find out who has this route. We need to know where that person is right now!"

O'BRIEN PUSHED THE JEEP, hitting speeds of near one hundred miles an hour through the back roads of rural Lake County. Dan Grant sat in the passenger side, hands gripped on the door and center console. He said, "Hey, man. If you kill us driving like this, who the hell is gonna stop this perp?"

"What's the next turn?"

"Should be the next left. Quarter mile up, tops. Dispatch told me that the post office says this mail carrier ends his route on River Lane, a long mile stretch. He might be done for the day."

O'Brien turned down River Lane and took out a plastic trash can someone had sat too near the street. "Whoa!" yelled Dan.

"There he is!" said O'Brien, looking at a slight incline where the white mail truck poked along. The postman was opening a mailbox when O'Brien brought his Jeep to a screeching halt directly in front of the truck. Both O'Brien and Grant got out and approached the frightened letter carrier. He reached for his cell. "I called nine-one-one! Cops are on their way!"

"We're here. Fast enough for you?" Dan said, flashing his shield.

"I didn't do anything!" the postman shouted.

"We know you didn't," said O'Brien. "Do you remember the Johnson residence? Lyle and Anita Johnson?"

"Sure. I got three Johnsons on this route, but I know their box."

"Do you recall making a delivery there today?"

"Yep. That's an easy one because Mrs. Johnson was at the mailbox to greet me."

"What'd she say?" asked Dan.

"Not a lot. Looked a little anxious. I remember the only letter she got today."

"How so?" asked O'Brien.

"Because it was a handwritten letter . . . large block letters with a guy's kinda handwriting. None of that stuff is the postal service's business. But I remember reading something right below the zip code."

"What was that?" asked Dan.

"S-W-A-K," he said, almost shyly. "You know, sealed with a kiss. Used to see that all the time. Now, hardly ever. Maybe it's because of e-mail."

"Did she say anything to you?" asked O'Brien.

"Not really. Mrs. Johnson seemed . . . seemed anxious, I guess is the best word."

O'Brien said, "Did you see anyone around? You know, maybe a delivery person . . . a car or truck that you don't normally see there?"

He thought a moment. "No. What happened? Is she okay?"

"She's dead," said Dan.

O'BRIEN AND GRANT were less than a mile away from the Pioneer Village when O'Brien's cell rang. It was Tucker Houston.

"Sean, state's refusing to hear it. I've got it hand-delivered to the Fifth Circuit. A clerk's ready to receive it."

"Good!" said O'Brien. "You can put this in that habeas corpus mix—we have another body. Wife of the prison guard who overheard Spelling's confession to Father Callahan. Neighbor found her murdered. Now I know Russo didn't do it."

"Then who did?"

"Buy me a little more time and I will find out."

"What this latest murder will buy us is coverage on the whole damn broadcast spectrum. If we can get the exposure, we'll get the ear of somebody's court."

EIGHTY-THREE

The yellow crime scene tape was still around the front porch of the old general store. O'Brien looked at the porch from a half dozen angles. He watched the windmill turn. He listened to the cluck of nearby chickens and tried to picture the scene the night Lyle Johnson died on the front porch.

Dan said, "They found his body sitting right there in that chair." He pointed to a rocking chair on the porch.

O'Brien said nothing. He knelt down in the Bahia grass next to the porch and looked at the surface of the old cypress slats. He stood and slowly walked up the three timeworn steps leading to the porch. He looked at the bloodstain beneath the chair and then at the wooden barrel behind the chair.

"Place has been gone over by a team, Sean. Except for the blood, Johnson's pistol lying next to the chair, they got nothing. I know you wanted to come here, but we might be wasting time we don't have."

O'Brien said nothing.

Dan said, "What do you do, man? Go into some kinda zone? Do

you put yourself in the vic's place or the perp's? Because the expression on your face looks damn funky right now."

O'Brien studied the pitchfork and looked across the porch, staring at a spot in the knotty wood. He pulled a paper napkin out of his pocket and used it to move the pitchfork from the back of the barrel to the front. He stepped across the porch, knelt, and looked at a small hole in the wood. O'Brien said, "Look at the angle of this hole."

"Lots of old wormholes in these planks. Some ought to be replaced."

"This is new, Dan. Rain and mildew haven't had time to set in, but there is rust in there. Wood doesn't rust. And look at the angle. That could only have been made by something coming from a trajectory near the rocking chair."

"What are you saying?"

O'Brien pointed to the far right prong on the pitchfork. "The rust on this point has been knocked off. The other three prongs all have a covering of rust on the tips. This one doesn't, and like the hole in the porch, the elements haven't discolored it."

"So," said Dan, "you think Lyle Johnson picked up this pitchfork and threw it like some kind of javelin at the perp, right?"

"That's exactly what I think. Maybe he made contact. Maybe not. But get a forensic team to check for any DNA that might be in the hole and on the pitchfork. Get this stuff to the lab quick as you can."

Dan looked out toward the windmill. He said, "O'Brien, you're like a bird dog. Wish I could have worked with you in Miami. Where to . . . Sherlock?"

"To where Sam Spelling was shot."

EIGHTY-FOUR

Grant led O'Brien up the side entrance steps of the U.S. district courthouse in Orlando, a forty-year-old building. Dan pointed to the top step and said, "Spelling had reached this point. The federal marshals escorting him said Spelling had turned around and asked if it would be okay to smoke a cigarette over there on the side before he went in to testify. He was nervous. The sniper's bullet caught Spelling about here"—he pointed to a spot between his heart and top of his shoulder. "Bullet was a .303 British."

Dan took half a dozen steps and pointed to the far left door. He said, "That spot on the door, the one that's been sanded, filled, and painted over, is where we dug out the round after it passed through Spelling. Clean shot. Didn't even hit a bone."

O'Brien looked in the direction of a parking garage across the street. Then he backed up and stood next to the door. He marked his height at six two with his right hand, made a small line on the door with his pen, and used his driver's license to mark off three-inch increments down to the spot that was sanded and painted. He looked at the place where Spelling was standing when he was shot.

Dan said, "I see where you're looking. I almost hate to say it, but they combed the garage. It's only nineteen floors. Spent two days up there. Metal detectors. Dogs. Nothing. Not even a sweat stain or boot mark left anywhere that we could see."

"How well do you think they checked the roof?"

"That's the first place they started."

"Should have been the last. How about the third floor?"

"Out of nineteen floors, the largest parking garage in the city, why the third?"

"The building is about one hundred yards from this spot. Spelling was five-eight. If he stood right there, and the round hit here, the bullet dropped about a half inch. The shot came from between the second and fourth floors. Let's go in the middle, to the third."

O'BRIEN PARKED HIS JEEP close to the opening of the third floor that provided a view of the courthouse. He got a pair of binoculars out of the glove box and said, "Let's try to see it from the shooter's perspective."

"I guess that would be the closest thing we got to a scope right now," said Dan.

O'Brien walked to the farthest right-hand corner. "I don't see any surveillance cameras in this vicinity."

"Most are in the high-traffic areas. We checked the tapes to see what came and went an hour before and a half hour after—on either side of the time Spelling was hit. Everything checked clean except the second vehicle to leave. Two minutes after the shooting. A blue van. Tag stolen."

"Who was it registered to?"

"Guy's name is Vincent Hall. Says it was stolen off his Mercedes."

"Where was his Mercedes parked?"

"Third floor."

"Where on the third floor?"

"Over there." Dan pointed to a far corner.

"I bet the blue van was right beside the Mercedes. Perp may have arrived early—first thing—got here early to find the best spot. Check that on the tapes. He laid low here. Waited for Spelling to be paraded up the courthouse steps and fired one shot. Guy's damn good, an expert."

O'Brien walked to the corner. A red Cadillac was in the spot closest to the corner and the large concrete pillars. He stared out the open breezeway across to the courthouse steps. He looked through the binoculars.

O'Brien surveyed the area. He found a crumpled cigarette pack. No sign anyone had been smoking. There was an empty five-gallon bucket of roofing tar. It sat adjacent to an opening between one of the concrete pillars and the steel girder. O'Brien squatted down behind the bucket. "Let me see the glasses from here." Dan handed him the binoculars. "I believe the shooter used this bucket to steady the rifle. The bucket's been left behind from some construction work. Have your department set up a laser right here. It should match the trajectory to the hole in the door."

O'Brien looked down at a gutter with half-inch grates spaced to allow the water in but to keep most of the leaves and debris out. The gutter ran the entire length of the floor. He looked in one of the slots and said, "Too dark to see anything."

"I'd doubt if you'd find a casing in there. Perp probably picked it up. Bouncing in one of these holes would be like hitting one of the ringtosses at the county fair."

O'Brien heard a car door close. He looked over and saw a woman locking her door. "Dan, give me your badge for a second."

"Sean, it's one thing to be out here with me impersonating a cop, but if you take my ID, you're busted. In case you haven't looked . . . our skin color is a little different."

O'Brien grinned. "They always look at the shiny badge first."

Dan sighed, handing O'Brien his detective's shield.

"Ma'am!" shouted O'Brien.

The woman, dressed in a business suit, turned to look. O'Brien approached her with the ID and said, "Police, ma'am. We're investigating a shooting. And we've run into a little challenge. Maybe you can help."

"I'm late for court. I don't—"

"May I borrow the mirrored makeup compact in your purse?"

"How'd you know I carry one?"

"Lucky guess." O'Brien smiled.

"Okay, I suppose."

She opened her purse and said, "Just take it."

"Thank you. If you can afford to wait thirty seconds, I'll hand it right back."

O'Brien took the compact, opened it, and angled the mirror so the sun would reflect through the slots in the gutter near the bucket. He dropped to his knees, trying to peer through the grates. He moved the mirror slowly, like a small searchlight in the dark. He saw loose nails, a dime, leaves, and something the color of polished brass near a leaf. "Dan, would you get a coat hanger out of the back of the Jeep?"

The woman watched as Dan got the coat hanger and handed it to O'Brien. He untwisted the hanger, fashioned a small hook, stuck it into the grate, and carefully lifted up the shell casing from the dark. O'Brien stood, the casing winking like gold in the late afternoon sunlight. "Hand me an evidence bag," he said. As he dropped the casing into the bag he said, "A .303, British Springfield. Sometimes you get lucky at ringtoss."

EIGHTY-FIVE

After O'Brien dropped Dan Grant off at the sheriff's office, he placed a call to Florida State Prison at Starke. He was transferred three times and finally got the deputy assistant warden on the phone.

"Mr. O'Brien, I understand you're on the approved call list, but each call has to be accepted by Charlie Williams. It's not up to us . . . who he talks to."

"I understand that. Can you get him to a phone?"

"Not a question of getting him to a phone, it's getting a phone to Williams."

"What do you mean?"

"Governor's signed Williams's death warrant. He's been moved from his cell on death row to a deathwatch status. Which means he's down to extremely limited phone calls."

"He still can speak with his attorney, right?"

"Are you his legal counsel?"

"I'm on his legal team."

Here was an audible sigh. The deputy assistant warden said, "Guess

301

we're gonna have to install a phone in Williams's cell. Media types are callin'. CNN, ABC, CBS, NBC, you name it."

"I understand your frustrations. Part of the state system in Florida is due process up until an inmate is in fact executed. No one wants an innocent man to go to his grave."

"Gimme your number. I'll see what I can do."

"Thank you."

O'Brien drove east on I-4 and took it to Highway 46 toward U.S. 1 and Ponce Inlet. His cell rang. It was Detective Ron Hamilton.

"Tucker Houston's the right guy for Charlie Williams," said Hamilton.

"For Williams's sake, I hope so. His other attorney sort of resigned after having all his petitions for a new trial denied."

"Sean, it might not be anything, but since you mentioned somebody was popping Alexandria full of heroin . . . something came up in a conversation I had with Joe Torres. Joe's working drugs and gangs in the area now. Torres was talking with Todd Jefferies, DEA. Jefferies was the lead investigator in the coke bust that sent Russo away. Jefferies worked with the FBI on that, and the one agent who's chief of the Miami office."

"Who's that?"

"Mike Chambers. I've met him. He's fairly aloof. Typical bureau. Other special agent was Christian Manerou, seems to be a stand-up kinda of guy. Anyway, although Todd Jefferies and the rest of the feds popped Russo on the coke charges, they'd found two kilos of pure uncut heroin in the pallet disguised as swimming pool chemicals. Jefferies told Torres that it was suspected to be the icing on a cake for a deal done between some Miami crime families with the New York mob. The heroin was found hidden at the bottom of the coke pile, all disguised as powdered chlorine. Russo, in a plea bargain, said he suspected the uncut stuff was "hidden" there by an unknown courier as a partial payoff for a mob hit. The trigger man was a lowlife called the Coyote, a.k.a. Carlos Salazar."

"What happened to the heroin?"

"Jefferies says it came up missing."

"Missing?"

"Somewhere between photographing the stuff, weighing, tagging and bagging, . . . and being tucked away in evidence storage, it was lost, probably stolen. This meant the heroin charges against Russo were dropped."

"I don't see how the DEA can lose evidence, or was it the FBI?"

"Don't know that we can blame the feds for this. The heroin was being stored in Dade County SO, locked away in their secure evidence vaults near an area where they keep the confiscated drug planes, cigarette boats, and whatnot. Jefferies says he suspects one of the Miami mob families associated with Russo had somebody inside, offered a hundred grand to drop the stuff in a canal out back. Let the gators have a heroin fix. Anyway, don't know if it can ever be traced to Alexandria Cole, especially now, but I thought I'd mention it."

O'Brien was silent.

"You still there?" asked Hamilton.

"Yeah, I'm still here. Just thinking. Did Jefferies say which FBI agent, Mike Chambers or Christian Manerou, played the bigger role in the investigation?"

"No, why?"

"Nothing yet. Would you ask him how things were divvied up during that case?"

"You mean between Chambers and Manerou, who was running the show?"

"Yeah."

"Okay, speaking of the feds, Lauren Miles had a break-in at her house."

"Is she okay?"

"Yeah, she wasn't home. Somebody walked off with her DVD player and a pearl ring. She'd called me about the Sixth Street Gym. She wants to work a co-op stakeout with Miami PD. Surveillance cameras, the whole nine yards to try and catch these freaks in the act of staging one of their kill matches. The Irish guy has a rap sheet that, if you included 'references,' would connect him to a few of Florida's finest hate groups."

O'Brien saw an incoming call with a 352 area code. The area code service for Starke and the Florida State Prison. He disconnected with Hamilton and answered.

"Mr. O'Brien?"

"Yes."

"I got Charlie Williams standin' here. You can have three minutes."

O'Brien waited a few seconds and Charlie Williams came on the line. "Hello."

"Charlie, it's Sean O'Brien. I wanted you to know that I'm close—very close to finding out who killed Alexandria. Did you know Alexandria was addicted to heroin?"

"I suspected she was on something real bad 'cause her moods changed so much."

"But she never admitted it?"

"Not directly, she just told me to stay the hell away because she said there were people that would take me out quick and they'd never find my body."

"But she didn't say what people or what person?"

"No. She was scared shitless. That's why I was tryin' to get her outta there."

"I understand, Charlie."

"I'm thankful for what you're doin'. That lawyer, Mr. Houston, is real helpful. He's doin' what he can to throw a wrench into this thing."

"He's the best. I just want you to hang in there, Charlie. Don't give up hope."

"Hope's all I got left, O'Brien."

"You've got more than that, Charlie, believe me, okay?"

"I wish I was as sure as you sound." Charlie laughed nervously and said, "This deathwatch thing has its upside. I got a little bigger cell. They moved me out of my eight-by-nine cage into a twelve-by-nine box. Had to leave my pictures behind. They wouldn't let me bring the picture of Mama and Lexie from the other cell to this. I got a cot and a blanket . . . and . . . that's about it. . . ." His voice broke, emotions rising in his throat.

O'Brien said, "You'll be out of there soon, Charlie. Then you can go home to see your mother."

There was a long pause and Charlie said, "They asked me what I wanted for my last meal. I feel like my life has turned into a movie with no good ending. I got about fourteen hours left. One of the guards told me the first drug they give to knock you out, don't always completely knock you out. Then, when they give the other drugs, you just lie there. You can't move. Can't talk. But you can feel, hear, and think. You feel the pain as your organs begin to shut down . . . one by one . . . especially your lungs. I don't want to go out like that. For God sakes, this is no way for an innocent man to leave this world. . . . Help me, O'Brien."

EIGHTY-SIX

It was dusk when O'Brien pulled his Jeep into the oyster shell parking lot at the Ponce Marina. A fog was building off the estuary, rising low over the boats. Through the old mercury vapor street lamps, the fog became flickering orbs of diffused light, like Halloween pumpkins glowing above the docks.

Max heard O'Brien coming before she saw him. She jumped up on an ice chest in the cockpit of Nick Cronus's boat and barked twice. "Hot dog, who you talkin' to?" came Nick's voice as he stepped from the salon.

O'Brien squatted at the stern and rubbed Max's head. He could see a television on inside Nick's boat. He said, "Thanks for keeping an eye on Max."

"I'm going to take her out fishing with me. When one gets off the hook, I say, 'Go get 'em, hot dog.' She jump in the water and bring the fish back to me."

"Max might turn into the world's smallest Labrador retriever, or shark bait."

"Wanna beer? You eat yet?"

"Yes and no. I'd like a beer and I haven't eaten. But right now, I don't have time for either. I need to sit on *Jupiter* in a quiet place and think. There's something I'm failing to see about the events surrounding this—"

"Sean, it's all over the TV. Fox News was just interviewing that Miami lawyer."

"Where's Dave?"

"Said he was going to the store for spaghetti fixings and wine."

O'Brien lifted Max up and set her down on the dock. She darted after a cricket. O'Brien said, "Thanks, Nick. Come on, Max."

Max trotted down the dock behind O'Brien. He picked her up to lift her over the transom. "No place like home, right, Max?"

She looked up at him, her eyes bright, her tail wagging. "We have to get back to our house on the river. The old dock needs a few new boards. Plus, I've been missing you—maybe missing our routine, too."

She barked once, almost nodding her head. O'Brien opened the salon door, Max following him inside. He poured some dry dog food in Max's bowl, opened the windows, set up his laptop, and spread the Alexandria Cole case files out on his small table. He looked at arrest and arraignment dates, hearing dates and times. Trial dates. Postponements and reschedules.

His cell rang. It was Ron Hamilton. "Sean, I spoke with Todd Jefferies, DEA. He told me that Mike Chambers played a big role in the Russo investigation and bust, but agent Christian Manerou worked the case hard and was damn good at it."

"I wonder if Manerou had any speculation as to what happened to the heroin."

"Don't know, but I do know you, Sean . . . and when you get this tone, it's usually because you're getting close."

"As in dropping the hammer."

"What?"

"Something Christian Manerou said. How difficult would it be for you to remember a dialogue from one of your interrogations more than a decade ago?"

"Depends, the bullshit lines and lies all run together after a while."

"I know."

"What are you tinkering with, Sean? You got something on Manerou?"

"Talk with you later. I have a little homework now." O'Brien disconnected and closed his burning eyes for a moment. Something wasn't clicking. What was it? He remembered what Judy had said that Alexandria told her shortly before she was killed, *You can put your trust in the wrong people . . . even those people paid to protect you.*

O'Brien leaned back in his chair, his eyes locked on the case files, his thoughts focused on Christian Manerou's face.

"You son of a bitch . . ."

EIGHTY-SEVEN

O'Brien jerked his cell off the table in front of him and hit Lauren Miles's number. He asked, "Why didn't you tell me you had a break-in at your place?"

"What?"

"Ron Hamilton told me. When was the break-in?"

"Tuesday or Tuesday night."

"Was it after I'd given you the second page from the notebook that Sam Spelling used to write his letter to Father Callahan?"

"Yes. That night I left work and joined some of my girlfriends at a watering hole. As I recall, I invited you to join us."

"Lauren, has Christian Manerou's lifestyle changed much since the Russo investigation and bust?"

"What do you mean? And please be careful with your answer."

"I know it's been a decade, everybody changes, but did you see anything tangible with Christian, not things out of character per se, but maybe a slight lifestyle change . . . maybe a few vacations to places that a special agent's salary might not cover, but things or places that wouldn't raise an eyebrow?"

"Not at all. And I don't care for this line of conversation—no, this questioning. What's this about? Christian is one of the finest, most ethical agents in the bureau."

"Did you take the Spelling paper, the file, home with you?"

"Yes."

"Did Christian know it?"

"I mentioned it to him in passing that afternoon."

"Lauren, did he ask you about it, or did you bring it up?"

"Let me think a second. . . . He mentioned it, why?"

"Nothing yet."

"Sean! Please, for Christ sakes, come on! Drop it, okay? I trust Christian with my life! You're way off base."

"You're right! I was way off base because Christian helped point me there. He pointed me in the direction of Russo, and he did it very well. Maybe because of the deadline in the race to save Charlie Williams, I didn't see it. Maybe, like you, I had no reason not to trust an FBI agent."

"No!"

"I'll call you back." O'Brien hung up and began looking through Alexandria's file. He started to glance at his watch to see the numbers of hours left for Charlie Williams; instead, he pored through the files in front of him. Where did he see or hear something that was incongruous with the time lines of Alexandria Cole's murder and Charlie Williams's sentencing? He closed his eyes and let the slate go blank in his mind.

Think.

Max sat at his feet and looked up at him.

When O'Brien had originally questioned Russo and Sergio Conti, Russo had already been arraigned on a drug charge, and his trial was not even on the radar.

As we were about to drop the hammer on a big bust, it looks, in retrospect, like his alibi may have been a fabrication, so he could have killed the girl the same night.

The words played back in O'Brien's mind. He could see Christian Manerou standing in Lauren Miles's cubicle, quoting Russo's alibi: *Ate them from his penthouse balcony and tossed the shells down to the beach below them. Called it "raining crabs."*

O'Brien leafed through the case files, found the spot, and read: "Subject, Jonathan Russo, stated he had dinner on the terrace of subject Sergio Conti's condo and said they picked up a jug of chardonnay, a few pounds of stone crabs from the marina, ate them from his penthouse balcony and tossed the shells down to the beach below them. Called it 'raining crabs.'"

O'Brien looked at the dates. Alexandria Cole's murder was Friday, June 18, 1999. He went online, typing fast. In a few seconds the arrest records of Jonathan Russo were on the screen. O'Brien scanned the information and stopped at the dates of Russo's arrest for possession of contraband—cocaine—more than two kilos with the intent to distribute in the United States of America. The date of the arrest: May 3, 1999.

Why was the FBI doing a wiretap after Russo was arrested and booked?

As we were about to drop the hammer on a big bust, it looks, in retrospect, that he may have killed the girl the same night.

O'Brien leaned back and his chair and whispered, "You didn't tie the wiretap alibi to Alexandria Cole's murder because you never heard it . . . you *read* it. You weren't about to drop the hammer. You didn't hear Russo's statement in a wiretap. You read it in *my* report. You bastard!"

EIGHTY-EIGHT

O'Brien called Lauren Miles. He said, "Lauren—"

"Sean." She was almost breathless. "I hope this isn't about Christian. He's gone out of his way to help me on things time and time again. I trust that man. You will, too. I just heard from Simon Thomas. He had some luck with Spelling's letter. He managed to make out another line before it faded into oblivion. Spelling wrote: 'Later I hid the knife in St. Augustine on Tranquility Trail . . . at my mother's.' At that point, Sean, the print was no longer detectable. When Simon called, I conferenced in Christian on the call."

"What! Why?"

"Because he'd offered to help you! I'll prove to you how far off base you are. Also, in view of your short time window, it was generous of him to offer and for Mike Chambers to authorize. As a matter of fact, Christian's in Lakeland doing a deposition, and said he'd head over to St. Augustine for you."

"He's here because he just killed a woman! If Sam Spelling's mother is there, he'll kill her to get the knife."

"Sean! Have you been drinking?"

"Christian didn't hear Russo's alibi with Sergio Conti in a wiretap. He read it in my case report."

"What?"

"Listen to me! Since the cases—the murder of Alexandria and the drug bust of Russo—overlapped, Christian, or the DEA, pulled information from my files, probably to add to whatever they had on Russo. But the bust and arrest of Russo happened more than a month before Alexandria's murder. Christian was investigating Russo close enough to know of Russo's associates and employees . . . and Alexandria. She was one of the most beautiful women in the world. He knew she was heavy into coke, threatened to arrest her and ruin her career unless she had sex with him."

"Sean, you're accusing a respected FBI special agent of having an affair with a subject he was investigating. That's very serious."

"So is murder. Two kilos of heroin, drugs found in the coke bust, were stolen."

"What's that have to do with Christian?"

"He took it, or he took some of it. Alexandria was addicted to heroin and I think it was because Christian forced the poison into her. Did it enough and she was addicted."

"I can't believe you seriously think Christian hooked a supermodel on heroin."

"Hooked her, sexually took advantage of her, and killed her."

"Sean! Enough! I can't allow you to ruin this man's career on speculation."

"Manerou was near Ocala silencing the last living witness that could tie him to Alexandria's murder, the wife of the DOC guard. The same guard that Manerou killed the day he murdered Spelling and Father Callahan."

"No! I can't believe this."

"It's true. If he hasn't tossed it, look for a ski mask in his car. Go to his house. See if he owns an all-black suit, something like a priest might wear. If it hasn't been cleaned, see if there's any blood, hair, or fibers that will tie him to the three vics he killed in one night. Also, pull some hair out of a brush, get his damn toothbrush. I don't care what you use, just get—"

"Sean—"

"Was Manerou in the service? The military?"

"Army, I believe. Why?"

"Check his records. See if he went to sniper school."

"Why?"

"Only somebody with an expert rating could have shot Spelling like he did."

"Sean, you need to—"

"The name—Manerou—what's that?"

"What do you mean?"

"Nationality!"

"Probably French or Greek. Why?"

"Where was Manerou born?"

"I don't know."

"Are you at a computer?"

"Yes, why?"

"Go in the FBI's bio on its agents. Wherever it is you people keep that, and see where he was born." O'Brien paced inside his boat. Max watched him.

There was an audible exhalation and she said, "Give me a minute."

O'Brien could hear her fingernails hitting the keys, then a long moment of silence. Lauren's voice dropped to above a whisper and she said, "He was born in Greece. On the island of Patmos . . . that's the same place you mentioned, Sean . . . oh my God."

EIGHTY-NINE

O'Brien called Detective Dan Grant. "Dan, FBI got a better read on part of the letter that Sam Spelling left behind. Spelling may have left the knife that killed Alexandria Cole at his mother's house. Tranquility Trail, St. Augustine."

"I'll see if I can get a search warrant."

"You don't have time!"

"Judge Franklin will sign it. His house isn't far from—"

"Dan, you don't have time. An FBI agent, Christian Manerou, killed Alexandria—and he killed Sam Spelling, Johnson, Johnson's wife, and Father Callahan. He knows Spelling's mother's address. You're closer to St. Augustine than I am. Take backup with you. Go!"

O'BRIEN CALLED TUCKER HOUSTON. "Tucker, FBI managed to pull an address from the sheet of paper under the letter Sam Spelling wrote. It's his mother's address in St. Augustine. The knife is probably there."

"Excellent, Sean! CNN is using Six's studio to do a live interview

315

with me. I'm getting Charlie Williams's name across the nation. It's now in the hands of the nine justices, or the Governor of Florida."

"Listen, Tucker. I believe an FBI agent, Christian Manerou, killed Alexandria Cole. He had a secret affair going on with her. I suspect he'd cut a deal with Russo. Once Manerou had access to her, he got her strung out on heroin, and when things became testy, he stabbed her and framed Charlie Williams. He's gone on a killing spree, eliminating anyone with a tie to his name."

"Can you prove this?"

"We've collected possible DNA samples from three of the four crime scenes. It's being processed now. All we need is a sample from Manerou."

"Is he here in Miami?"

"He was. But one of the agents in the bureau shared Spelling's mother's address with Manerou before she knew he was the killer."

Tucker was silent for a moment. "What are you going to do now?"

"I'm going to get to Spelling's mother's place before Manerou does."

"I can't incriminate this Manerou until I have something solid. But, Sean, you've given me a lot to throw at Governor Owens."

"Throw a fast pitch because they strap Charlie to the gurney in eleven hours."

NINETY

D ave Collins was about to open a bottle of wine when he looked out toward his cockpit and saw O'Brien walking fast with Max under his arm. Through the open sliding-glass doors, Dave said, "Come on in, Sean. Cracking a bottle of cab. A Foxen Canyon, ninety-nine vintage. A good year for California cabernet."

"A bad year for Charlie Williams. But now I know who did do it."

"Who?"

"An FBI agent. Name's Christian Manerou."

"Good Lord, Sean. Every crime talk show in America's running stories about the case. You must have just spoken with Tucker Houston. With his Texas tie and slight southern drawl, he's become the darling of CNN. He was just saying how a new development in the case would definitely point toward a killer who used his position to shield the truth. He called it a 'legal, moral and ethical obligation to seek the truth in Williams's case.' An FBI agent. Who would have thought?"

"It explains why I jumped to conclusions during the original investigation. I wasn't following a sloppy trail left by Charlie Williams,

I was following a well-thought-out trail laid by a man who knows forensics. He probably used a Ziploc bag to collect a few drops of Alexandria's blood after he killed her. Sprinkled them into the front seat of William's truck . . . it was a trail that made it a slam dunk in Charlie Williams's face."

O'Brien told the story as Dave sipped from a glass of cabernet. O'Brien concluded by saying, "If we can find the knife he used, the one that Spelling found and hid, we might find something on it to connect Manerou. The location of Sam Spelling's written statement lies in the bloody message, or code, Father Callahan left behind."

Dave sat back in his chair and looked at the fog drifting over the docks like smoke from a smoldering fire. He said, "The name Christian Manerou. Sounds French, could be Greek, and you said he was born on the island of Patmos in the Greek Isles. The same place depicted in Hieronymus Bosch's painting—*Saint John on Patmos*." Dave paused, sipped some wine, and said, "If we go back to Father Callahan's hieroglyphics, if we look at them now in light of what we've discovered about Bosch, the painting, omega, and Patmos . . . that leaves us with one thing."

"The six-six-six," said O'Brien.

"Precisely. Can we connect our latest eye-opener, Manerou, to these numbers?"

"You mean is Christian the devil? As oxymoronic as those terms sound . . ."

Dave wrote Christian Manerou's name in large block letters on a piece of white paper. He said, "Since we're talking numbers here . . . the ancient Greeks used numerology a lot in connection with their alphabet. They gave letters a numerical value. In the case of omega, the last letter, it had the greatest value, eight hundred. You mentioned an oxymoron. Well, as we said the other night, today our scientists give omega the value of one in trying to find the equation to the fate of the universe, but two thousand years ago, the Greeks gave omega the princely weight of eight hundred."

O'Brien said, "Alpha was the value of one."

"Absolutely." Dave sipped and smiled, his teeth purplish from the dark wine, his eyes alive with discovery. He said, "I'll go online to find the numerical value of the twenty-four letters in the Greek alphabet." Dave typed, and the Greek alphabet and the story of Greek numerology appeared. "Take a look at this, Sean." Dave positioned the laptop screen so O'Brien could get a better view.

Greek letter	Numerical Value	English Equivalent	Greek letter	Numerical Value	English Equivalent
alpha	1	A	nu	50	N
beta	2	B	xi	60	X
gamma	3	G	omnicron	70	O
delta	4	D	pi	80	P
epsilon	5	E	rho	100	R
zeta	7	Z	sigma	200	S
eta	8	H	tau	300	T
theta	9	Q	upsilon	400	Y, U
iota	10	I	phi	500	Ph
kappa	20	K	chi	600	Ch
lambda	30	L	psi	700	Ps
mu	40	M	omega	800	Ω

Dave stared at the screen, his brow furrowing, the light playing off his eyes. He picked up his pencil and began writing. "The numerical value of your first name, Sean, could be S at 200, plus E at 5, plus A at 1, plus N at 50 equals 256. There was always a lot of ancient mysticism with numerology. Some alleged it could be tied with fortune-telling; as in omega, it can be connected to the universe. A Greek philosopher named Pythagoras was convinced the entire cosmos could be expressed with numbers . . . which brings us to the elusive number six-six-six." Dave wrote the numbers on the paper. He said, "To this day, many people, even those high up in the Catholic Church, believe six-

six-six is synonymous with a guy who killed a lot of Christians—Nero. Nero alone won't equal six-six-six in value. But the ancient Greek spelling of Nero was Neron. If memory of Greek numerology serves me well"—Dave wrote NERON CAESAR—"if you add Neron and Caesar together, they total six-six-six."

O'Brien stared at the names and said, "Dave, look at this." He wrote out MANEROU in block letters and underlined four letters. "There's your Nero today: MANEROU."

"Interesting," said Dave. "Let's add them up to see if it gets even more interesting."

M	=	40
A	=	1
N	=	50
E	=	5
R	=	100
O	=	70
U	=	400
		666

NINETY-ONE

Nick Cronus stepped onto *Gibraltar* with three Greek sandwiches wrapped in aluminum foil. He carried a six-pack of Bud, one of the six MIA. His dark hair feathered out from a baseball cap, his red swimsuit faded to the color of salmon. No shoes. He said, "I smell no spaghetti comin' from your boat, so I say to myself, tonight would be a good night for grouper, lettuce, tomatoes, Nick's special sauce, all folded in warm pita bread sandwiches."

"Big fat Greek sandwiches," said Dave. "Very nice!"

Nick said, "Hot dog, I save some fish for you, too." Nick had a small piece of grouper wrapped in foil for Max. "Sean, you want a beer? Looks to me like you need one, real bad, man." As Nick ripped off a can of beer, O'Brien's cell rang. It was Detective Dan Grant.

"Did you reach Spelling's mother?" asked O'Brien.

"Feds may have read the imprint, but somehow they missed the message."

"What do you mean?"

"I mean Tranquility Trail. It's not a house. It's a freakin' cemetery."

"What?" O'Brien paused. "Maybe Spelling's mother is buried there. Evidence could be buried with her."

"Sean, I might have blown off a judge's signature for a search warrant, but to start diggin' a coffin out of the ground we need a court order. I know we're under the gun for Charlie Williams. The death penalty crowds are already gathering at Starke, those for and against. But I'm not about to start diggin' up graves to find something I don't even know is buried in one of them."

O'Brien said nothing.

Dan said, "Keep in mind, that's a damn old graveyard. Goes back to the Spaniards and French Huguenots settling Florida. Finding her grave at this hour—with a storm coming through—would be like a needle-in-a-haystack thing."

"I'll call you back, Dan." He disconneted. "Nick, you said you were on Patmos as a child."

"Yeah, man. It's a religious experience. I feel the need sometimes to return."

"The Bosch painting—*Saint John on Patmos*—looked like John was taking notes. The Virgin descending, an angel pointing to her, a ship burning in the harbor."

Nick took a long pull from his beer. He said, "Domitian kicked the holy man out. He lived on Patmos. God told him, either mankind—we get our shit together and learn to get along, or face the end—omega. Apocalypse. It's all there in the Book of Revelation."

"That's it!" O'Brien said, his fingers flying on the computer keyboard.

Nick said, "Sean, relax. You need to go to Patmos, learn to find you inner peace."

"Right now I'd rather find Sam Spelling's letter. I know where it is!"

"Where?" Dave asked. He and Nick looked at the computer screen.

"It's where Father Callahan hid it. He left a direct key to the last book in the Bible: The Revelation of Saint John. Father Callahan

322

somehow knew Manerou was born in Patmos. Look at the screen." O'Brien pointed to a passage from Revelation. He said, "In Revelation 13:18 it says: 'Here is wisdom. Let him that hath understanding count the number of the beast: for it is the number of a man; and his number is six hundred sixty-six.' Manerou's name totals six-six-six in Greek numerology. Father Callahan, an art expert, drew a symbol from Bosch's painting as he lay dying. Saint John on Patmos. He tried to write Patmos, getting out the first three letters before he died."

Nick said, "I'm going to pray. This is spooky stuff, man."

O'Brien pointed to the screen. "The sign of omega that Father Callahan drew, it's right there in Revelation 22:13. 'I am Alpha and Omega, the first and the last, the beginning and the end.' Again, The Apocalypse—the end of the Bible. Omega—the end. I was looking everywhere but there. I bet that Father Callahan hid Sam Spelling's letter in The Revelation of Saint John—in the Bible on the sanctuary dais. Less than fifteen feet from where he was killed."

Dave said, "Maybe Father Callahan didn't write out the location because he thought the killer might return. He put a lot of stock in you, Sean, to figure this out."

"I almost didn't."

"But you did it, man!" Nick said, tossing a piece of pita bread to Max.

"Charlie Williams has six and a half hours left. I have to go."

Dave said, "Sean, the riddle of the Sphinx was less of a challenge, but you, my friend, had to travel through all nine circles of Dante's hell to get to the Elysian Fields."

"I'm not there yet," said O'Brien, getting up to leave.

Nick said, "Man, it's eleven thirty—where you gonna go at this hour?"

"To church."

NINETY-TWO

It was almost midnight when O'Brien parked his Jeep in the back lot at St. Francis Episcopal Church. The fog had cleared and in its wake a cold front was building, the smell of rain coming across the sea of urban sprawl. He took a small flashlight and a leather pouch out of his glove box. O'Brien searched the exterior of the building, found the electric breaker box, and shut off the power, killing the alarm.

At the back door, he held the flashlight in his teeth, took a pick from the leather pouch, and worked the lock. There was an audible *click,* and he opened the door. The inside of the church smelled like candles, incense, and old books. He shined the flashlight on the marble floor, the area where he'd found Father Callahan's body. The bloodstain was gone but the memory was there. Father Callahan dead in front of a podium where he had stood for sixteen years. Stood and spoke of the love of God. Spoke about the line between good and evil. The temptation to cross the line—the will not to, the bridge to come back. The bridge over the river Styx, thought O'Brien.

He stepped up on the platform and stood behind the large Bible, its pages lying open and turned to Psalm 23. O'Brien flipped the pages to the reading of The Revelation of St. John. He turned to 13:18.

The letter wasn't there.

Lightning flashed through the skylights, and thunder rolled in the distance. O'Brien found Revelation 22:13. There on the page opposite the verse, on a single sheet of folded legal paper, was a letter. O'Brien opened the paper and read Sam Spelling's words:

To Father John and God–

My name is Sam Spelling. I am real sorry for my sins. I wish to ask God for forgiveness . . . and I know now I done some bad things in my life. I hope to make amends. On the night of June 18th, 1999, I was working a deal, trying to score some cocaine at the Mystic Islands condos in Miami. I was supposed to meet a dealer there. It was the same night Alexandria Cole was stabbed to death. I was sitting in a car in the condo lot, waiting for the dealer to show when I seen a man come out of Miss Cole's condo. But before I go any further in this letter, I want to say right now where the knife can be found in case I get too tired to finish this letter.

It's in the town of St. Augustine. Tranquility Trail . . . my mother's grave is there. She always loved that old cemetery, wanted to be buried there. I put the knife in a plastic Tupperware box and buried it right across the road from her grave. It's about one foot directly in front of a statue of an angel with wings. I buried it under a rock. The angel is next to a pond in the cemetery. The angel is pointing with her right hand.

Back to what I was saying. I was sitting in a car in the condo lot, waiting for the dealer to show when I seen a man come out of Miss Cole's condo. He didn't see me on account I was hunkered down in the car. I could tell he was drunk, almost fell a few times walking toward a truck I figured was his at the far end of the parking lot. I was curious as to what he was doing, and I got out of my car to see what was going on. The man looked like he was getting something out of the truck, then he walked across the street to the Whales Tale Tavern. I didn't think much about it. Went back to my car and I seen another man go into Miss Cole's place. Wasn't but a short while before I heard a scream. I saw the man running from her condo. He ran and stopped behind a breezeway, then I watched him go on down to the truck, the same one the other feller opened earlier. Looked to me like the second dude put something in the truck. I got back in my car and followed him as he left. He went a block and tossed something wrapped in a newspaper . . . tossed it in a dumpster.

I looked in the dumpster, found the newspaper, opened it, and found a plastic bag with a bloody knife in it. When I seen the knife in the bag, I knew he'd put some drops of blood in the truck. The man that killed Alexandria Cole is Christian Manerou, an agent with the FBI. I recognized him from a picture in the paper. He was part of a drug bust earlier involving Miss Cole's manager. I made a call to him, told him I seen what he did and said for a hundred grand I'd go away and never come back. He agreed. I was sort of surprised he had that much cash, because I would have took less. He wanted the knife, but I told him I'd bury it and keep it as my little secret insurance policy. I pray for Charlie Williams' soul, and I ask God to forgive mine for what I done.

Sincerely,
Sam Spelling.

O'Brien looked at his watch. Midnight. It was now Friday. The day Charlie Williams was scheduled to die. At 5:30 A.M., he would be brought to the execution room and strapped to a gurney. At 6:00 A.M., they would pump the first of three chemicals in his bloodstream. At 6:03, Charlie Williams would be dead.

NINETY-THREE

O'Brien drove to Ponce Marina, sealed the letter in a Ziploc bag, got a high-power flashlight and extra rounds for his Glock. He called Lauren Miles. "Have you heard from Manerou?"

"About an hour ago. He doesn't know you're onto him. He said he would do what he could to 'help O'Brien' find Sam Spelling's mother."

"Get your guys to run a cell tower location on his last call."

"Okay. Sean, I checked, Christian is rated as an expert marksman, too."

"No doubt. The information your lab got off the letter faded out at the point where Spelling gave the town and street name and said it was where his mother is. . . . What you didn't get is the fact that it's where his mother is buried."

"Dead! Do you think Spelling buried the knife with his mother?"

"No, it's in front of a statue—a winged angel, across from his mother's grave."

"How do you know that?"

"I found Spelling's letter."

"Where?"

"Before his murder, Father Callahan hid it in a large Bible—in The Revelation of Saint John."

"Let me guess: Saint John, the disciple who wrote Revelation as dictated by God."

"The same."

"Incredible. Where are you now?"

"I'm heading to St. Augustine. I'm calling Tucker now."

O'Brien drove through the rain, the wipers doing little to remove the torrent from the windshield. He punched in Tucker Houston's number and said, "Tucker, I found Spelling's letter. He names FBI agent Christian Manerou as the killer and says the knife can be found near a grave—Spelling's mother's grave."

"Where are you?"

"Driving to the Old City Cemetery near St. Augustine. Spelling left directions to the spot where he buried the knife in a plastic box. If we're lucky, it's still in the original plastic bag Manerou used to carry Alexandria's blood."

"The letter alone may be enough to stop the execution. I'll call the attorney general. He's got Governor Owens's cell number. They're all on standby. Standard procedure during a routine execution, but this thing's proved far from routine. Governor Owens knows the nation is watching. We're counting on you to find it, Sean, and then Charlie Williams walks."

THE TRIP FELT LIKE it had taken forever as O'Brien drove up to the gates leading into the Old City Cemetery. He checked his watch: 4:39 A.M. He tried not to think about what Charlie Williams was going through, with less than two hours left on earth, his final meal and his final words. *No!*

The wind blew through the branches of ancient oaks and the wrought-iron gate at the cemetery entrance. There was a plaque in one of the old coquina stone pillars. The cemetery was designated as a national historic place, founded circa 1598.

O'Brien drove through the open gate, down a twisting road that wound its way through graves more than two hundred years older than America. It was lined with live oaks almost as old, their long branches laden with Spanish moss that stood like sentries to time, the boughs offering canopies to the dead. Through the flashes of lightning, O'Brien tried to make out the names of the small roads that seemed to come around every turn. He pointed his flashlight toward a bent metal sign, paint as faded as an old gravestone. He could read: TRANQU L . . . TRA L. O'Brien turned left and followed the road more than a half mile.

His cell rang. It was Lauren Miles. She said, "Sean, we got a fix on Christian's call. Came from a cell tower south of St. Augustine, near the cemetery. Be careful, Sean. If Christian's not there, he soon will be."

NINETY-FOUR

O'Brien was silent. He turned off the Jeep's headlights.

"Sean, are you there?" asked Lauren.

"I'm here."

"I could only hear the rain on the roof of your car. We're sending backup."

"You can't get here in time! The local PD would turn it into a circus. All I need is to find the buried box. Manerou doesn't know where Spelling hid it. I'll call you when I find it."

The rain turned to hail. The stones were the size of peanuts, ivory-colored rocks bouncing off tombs of gray. They pounded the canvas roof of O'Brien's Jeep. He drove slowly, straining through the bursts of lightning to follow the narrow road. At the end of the road, before it hooked left and turned into a coquina shell path, O'Brien saw the statue of the angel. Even in silhouette, he knew it was the one Spelling had described. O'Brien drove the car over a half dozen graves to get it off the road, to hide it behind a mausoleum. He shut off the interior dome light, picked up his Glock, took a small utility shovel out of the back, and walked toward the statue.

O'Brien stood behind a giant oak tree, out of sight from the road, and waited for the next burst of lightning. It came within seconds. He looked the length of the road to see if anyone was walking toward him.

Nothing. As O'Brien stepped around the tree, lightning hit the treetop. A branch broke off, crashing through the limbs. He dove out of the way, coming up next to a headstone. His vision blurred. His heart felt like it had stopped for a moment before the hammering started again in his chest. The hair on his arms and the back of his neck stood. His vision floated for a second, the words on the headstone coming into focus:

DOTTIE SPELLING
LOVING MOTHER
BORN 1940–DIED 1996

Broken limbs and leaves rained down on O'Brien. He covered his head with his arms and slowly stood. He darted across the cemetery road and approached the statue. He looked at the statue of the winged angel and thought about the Bosch painting—*Saint John of Patmos.* The angel in that painting was similar to the statue, her right arm out, hand pointing up, wings extended, and a look of peace on her face. In the white shimmer of lightning, O'Brien could see a small lake less than fifty feet from the statue.

There was a granite rock about the size of a loaf of bread in front of the statue. He lifted it and set it aside. O'Brien looked at his watch. 5:29 A.M. About thirty minutes left.

NINETY-FIVE

Two Department of Corrections officers led Charlie Williams out of his deathwatch cell. There was an awkward silence. One, an older staff member, said, "Son, I hope you've made your peace with the Lord."

"And I hope y'all know you're killin' an innocent man."

They escorted him into the death chamber. The room was bright white and the gurney was in the direct center. Two more guards stood there, hands clasped in front of them, somber expressions on pinched faces. The warden stood in a corner next to a black phone on the wall. A white curtain on the left side of the room was closed.

"We need to get you ready, son," said the older guard. "Just go on and make it easier on yourself. You need to lie down on the table."

Charlie looked through the curtain, his lower lip quivering, his jawline popping, and said," I don't want nobody to watch me die. It's not right."

"State law," said the warden. "The department has nothing to do with it. There has to be witnesses in case somebody tried to say we did something wrong."

"You're doing something worse—you're killin' the wrong man!"

The warden motioned with his head and three guards surrounded Charlie Williams and led him to the gurney.

Charlie said, "I can't just hop up there like I'm crawlin' in bed to be killed."

The warden said, "Put him up and strap him down."

"Noooooo!" Charlie screamed as urine trickled from his full bladder, a wet spot growing in the shape of a leaf on his pants. "Don't let them see me pissin' in my pants! Please! God, don't let them! Don't open that curtain! I didn't kill Alex!"

"Hold on, son," said the older guard in a soft voice.

When they finished the last leg strap, they readied the first chemicals and the needles, then they opened the curtain. Charlie Williams turned his head and looked at the glass. He thought he saw the head movements of people sitting, like seeing a school of fish beneath the water. He saw his reflection in the glass. He didn't recognize his own frightened face. And he couldn't hold back the tears.

NINETY-SIX

O'Brien began digging, holding the small flashlight in his mouth as he dug. Quick movements of the shovel in the wet earth. The wind whipped through the trees, the rustling sounds of leaves and of gnarled oak branches slapping each other, the creak and groans of wood against wood in the night.

Then there was the sound of metal hitting plastic.

O'Brien dug with his hands, furiously, wet dirt flying. He brushed the dirt off the top and sides, carefully lifting the Tupperware box out of the hole.

He sat it down at the foot of the statue and opened the lid. O'Brien lifted the plastic bag. It held an eight-inch kitchen knife and, in one corner, the bag still contained the ruddy creosote deposit of blood.

Thunder rumbled. There was the feel of cold steel on his neck under his left ear.

"Stand up!"

O'Brien stood and in a flash of lightning saw pure evil, the face of Christian Manerou. The eyes bore through the night like heat lightning behind pockets in a cloud. He wore a dark raincoat, the hood over his head, the pistol now aimed directly at O'Brien's heart.

"They know you're here, Manerou. The smart thing to do would be to give up, cop an insanity plea, and live the rest of your sick life in a padded room on Thorazine."

"Is that the 'smart' thing to do, O'Brien? You're nothing but a burned-out homicide detective, a puny little man who couldn't solve Alexandria's death eleven years ago, and nothing has changed. I'll destroy the evidence in your hand, bury you in this cemetery, and it'll be the end of a weak man's life. A cop who couldn't cut it against an esteemed federal agent. You picked an interesting place to die, in front of an angel."

O'Brien's mind flashed back to his dream—he'd touched the Bosch painting, the paint wet and sticky on the tips of his fingers. "Why did you kill Alexandria?"

"Why? I would not expect you to understand. She was extraordinary, the epitome of what a woman should be—a goddess, the embodiment of the most exquisite in the form of flesh."

"Then why kill her?"

"Because she fought me! She dissented. Alexandria did not understand how we were destined to become one. And if I couldn't have her . . . then no one would."

"Is that why you kept her flying high on heroin?"

"So you discovered that, O'Brien? Regardless, people called her a supermodel, but inside she was an artist. Alexandria loved to work with her hands and heart. . . . The heroin helped her self-actualize. I was her teacher."

"The heroin was your only way of controlling a woman who was far beyond your capabilities—"

"Shut up! You know nothing, O'Brien."

"Now I know that Jonathan Russo was the ultimate pimp."

"What are you talking about?"

"You cut a deal with him, didn't you? In working the Russo coke investigation, you became infatuated with Alexandria Cole. You found the kilos of heroin along with the cocaine and decided to cut Russo a little deal. When Todd Jefferies and his DEA agents weren't paying close attention, you stole the heroin. This ensured Russo's charges would be cut to almost nothing, meaning his jail time would be very little. And all you wanted in return was to take Alexandria's body and own her soul. You wanted a trophy, and Russo was willing to hand the ultimate one over to you for a steep price—he bartered her off to you in exchange for the deal. You kept some heroin to use on people like Alexandria, and then you managed to sell the rest. That's how you paid cash to Sam Spelling after he blackmailed you. You knew the cash couldn't be traced—"

"Shut up!" Manerou raised the pistol toward O'Brien's head.

"You knew it would be easy to frame Charlie Williams in the death of his former girlfriend. All you had to do was watch, wait, and strike. And you knew if you could put enough degrees of separation between you and Alexandria, you might never be caught. That's why you pointed me toward Oz and your pimp, Jonathan Russo. You believed either I'd kill Russo, silencing him, or he'd kill me, stopping the reopened investigation into Alexandria's murder. And all of this started when Sam Spelling started thinking about how he'd make money after he was released. He contacted you. Your plan almost worked, Christian. You almost killed him on the courthouse steps. If you'd succeeded, your dark secret would have been buried with Spelling, and Charlie Williams would be executed for your original crime."

Manerou grinned and said, "Impressive, O'Brien. But none of that detective work matters now because I have the gun pointed at you. I'm in control and you're standing there helpless while they prep Charlie Williams for the needle. It's been nice knowing you, Detective."

O'Brien glanced at his watch. 5:51 A.M. Nine minutes left.

Manerou mimicked a grin, his face shining and wet from blowing rain, villainous eyes inflamed with hate. He said, "Too late for Charlie Williams! Like it's too late for that dumb guard and his wife! Then there was greedy Sam Spelling. He accepted death without much more than a hiccup. Then there was the priest. You, O'Brien! You made me kill these people. It was your meddling after all these years. Now it's your turn to die. I'll make it quick and painless for you."

Manerou pointed the gun at O'Brien's forehead as headlights swept over the statue and tree line. Manerou looked away for an instant. It was enough time for O'Brien to grab Manerou's gun hand and slam it against the statue. The pistol dropped, and Manerou pulled a knife from his belt. He lunged at O'Brien, the tip of the blade cutting his shoulder. O'Brien hit Manerou square in the mouth. The blow knocked him to the ground. He got up and moved the knife to his right hand.

"Do you really think you can defeat me?" He jabbed at O'Brien, the knife coming inches from his stomach. O'Brien dropped quickly. He picked up two fistfuls of wet dirt and threw it into Manerou's wild, mocking eyes. "Throw dirt, little man!"

O'Brien grabbed Manerou's wrist and held the knife hand in his left, pushing Manerou to the statue. O'Brien's right forearm smashed into Manerou's face, causing his head to crash against the statue. O'Brien maneuvered the knife closer to Manerou's neck. The arms of both men shook as they pushed, muscle and bone, the rain pelting their faces. O'Brien turned the tip of the blade toward Manerou's throat.

"Sean! Don't! Don't kill him! Let the state do it!" Detective Dan Grant screamed. Grant and two deputies pointed guns and flashlights at Manerou's face. Grant pushed a pistol barrel inches from Manerou's forehead and said, "Drop the knife!"

O'Brien twisted the knife out of Manerou's hand and let it fall to the ground.

"Hold him right there!" O'Brien shouted over the rain.

"This guy's not going anywhere except to the death chamber," Dan said. "Put the bracelets on him, Bobby."

NINETY-SEVEN

O'Brien looked at his watch: 5:57. He called Tucker Houston. "Tucker, we have Manerou in police custody. We have the knife he used in the Cole killing. He admitted he killed her and the rest. And he just tried to kill me."

"I've got the governor's office on hold. Stand by. I'm putting you on hold. I'll be right back.

AT 5:59 A.M., the black phone rang in the Florida State Prison death chamber. The warden answered, "Warden Stone."

"This is Governor Owen. What's the status of the prisoner?"

"We're ready to begin, sir."

"Don't. I'm issuing an oral executive order to halt the execution. You'll have it faxed over momentarily."

"Yessir."

"And Warden Stone, please convey to Mr. Williams our apologies for what he's been through."

"Yes, sir." Warden Stone turned to Charlie Williams and said,

"Mr. Williams, you are being removed from death row. The State of Florida will be reviewing your case, sir. Governor Owen sends his apologies."

Charlie Williams wept. He looked at his reflection in the glass window. He recognized the man he always was.

An innocent man.

"SEAN," SAID TUCKER, "the execution has been stopped. I told Governor Owens everything. Charlie Williams is alive. We'll get him out."

"Thank you, Tucker."

"You're the hero in this, Sean. I'm glad I was able to play the man behind the curtain for you, the guy to help pull strings to get a few political ears to listen. Talk with you later."

O'Brien turned to Dan and the deputies. He said, "Execution was stopped. Charlie will be walking soon." To the two deputies, O'Brien said, "Lock this animal up."

They nodded and led Manerou, hands cuffed behind his back, to a squad car parked behind Dan's unmarked car.

Dan said, "Sean, you need to get to the hospital. You've lost some blood out of that shoulder."

"I'll be okay. Thanks for everything, Dan. I have my Jeep just over there. I can drive myself. Here's the knife that Manerou used to kill Alexandria. Take it to the lab."

Dan nodded, took the Tupperware box, and walked to his car.

O'Brien stood in front of the statue for a minute. The rain had stopped and the dark clouds rolled across the moon like tumbleweeds. It would be dawn soon. The moon was full. It sat in the sky directly above the angel's arm, near the tip of her pointing finger.

O'Brien was exhausted, weak from the loss of blood. He tried to blink away hallucinations as he stared at the statue and the moon in the background. In his mind's eye, he saw the painting, excerpts from his dream, the angel, Saint John, and the Virgin Mary. He held his bleeding shoulder, shook his head, and tried to concentrate on the statue and the moon in front of him, but within a few seconds, a white cloud folded over the moon like a silk handkerchief.

It was fine, O'Brien told himself. The moon will be back tomorrow night.

Now Charlie Williams will live to see it.

NINETY-EIGHT

Charlie Williams was now a free man. He was going back to North Carolina. Back to reclaim eleven years of his life he would never retrieve. He would forever be suspicious of cops, crowds, the system, always looking over his shoulder. O'Brien was there when Williams walked out of prison. He met Williams in the hot parking lot after the reporters had done interviews and filed their stories. O'Brien said, "It's good to see you, Charlie."

"Good to see you, too. I appreciate all you did for me."

O'Brien nodded. "I'm sorry it took so long to do it."

"But I'm alive, O'Brien. And I'm going home, back to North Carolina."

"How are you getting there?"

"Catch a bus, I suppose."

"How'd you like to ride there in a convertible?"

"Huh? Convertible?"

"Yeah," O'Brien pointed to the T-Bird parked next to a high fence. "That's your car, Charlie."

"You got to be kidding me!"

"No." O'Brien tossed Williams the keys. "It has a full tank of gas. Take care of it. It'll be a classic someday."

"Man, how'd this happen?"

"I bought it from an old friend of mine. Thought I liked convertibles, but I'm more of a Jeep kind of guy."

Williams smiled. "You're okay, O'Brien. One of the good ones." He walked to his car, got in, and turned the key.

O'Brien stood in the lot and watched as Williams pulled away from the prison, the wind tossing his hair, a country song on the radio. In less than a minute the T-Bird was a dot on the horizon.

A STATE SENATOR was proposing a resolution to compensate Charlie Williams with a payment of two million dollars for eleven years in prison and four minutes too long strapped to a death chamber gurney.

After a month, O'Brien's shoulder was healing well. Most of the movement restored in the muscle and tendons. The stitches had been removed. He was lifting weights, eating fish and lots of salads. He ran every day from his river house along an old Indian trail by the river.

He sat at the end of his dock. Max was curled in his lap, sleeping in the late-afternoon sun. O'Brien watched a baby alligator crawl up on a log, its yellow eyes catching the last warmth of the day. He thought about the events of the last few weeks and what would await him. The state attorney in Volusia County would prosecute Christian Manerou for the deaths of Sam Spelling, Lyle and Anita Johnson, and Father Callahan. In Miami, DA Stanley Rosen had held a press conference and said Manerou would be brought back to Dade County to stand trial for the death of Alexandria Cole.

Forensics had found her blood in the plastic bag along with a one-inch strand of hair that matched Manerou's DNA. The same DNA matches the lab got from the wool fiber found on Anita Johnson's ring. Rosen filed accessory-to-murder charges against Jonathan Russo, reminding the media that there is no statute of limitations in a capital murder case.

Father Callahan and Sam Spelling had been buried next to each other. O'Brien went to their graves right after he had his shoulder stitched. He'd left flowers and silent prayers. He sent a gift certificate to Barbie Beckman for two dinners at Joe's Stone Crab. She was enrolled in college. Tuition paid for. O'Brien would be the prime witness in the separate trials of Christian Manerou and Jonathan Russo. In the meantime, O'Brien needed an income. Maybe he could actually learn the charter fishing business from Nick.

There was the sound of a car door shutting.

Max perked her head up, looked toward the house as a woman walked around it, a picnic basket in hand. She approached the dock. Lauren Miles was dressed in shorts and a white cotton top, and her long brown hair was down.

O'Brien smiled and said, "You're right on time. No problem finding us."

Lauren set the basket down on a wooden bench seat. She petted Max and said, "You gave good directions."

"You brought food, which means you're won Max's heart for life."

"She's adorable. Hi, Max." Lauren stood and looked across the river. She watched two roseate spoonbills stalking the water, their pink feathers reflecting off the river's surface. "It's beautiful here. No wonder you left Miami. So this is the St. Johns River. It's breathtaking . . . peaceful. I can see why you love it."

"It grows on you, gets in your pores, seeps in your blood, and changes you."

"One day you can tell me how it got its name. Not now. No more work, it's time for a picnic on this beautiful river, and as I recall, you promised me a boat ride."

"My boat, *Jupiter*, is over at Ponce Marina. A boat ride might result in a few days of finding the right fishing spots. Lots of remote places up and down the Atlantic coast."

"I have a whole week off." Lauren smiled.

"Okay, tonight after I show you a sunset on the river, we'll head to the marina, stock up on groceries, some choice wines, and get lost at sea, at least for a while."

"Sounds like a marvelous plan."

"One thing, though."

"Oh, what's that?"

O'Brien looked at Max, and she raised her brown eyes to meet his. "I'll be bringing another lady along."

"Pardon me."

"She weighs about nine pounds."

Lauren smiled, the golden light from the setting sun caught in her brown eyes, a breeze across the river's surface touching her hair. "Would that other lady be Max?"

"It would. She's my first mate. Max is not a Labrador retriever, but she looks great balancing on the bowsprit with the wind lifting her ears like the wings of a little angel."